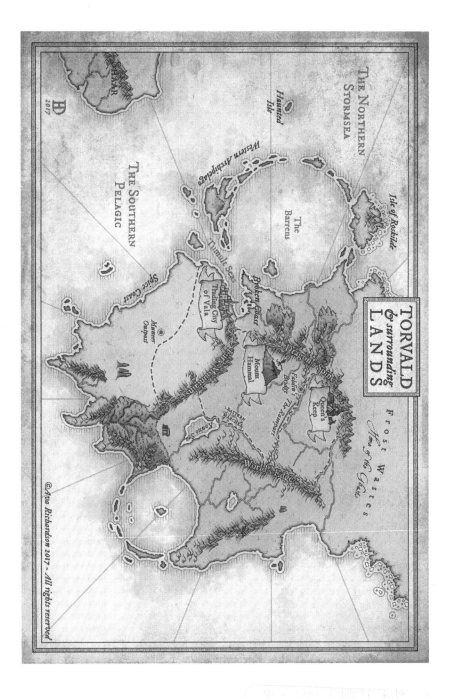

TORVALD
& surrounding
LANDS

THE NORTHERN
STORMSEA

THE SOUTHERN
PELAGIC

SARHAAR
2017

Haunted
Isle

Western Archipelago

Isle of Roakilde

The
Barrens

Tumult Seas

Spice Coast

Manter
Outpost

Broken Glaxer

Dragon Spine

Trading City
of Vala

Mount
Hammal

Stranhallow Mountains

Kerns Sea

Paldin's
Bridge

The Rampart

Queen's
Keep

World's Edge

Frost Wastes
Arms of the Glace

DEADWEED DRAGONS

Dragon Called

Dragon Magic

Dragon Song

Cover Design by Joemel Requeza

www.relaypub.com

AVA RICHARDSON

DEADWELD DRAGONS BOOK ONE

BLURB

Life and death is a delicate balancing act—and only the brave survive.

Dragon eggs are disappearing from the High Mountains aeries. The South Kingdom seeks to replicate the dragon riders of Torvald to stem the Deadweed that strikes out like living beings. They'll pay the Dragon Traders handsomely for every egg they capture, for only dragon fire has proven effective at turning back the invasive plant.

Until the deadly scourge magically returns with a vengeance.

From the moment fifteen-year-old Dayie washed ashore as an infant, everyone recognized she was different. Animals took to her instantly. Wounds healed and plants grew larger in her presence. But after she's blamed her for the vicious Deadweed attack, the villagers sell her to the ruthless Dragon Traders for fear of her powers and mysterious origin.

When Dayie makes the dangerous mountain climb and steals a dragon egg, she winds up with more than she bargained for when the dragon hatches and bonds with her before she can return. She's forced to hide the hotheaded young dragon or risk losing him to merciless patrols or the Deadweed creeping ever southward.

But he's soon discovered when the Deadweed attacks and their rescuer reveals the magic behind the ever-spreading menace. Now Dayie must either give up her dragon or take her place in the Training Hall of Dagban, where bonding is misunderstood and discord between dragon and rider reigns.

In order to embrace her destiny, Dayie must find balance in this epic dragon fantasy.

MAILING LIST

Thank you for purchasing 'Dragon Called'
(Deadweed Dragons Book One)

If you would like to hear more about what I am up to, or continue to follow the stories set in this world with these characters—then please take a look at:
AvaRichardsonBooks.com

You can also find me on me on
Facebook.com/AvaRichardsonBooks

Or sign up to my mailing list:
AvaRichardsonBooks.com/mailing-list

ACT 1: THE DRAGON TRADER'S SLAVE

CHAPTER 1
DAYIE, WHERE SHE SHOULDN'T BE

"Go, quickly now, girl!" hissed the stocky and shrouded shape of Fan Hazim; my mentor, boss – and owner. She didn't waste time on the niceties, I noticed, but then again, she never had in the eight years I'd been in her 'employment.'

Employment. That was a joke. As if cleaning pots and folding canvas and doing the thousands of other things I had to do for Fan's travelling crew was really a job. I never saw any money, all of it going to work off my 'debt' for having the misfortune to be sold at age seven to this woman.

"Well, what are you waiting for? I have to get back to the Festival, and we can't let the Torvaldites suspect what we're up to!" Fan flicked her dark hair over her shoulder and gestured to the small crevice with one tanned arm, heavy with the deep blue inks of her tribal tattoos. She called herself a Headwoman of her tribe of itinerant wanderers – but I had never seen her join in with the old Gypsy songs with the others around our caravan campfires.

Another glare from Fan and I knew that I had dawdled enough. "Fine. Just don't leave without me," I muttered, hunkering down to crawl into the crack in the rocks of Mount Hammal.

"We'll be gone before morning, child – so you'd better be back before then – unless you're already dragon meat!" Her cackle echoed behind me as I crawled and scraped my way through the stones of the sacred mountain of Torvald and into the home to their infamous dragons.

The tunnel was tight, and it smelled slightly of old mouse droppings or perhaps fox. Nothing seemed to live here now though, and I wondered if the great lizards that I was climbing towards had eaten them.

No, they're far too small, aren't they? I thought glumly, remembering Fan's ghoulish words just last night, in out camp outside the walls of the citadel of Torvald. "Dragons eat sheep and cows and deer – and most of all, they like the meat of young women!"

Ha. I'd never heard that the Torvald Dragons – those noble beasts that were ridden through the sky by the Torvald Dragon

Riders – ate people. The wild mountain blacks, and the Sand Dragons yes, but not the Torvald ones.

Back home in the southlands, our dragons came in just three sorts – and all of them were as mean as a hungry desert cat, or so I had been told. We had the blacks, the orange and yellow Sand Dragons, as well as the much smaller Orange drakes, whereas up here in the north they had the Sinuous Blues, the Stocky Greens, the Giant Whites and of course the Crimson Reds. I'd seen the Torvald Dragons many times as a part of Fan's surreptitious travels, but I had never been as close to them as I was about to be now.

This was a dumb idea, I thought once again as I teased out the tiny bit of earthstar crystal on its chain that Fan had given me and knocked it a few times on the rocky walls to get it to wake up. I didn't know how it worked, but I was very pleased when the little shard of blue crystal started to glow a faint blue-white light, allowing me to see a few feet ahead. The tunnel rose unevenly over rounded rocks and jagged piles of rockfall littered its course.

Please don't collapse on me, I thought as I pulled myself up over the hump of stone and squirmed under the next shelf of rock. But I was light – I wasn't stocky like the others – Fan and her husband Rahim, their only son Naz, and their small crew of other Gypsy travelers. I stood out like a string-bean in a field of potatoes with my thin body and my long, platinum-white hair. Another reason I had ended up with the Hazim family, I guess. The villagers who had adopted me had been certain that I was a witch.

A few fragments of rock scraped and moved under my grasping hands and I froze, my heart hammering even as my breath stilled in my chest. I waited for the ceiling to shift, but it never did.

"Come on, get this over and done with!" I whispered at myself, knowing that even if I failed, it would still be a long trek back down the sides of the mountain to where the Festival of Summer was in full swing.

That was the reason why Fan had driven us all the way up here – or I guess you could say that was the cover that she had used to get us here. The rest of the Hazim troupe had transformed our caravans into show booths, and, Fan Hazim was no doubt returning to one of them to dispense made-up fortunes from tea leaves and playing cards. The others would be playing instruments or performing tumbling tricks for the fat, complacent people of Torvald. We would be just one more troupe of performers in a sea of others by the outer walls of the Citadel – easily overlooked, and hopefully just as easily forgotten.

"It has to be tonight," Fan had told her husband Rahim, her husband, just last night. "The Festival offers us the only opportunity to sneak into the Dragon Enclosure and get our hands on some ACTUAL dragon eggs from Torvald stock."

Rahim, ever the avuncular, and friendly one that I had liked far more than his wife had surprised me by nodding his agreement. "And it has to be Dayie," he had said about me.

Cheers, Rahim.

I was the thinnest, and I was the only one of the troupe who looked like I might have actually grown up in Torvald (which I hadn't – I had far too many scars and bruises for that) with my fair complexion. If I was caught, I might be able to lie and say that I was just a stupid city-girl who had thought to have an adventure. I'd probably still be punished, but not as badly as a foreign emissary from the Southern Kingdom, sent to steal Torvald's most valuable asset.

The rocks moved again, but this time when they shifted a little, they let in a chink of fresher air. I was close!

"Now, where are you?" I whispered, holding up the light. This tunnel I was in continued on into the darkness, but the shifted rocks had opened up a smaller, narrower cleft in the rocks above from which was *definitely* flowing a river of fresh, cool night air.

Do I continue, or try for up? What had Fan told me – that these tunnels were ancient, and that the dragon mountain was riddled with them? I could be stuck in here for days if I didn't take the chance now!

Gritting my teeth and wiping the sweat from my already dirt and dust-smeared brow, I chose up.

"Almost…" my fingers (bound with strips of linen to stop the sweat and help me grip) searched and dug at the walls until I found a crack big enough to haul myself up from. "There!" The muscles in my back ached as I pulled and kicked until I could brace with my soft-booted feet against either side of the chimney walls and reach up a little further.

In this way I climbed up the rocky walls of Mount Hammal, following my nose.

Maybe I should have chosen the other route, I had a moment to think just as the rock I was shoving at gave way, and I burst to the surface, scrabbling quickly hand over hand, seizing at handfuls of tall, whip-like grass and panting as I collapsed. Above me, the vegetation waved in the night, the thick-leaved trees making a sighing sound as their branches shook a little – and between them they revealed the brilliant stars of the night sky.

There was the Hog, and the head of the Serpent. I recognized the stars that could be seen even down in the southlands, but the rest of them were a mystery to me. These strange north-erners and their strange stars, I groaned as I flipped over, and found myself staring at a giant dragon claw.

Holy crap. I blinked, staring at the sleek black sheen of the claw. It was curled like a cat's but whose inner edge had small serrated burrs that I knew would be able to rip leather and wood and even metal. It was also about as big as my entire torso.

But thankfully, there currently wasn't a dragon attached to the other end of it. I was looking at an old talon from either a long-dead dragon or the result of a horrible injury to the Enclosure dragons. From the size of the thing, I suddenly understood why the Southern Kingdom were so keen to have another Torvald dragon.

Okay, Dayie, think... I folded myself back into a crouch, searching my travelling pouches attached to my broad belt for the little thick brown glass pot of salve that Fan had given me. She had watched as I had slavered it all over every possible bit of exposed skin just before sending me down the tunnel, but I didn't want to take any chances, and so reapplied the thick, goopy paste again.

"This will hide your scent. The dragons will think that you're another dragon," Fan had told me, which made me wonder at what under the stars she had used to make this vile stuff. Nope. Actually, I really didn't want to know.

It was only after I had managed to walk a few meters down the sort-of trail between the thick vegetation that I stopped to wonder: *Aren't dragons insanely territorial?* Had Fan meant that I would smell like one of the *Torvald* dragons, or *any* old dragons? I stopped, waiting for the shrieks and chittering of alarm from the Enclosure around me – but nothing happened.

"Phew!" I whispered, and then clamped a hand over my mouth. *And didn't dragons have the best hearing in the world?*

But no one had managed to get this far, that I knew. And so I took another few hesitant steps. The ground underfoot was damp and thick with the hummus of this strange place. It looked a little more like the oases that scattered the southlands, spiky-leafed plants or trees with strange, fibrous barks next to spreading leaves. Past the vegetation, the silhouette of the high walls of the Enclosure cut across the skyline. The Dragon Enclosure of Torvald was huge and sat inside the same mountain that the Citadel of Torvald climbed. It was here, in this ancient crater that the Torvaldites bred their dragons before sending them up to train at the famous Dragon Academy, to be their fire-full steeds, dominating the skies.

"Sussussuss-r!" The sound of the hissing whistle—close by—made my heart skip a beat. I waited for the alarm call to start, but only that strange, wheezing sort of hissing noise returned.

"Mamma-la, mamma-la…" my voice quavered on the words of the song that I used ever since I was a little girl. A song that I don't even remember learning, but one that I knew was a part of my heritage.

I had been adopted by the villagers of Happa when I was just a little girl, and even though they did not know where I had come from, (a shipwreck, they thought, because they found me on the beach there) I had arrived with just one thing to call my own: this song ingrained in my memory. My adoptive parents had said that it must be the nursery song of my real mother, and that my mind had clung onto it because of the terrible events that I must have been put through. All I knew, was that when I sang it, I felt safe, and it seemed to calm the Gypsies' horses and dogs too. I don't know whether it worked on dragons, but I was willing to try anything in order to not get eaten.

"Mamma-la, mamma-la," I sang, my voice sounding thin and stupid in the night air.

"Sussususs…" the whickering hiss eased a little, and, as I pushed aside the foliage to step forward, I saw why. I wasn't dealing with an angry, territorial dragon but with a sleeping one.

It was beautiful. The Great White was curled up around itself, nose to tail like a giant, house-sized cat. Its bulk had flattened and crushed the trees and bushes around it, making a sort of nest for it to sleep in. Its scales gleamed dully in the starlight, looking almost milky and translucent, and my heart squeezed in awe at the sight.

I had never seen a dragon this close, and I didn't think any of our retinue had seen one like this either. The dragon was massive, larger than all our caravans stacked end-to-end – but it also looked serene and comfortable; cute even in the way that it huffed and sighed in the night. Its scales were a blanket of armor that fitted naturally and perfectly, some of them burnished and smooth like mirrors, others smaller and hard like nails. I had never known that there was such variation in their skin, I thought as the Giant White went from ash-colored, to chalk, marble, milk and silver.

"Mamma-la," I whispered once more, and the Giant White's lungs sighed a deep breath. It made me feel honored and special in a way that I had never felt in all of my years with Fan Hazim.

Maybe I *can* do this, I thought, seeing where a small trail led out, behind the nest of the Giant White and up the near slopes of the Enclosure wall and to where a line of caves was bored into the rocks.

All dragons lay their eggs in caves, right? At least, that is what the wild southern dragons do… With a last, lingering look at the sleeping dragon, I picked up my pace and skipped up the slope, towards the dragon caves.

The air from the mouth of the cave was warm and tinged with a scent that I did not recognize—somehow fragrant and slightly bitter at the same time – a little soot, mixed with rose or jasmine, perhaps?

Now standing on the ledge in front of the line of caves, I could look out across most of the Torvald Dragon Enclosure to see that the entire caldera wall was marked with them. Fan had been right that this place was riddled with caves, it seemed –

and from a couple I saw thin ribbons of smoke curling sluggishly into the night air. Those were the occupied ones, clearly.

But which one to choose? I regarded each of the nearest entrances in turn. None of them had smoke – but that didn't mean that they weren't occupied, right? For some reason, my steps were drawn to the last, smallest of the three caves. As I crept forward, my soft boots crunched a little on the layer of grit and sand, I noticed that the opening was smoothed as with the passage of many feet. *Claws, Dayie – they're called claws,* I reprimanded myself.

I pressed on, to the mouth of the cave, my heart in my throat as I peered in…

The starlight reached into the cave over my shoulder, illuminating a large mound of fibrous material. Hay and straw and leaves. The Dragon Riders must stock these caves with bedding material, I realized.

They're here. They're close. I knew in my heart in the same way that I would know when one of Fan's horses was slowing down because she was about to throw a shoe. I had never questioned these intuitions before, they had always just come naturally to me in a way that my adoptive parents Obasi and Wera had said was a gift, though it was a gift that other people wouldn't understand.

My feet moved closer into the murk. I didn't use the earthstar crystal this time, not wanting to accidentally wake up a mother dragon on her nest!

But there was no mother dragon here on this mound of nesting materials. The stones underfoot and the rocky walls already radiated heat, and the large eggs that I could now see were already packed down, deep into their home. There were three of them, each the size of a large melon, but egg-shaped, not round. They were each speckled with dots, some of which gleamed in the starlight.

Without thinking, I reached out a hand to the nearest egg, to find it warm underhand. This one would hatch soon, I knew without understanding how, and the egg quivered just slightly under my skin. There was a baby dragon in there – *what did they call them, newts?* – and I had never felt so elated in all of my life.

It wasn't the achieving my mission. It wasn't the joy that this would bring to Fan, or the money that it would earn, or the hope that it might eventually bring to the Southern Kingdom itself. It was just the fact that it was me, little Dayie, here with such a new life that was fragile and strong all at the same time.

I didn't need any more encouragement. I drew out the padded egg-sack that Fan had made for this purpose, and, very carefully tugged it down over the egg and lifted it up.

It was done. I was now a Dragon Thief.

CHAPTER 2
DAYIE, DRAGON THIEF

"Day!" the voice surprised me as soon as I backed out of the dragon birthing cave.

"Nas?" I hissed. It was Fan and Rahim's son, short and stocky like them, wearing the tight-fitted and sleeveless leather jerkin that Fan had got him for his Name-Day just this year. Like all of the presents they showered on him, it was finely-tooled with brass buckles and green embroidered thread. He was perched on the rocky ledge a little way from me and beckoning me up. "What are you doing here?" I said urgently as I accepted his hand to scramble up to the rock above – to be engulfed with the smell of his own dragon-salve lotion, all acrid and bitter.

"You don't think Mother would put all her faith in you to get the job done, do you?" Nas sneered at me, already turning to jog down the ledge. "Come on, we haven't got long!"

I looked at his disappearing back, and it was hard to describe quite how crushed I felt. I knew that I shouldn't. He was their true-born son, after all, and I was just an indentured servant (*ha*) – but this was to have been *my* ordeal. I guess a part of me had been perversely proud of the fact that Rahim had thought that *I* would make the best egg thief of our troupe.

Only he hadn't, had he? I instantly felt stupid and disgusted at myself for my simpering gratitude at what was just another challenge that the troupe had wanted to put me through.

Fine. That was how it was, was it? Still, even if I wasn't so special, getting a dragon egg would surely knock a few years off my indenture, right?

The egg on the sack at my back was heavy, but every time I thought about it, I felt a reassuring wave of warmth. It was just one small and frail life, I realized, which made me want to keep it safe all the more.

"*Day'!*" Nas reappeared around the bend in the ledge, looking frustrated at my slowness.

"Alright, keep your mustache on," I hissed back, before masking my grin as I kept my head down. Nas was trying for a mustache this year – and so far, he had managed two patches of wiry hairs to either side of his mouth. It made him look like a ground gerbil, but I daren't say it to his face. I set off after him, carrying my heavy load.

"Keep quiet and keep your head *down!*" Nas bickered at me as we approached wherever he was leading me, despite the fact that it was *him* who was making all the noise with his heavy, hobnail boots. The guy was a brute. "I don't want you ruining this for both of us…"

"How am I-?" I started, but one dark-eyed look from my colleague shut me up. There was no arguing with him when he was like this.

"There, we're almost out…" he said, crawling a little bit further.

Fan had known there was another way in and out of this place? I realized as I followed his example (only better, and far more quietly). Then why had she forced me to crawl through the mountain? Was it because she had expected me to fail – or had *wanted* me to fail? Or so I would be the distraction that would allow her son to cart off the eggs?

Our ledge of rock was sheer below us, with the tall, strange trees growing thick from the incline below us just a few meters from my right shoulder. The cliff walls of the Dragon Enclosure were on our left and they looked very high indeed. Had Nas climbed over them to get his way inside?

"We've got just a bit of time left before the watch changes guards, so don't mess this up for me," Nas said, nodding down to where there was a large gated tunnel sunk into the walls, with a smaller gate door set inside the larger. Nas pulled from his pockets a small iron key, and shame and embarrassment burned up my cheeks. *He had a key? And yet Fan had sent me to crawl through the tunnels.*

Scrambling, Nas hit the dirt floor outside the gate first, and proceeded to unlock the door, then reached under some of the nearby vegetation to pick up a bundle that he had hidden there. It was another of the egg sacks, and this one was bulging, much heavier than mine.

"Yeah, I managed to get two–how many did you manage?" Nas said with another cruel grin, swinging the bag onto his back, when he could already clearly see that I had only managed one egg.

"But Fan said to just get one!" I pointed out, following him through the smaller door-gate and into a wide, dark and echoing tunnel.

"She told *you* to only get one," Nas instantly relaxed, even swaggering as he walked briskly towards the semicircle of slightly lighter night-sky at the far end. "Probably knew you couldn't carry *that* many," he said with an arrogant shrug.

Pig. It was hard not to feel angry with him, and the rest of them, but my thoughts were wiped away by the sudden thump from my back. It was the egg. It had moved.

"Uh..." I said uneasily as I could feel the egg growing

warmer, and something writhing inside of it. Well, it wasn't something – it was to be a baby dragon, wasn't it? How long did they stay in the egg again? All I had to go on was what Fan had told me-- that it was just after laying season, and so the eggs wouldn't hatch until we got them all the way back to the Southern Kingdom and their ultimate destination – the city of Dagfan. But with every step, and every hammer of my heart – in time with the little newt's insistent thumping – the certainty inside of me grew: this egg was going to hatch, right here and now.

"Nas, I think we've got a problem..." I managed to say. We were by now halfway down the tunnel, which I could see was made of natural rock and smoothed from the passage of many reptilian bodies.

"You *are* the problem!" he whispered, as he neared the far end and a silhouette appeared across the distant opening.

Oh crap. The silhouette was taller than either me and certainly Nas, wearing a cloak and who was clearly holding a tall spear.

The sorts of spears that the Dragon Handlers of Torvald used.

"Halt!" the guard said in a thick bark of a voice.

What are we going to do! I thought as Nas sauntered towards the guard in an amiable gait.

"Nas!" I was about to scream at him, when *thump* – the egg jostled against my back once again.

"Easy there, friend," Nas said, his voice friendly and enticing, holding out one hand from which dangled a leather coin purse. "See? I wouldn't forget you."

"You ungrateful idiot," the guard muttered as we approached, and I suddenly realized Nas and the guard knew each other. He was an older man with a blonde-chestnut beard and a gnarled face under the pointed Torvald helmet. "You never told me there was another of you in there – and that you had taken two yourself!" The guard moved the spear across Nas's path. "That's too much. One egg I can explain away – maybe one of the dragons crushed it, or we did the count wrong – but not three."

"Aww, c'mon, friend! There's enough in here to buy that little cottage you were telling me about." Nas dangled the coin purse once again. "Real southern rubies, fresh and uncut."

"I doubt that entirely," the guard grumbled, reaching with one hand to snatch at the offered bag, but Nas moved it out of the guard's reach.

"Uh-uh, not so fast. I don't want you to take the rubies and then blow that silly horn thing of yours anyway. I want to be far away by the time that *you* get paid." Nas laughed, making a move around the guard.

"I said *halt!*" The guard shoved his spear across the entrance to the tunnel, thumping against Nas's chest. "I want my *money*, you little squirt – and if you don't give it to me, I'll run you through, right here and right now."

"Oh, you will, will you?"" Nas's eyes flashed

Thump. I didn't know just how much time I had – should I go back? Could I leave the egg with the guard? "Nas. Just give the guy his money," I said urgently.

"There, listen to the prettier one." The guard laughed, darting his other hand to snatch at the bag of coins. He didn't have enough hands to open it *and* hold the spear, but he threw it and caught it a few times. "Only feels like *two* eggs to me, not three."

There, I guess my choice was made. I started to lever the heavy egg bag from my shoulders. At least the newt could grow up here in its nest, I thought, wondering at how guilty I suddenly felt. It had been an adventure, before. It hadn't been real. But now that I was standing out here in the cold with the warmth of a young life on my back? Then that was all of a sudden *very* real indeed. "Take mine."

The guard looked me over, nodding back the way that we had come. "Nah, not you." The guard glared at Nas. "This one here has got two. *He* has to take one back to the nest he got it from. *Then* we'll call it even, okay?"

"What?" Nas snapped at the corrupt guard. "I'm not going back in there – I don't care what you say. *Neither* of us are going back in. We got three, and that's what we're walking out with. Day?" he barked over his shoulder at me to follow him.

"It's alright," I said. "Maybe it's for the best that my egg goes back to the Giant White."

"I said *you* lose the egg, short stuff." The guard thumped Nas's chest with his spear one more time, obviously having taken a disliking to him. Not that I blamed the guard for that, but still…

"Get off me," Nas said, and that was when he made his mistake, shoving the spear and the guard back a few feet and taking off.

But Nas was not fast enough. The guard was surprisingly quick for an old man, springing forward to snatch at Nas's egg bag and hanging off the end. There was a brief grunt of exertion and I watched in horror as the fabric ripped, and one of the large, cream and white speckled eggs from Nas's pack slid out.

"Oh, stars!" The guard instantly dropped the spear to catch the egg, releasing Nas as he spun around, his hands scrambling to save the egg before he fell onto the floor. I stood still in the mouth of the tunnel between the bickering and fighting two, frozen with my heart in my mouth. This was too much. Too dangerous.

"By the sacred mountain…" From where he sat, the guard looked at the captured egg in his hands. There was a large crack radiating along one side of it. For a wild moment I had hoped that it was about to hatch, and that the newt inside must have been awoken from all of the jostling (*thump,* went my own egg) but no. The egg did not shake or wobble. The crack had been caused by the fall.

Oh no. I looked in horror from the egg to the guard, whose face was now screwed into a ball of fury. "I'm going to get into a *lot* of trouble for this, you two little..." he hissed, before taking a deep breath.

"Guards! Treachery! THIEVES!" his thin voice rose in the night air.

"What!?" Nas leapt to his feet to shout at the old guard. "You're double-crossing us?"

"STOP! THIEEEEVES!" The guard was grinning cruelly as he cradled the cracked egg to his chest and howled at us.

I was still frozen to my spot, looking from the sadistic Torvald guard to the cracked egg in his gloved hands, and then over to Nas, who was already high-tailing it down the mountain slope, straight towards the thick woodlands below.

I ran.

"Nas – wait up!" I shouted after him as he crashed through the undergrowth ahead of me. This entrance to the Dragon Enclosure faced out towards the ridge of the mountain leading to the fabled Dragon Academy on the other side of the mountain to Torvald Citadel. On this side of Mount Hammal there appeared to be deep forests and ravines, perfect to let the dragons hunt in.

Branches and leaves whipped and slapped at my face and arms as I tried my best to protect the egg on my back. There was a sudden scream to our right as a covey of birds swept into the night airs.

"We're going the wrong way! We have to arc back around to the Citadel Gates!" I called out at the thrashing and crashing undergrowth, but I had no idea whether Nas even heard me. He was gone, and I was alone in the Torvald wilds.

What had happened back there? I wondered, my heart hammering in my chest as I tried to make sense of the last few hours. I had stolen a dragon egg. Nas had been greedy and stolen two – and had managed to annoy the crooked Torvald guard so much that the guard wanted *him* to make amends for it.

Wasn't this a good thing? I thought shallowly. That meant that both me and Nas had one dragon egg each – he couldn't claim that he had done better than me. But any joy that I might have found in that realization quickly faded as I considered the newt on my back, *thump.* It really was near hatching, and our troupe had no facilities to care for a baby dragon.

We were supposed to get them to the Training Hall in Dagfan. Where they would be forced to bond with one of the specially-trained Riders that the Southern Kingdom had. It wasn't supposed to hatch out here in the wilds – and who knew if the Training Hall would even *pay* for a newt dragonet?

'They want eggs, and so eggs is what we'll give them!' Fan had said victoriously over the campfire just last year. The idea was, that the Training Hall would raise them from eggs as Torvald raises their dragons. These larger, less vicious northern dragons would be perfect – and now it looked as though I had ruined all of that, and was about to release a baby dragon in the wilds somewhere!

"Maybe I could get you back home," I thought, crooning to my egg as I turned to look back up the slopes of Mount Hammal to where the tall walls of the Enclosure soared above us.

BWAARRRM! In that moment, the air was split by the sonorous sound of a horn – but it was unlike any flute or battle horn that I had ever heard before. This was more like listening to a dragon roar, on an elephant call, but more melodic. It was a deep and full sound that made my stomach turn upside down, as the sound echoed down from the heights to double and triple in the ravines around me.

"The Dragon Horn of Torvald?" I muttered. I had heard of it of course, Rahim had told me stories of generations gone past, when the mighty golden horn – so big that one of our caravans could supposedly park quite comfortably in its mouth – would warn the citadel of imminent attack from wild dragons, foreign armies, or evil sorcerers. But there had been so few wars now in the north at least, I had thought that the Dragon Horn was a fanciful legend.

Well, it clearly wasn't, was it? "But maybe it's not for us…" I tried to tell myself, not sure if I was talking about me and Nas or me and the egg.

Clearly the time for wishful thinking was, however. Just a moment later the deep angry cries of hounds erupted from the ridgeway. Hunting dogs. "Great," I said, looking around me. I should be heading left, around the mountain and back to the front gates of the Citadel to meet up with Fan and Rahim (and Nas, if he ever showed up again) but that way would mean I had to climb *up,* toward the dogs.

"I guess I'm not going that way, then." I turned instead and set off north, and down the mountainside, and into the wilds.

What had Rahim told me about hiding? He had said that it was an art, and one that he and his family were trained in, along with, it seems, playing musical instruments, bare-knuckle fighting, and charming people out of their money.

"You have to make sure you are where they would least expect you to be," I could remember the man saying, which right now for me, meant that I had to wade out to that waterfall.

The ground had levelled off a little before sloping down once more, and my steps had taken me through woodlands and over fast-flowing mountain streams. Always, with the sound of the dogs howling behind me. *That guard must have told them that he had caught us stealing,* I thought in dismay. I don't know how long I had been running for, but I was now exhausted, and the eastern sky had turned from a deep blue into a washed-out sort of grey, which meant that morning couldn't be far behind. The only thing going for me, I think, was the fact that I was still wearing that stars-awful dragon lotion, which I hoped was at least confusing the hunting dogs above me.

My feet had taken me to the shores of a long and narrow lake whose surface rippled with starlight. On either side, trees marched almost to the very edge of the slate and pebble beaches. At one end a waterfall fed the lake, and the ravine walls there looked cracked and broken. I could climb it, and it would be the last place that the dogs would want to go.

My soft leather boots did nothing to protect my feet as I sloshed through the breakwaters of the lake, and within just a few moments was up to my calves in freezing lake water.

Don't think about how deep it might be. Don't think about what might be in it. I grit my teeth to stop them from chattering, and not just from the cold. I had never been that good with water – quite clearly, since Obasi and Wera had said I must have been washed ashore after a shipwreck. I don't remember any of that, of course – I was young, and, in the words of my adoptive mother Wera, I had given myself 'the blessing of forgetfulness' about that time. I don't know why I would have been on a boat in the first place, or even where I might have come from at all.

Or who my real parents were, I thought once again; that old wound. Not that I had ever wanted anything *more* than Wera and Obasi. The two fisherfolk of the little southern spit of a village had been kind and patient parents to me. They had defended me and protected me when the other villagers poked fun at me, or, in my later years there – made the evil eye as I passed.

Was it my fault that I was taller and paler than the southerners of that region? Was it my fault that the village's ponies and scrubby goats seemed to like me more than any of the others? The ponies never got lost or threw a shoe if I was with them, and the goats always let down their milk for me, and never broke into the small gardens we kept when I was tending to them. (Well, that last bit isn't entirely true, but they only got into the Old Man Harris's when I would get to daydreaming; I generally found that if I just spent time with them, they were more interested in me than going off to make mischief).

But all of these things, and the fact that I didn't catch the Coughing Pox or the Red Spot when all other kids my age in the village caught it, was enough for the small backward village of my childhood to think that I must be some kind of foreign witch. *If only!* Then I would've magicked away the terrible Deadweed as soon as it came to our shores.

Deadweed. Just thinking about that horrible – *thing* – made my nighttime wading through the dark waters about a hundred times worse. The weed, a type of plant that grew along the waterways of the Southern Kingdom, had thick vines that could whip and envelop entire villages in days, and whose thorns have been known to pierce even the toughest studded leather. It was deadly poisonous, and it was to that foul stuff that I lost Obasi and Wera, the summer before I was sold by the rest of the surviving villagers to Fan Hazim.

Yeah, thanks, I thought miserably as I waded, feeling the round and slimy stones of the lake bed shifting underfoot. I hoped the goats got out often and ate *all* of their gardens these days.

Thump. The egg on my back shifted, almost making me fall over into the murk of the water.

"Hey, watch it!" I hissed to it, glad that there was nothing near to hear me talking to an egg. *What an idiot*, I could imagine Nas saying about me.

BWAAR! BWAAARRM! The Dragon Horn was still blaring far above me, still loud enough to be heard past the roar of the waterfall that I was nearing. I couldn't hear the dogs though – was that a good thing or a bad thing? What if the Torvald hunting dogs were like the Hunting Lynx of the Binshee Tribes of the south, who fell into a deadly silence before they killed?

Don't think about that, either, I thought as I sidled into the spray, shivering and quaking as I ducked under, towards the far ledges in the rocks. There was no way that I could stop my teeth from chattering now, and my hands were shaking as I reached up to the walls of broken boulders.

Damn. My hand slipped on the first attempt, and on the second as well. I couldn't even feel my skin anymore, and everything felt numb with the cold.

You WILL get up that waterfall. You WILL! I told myself, finally managing to haul myself up the first few boulders through the freezing spray. *The egg is getting wet!* I thought in alarm, shifting so that I clutched it to my chest and not on my back. *Did that matter with dragon eggs?* I didn't know. I still didn't want it to get cold, though.

My hand slipped as I tried for the next crack in the rock, and I was almost about to give up when my reaching hand encountered an opening just above me. There was a cave behind the waterfall. Big, too.

"Puh-puh-please n-n-no bears..." I hissed as I reached up to haul myself into the dry of the cave. I was too tired to do anything else and knew that I wouldn't be able to stop a bear or a wolf or a pack of giraffes or whatever wild things they had up here in the blasted north, anyway.

I groaned, looking up at the dark ceiling of rock as I lay on my back, cradling the egg in my arms. To one side the waterfall was a silvery curtain and a fierce roar, and to the other I saw that the cave seemed to go back a fair way into the dark.

"I don't care. I just want to sleep." I once again told the egg, but something forced me not to accept that. I had to get warm, for the egg's sake if not for mine. I grumbled, rolled, and stumbled deeper into the cave, my shaking fingers teasing out the earthstar crystal only to drop it on the floor, but that still worked. The mineral's dull blue glow illuminated quite a high and deep cavern that was surprisingly dry and airy, and at the back there appeared to be humps of rock next to a heap of material....

Was that an old horse blanket? I wondered, seeing that yes, it was a very tired, very threadbare and dusty blanket in coarse homespun which had surprisingly held its shape. I guessed that the waterfall stopped the moths and other creepy crawlies from flying in here and eating it, and it was cold, as well.

Some other pilgrim slept here, I thought, remembering Rahim's campfire tales of old 'Dragon Monks' many hundreds of hundreds of years ago who had flocked to this mountain to be near what they thought were sacred beasts. The blanket couldn't be that old, I was sure, but I didn't care right now as I curled up to wrap myself around the egg, and then wrap the blanket around both of us.

"Yuh-you'll guh-guh-get warm soon," I promised it, holding its finely pebbled sides tight against my belly, and feeling an echo of its warmth spread through me. It was just enough to let me sleep, and so I did.

CHAPTER 3
DAYIE, THUMP

"Skreeyargh!" The sound of a very angry dragon burst into my dreams of clashing waves and dogs with glowing eyes, making me startle.

Where am I? Where are the others? I was confused for just a moment, not being able to remember why I couldn't smell the Rahim family's campfire, or the cinnamon and nutmeg they loved to season their food with.

Oh yeah. Torvald, and the Festival of Summer. The Dragon Enclosure. *The dragon egg,* I patted the warm and snugged form against my belly, only for it to jerk with the movement of the creature inside. *Thump.*

"Maybe that is what I'll call you, *Thump,*" I said with a yawn, before remembering what had woken me up. Dragon sign. I had stolen a dragon egg, and the dragons were angry.

"Skreych!" The call was insistent and sharp, but so far above me as I huddled around Thump, and muffled by the waterfall's rushing. *Maybe I should give you back,* I thought, not for the first time. "I could plead for mercy," I whispered to the egg, wondering what counsel it might be able to give me. None, as it turns out, as the egg remained stubbornly inexpressive. *Who am I kidding. You're an egg.* I shook my head. Who was I kidding about Torvald, either? Everyone in the south knew that if there was one thing that Torvaldians took *very* seriously, it was anything to do with their precious dragons.

That was why the south paid us to steal them, after all. Them and their precious bloodlines.

No, I couldn't take the egg back and expect anything better than a lifetime as a prisoner or a slave up here instead of an indentured servant with Fan. At least with Fan, I might get free… I was halfway through this thought when it was like I actually heard the words and understood what they meant for the first time.

"*When* I get free…" I said out loud, looking around me. I was in a cave in the middle of nowhere— in hostile territory, I had to admit—but still. *No Fan. No Nas. No troupe at all.*

Would I be able to make it all the way to the south myself – without the Gypsies? At least if I made it back there I would know the people – and there wouldn't be trained Academy dragons hunting me. The thought filled me with a bit of trepidation. But much more than that – with hope. Maybe I didn't have to see Fan Hazim ever again! I could take this egg to the Dagfan Training Hall myself, and that would surely be enough money for me to—

To do what? I had never seriously asked myself this question before. What did I really want to do for myself? I didn't know. I had enjoyed looking after the goats and tending our little garden, but I had hated always having to duck out of the way and hide from the other villagers. There was even a part of me that enjoyed the travelling with the Hazim Troupe… Just not the having to do all of the chores and get shouted at or cuffed around the back of the head by Fan.

Maybe I didn't have to be a servant anymore. I didn't know what I would do instead, but the thought was delicious.

BWAAAAARRM! The call of the Dragon Horn shook me from my reverie, sending my dreams collapsing and crashing back down to reality. I still had to find a way to survive Mount Hammal first.

"Skrech!" A sharp cry from outside made me startle and look up to see that something was happening to the waterfall. The silvery curtain of the walls was being flecked with color: sunshine yellow, rich gold, and even flecks of royal blue. It was the sun, it had risen over the far mountains and was streaming onto Mount Hammal.

And that was when I heard it: the call of the dragons.

The shouts and twitters started to coalesce, rising in a song that was made up of many voices, hooting and ululating as they greeted the sun. Rahim had told me about this once. All dragons welcome the sun in the morning, and bid it farewell at night. The sound swept over me, filling me with warmth and a sense of grandeur and space. I had never heard anything so beautiful, and for a while I was lost in its flows and eddies.

Thump. Another jostle from the egg, and then the sound changed. *Tock-tock.* A hard, tapping sound.

"Are you responding to them?" I asked it, and something made me pick up the egg with both hands (it felt heavier this morning, I wondered. Maybe I hadn't noticed how heavy it was in last night's frantic flight) and carried it to the edge of the waterfall, were the glows of the refracting water-light could reach its textured shell.

Tock-tock. And then, to my surprise there came a tiny sound, only audible because I was so close. *"Peep!"*

It was talking. The newt inside was talking.

"Hello?" I said hesitantly.

"Peep!"

My hands shook. I didn't know what to do. *But no, I do, don't I?* I thought, remembering when the Oberas' kid goats were born, back before this life. I had always known how to be with animals. Wera said it was my gift. I stroked the egg with one hand, feeling it radiating with warmth as I sang under my breath to it.

"Mamma-la, mamma-la..."

Tock-tock. The newt knocked, and my own song joined in tone and harmony with the dragons, and I felt – *something* – pass between us, my egg and me. A sense of hope, and gratitude and safety. When I opened my eyes again (I hadn't even realized that I had closed them) the dragon song of the morning was fading to little more than a few strains, hanging in the air, and the air was still apart from the rush of the water outside. Thump was quiet, and I imagined that it must be asleep. *Do dragons still in eggs sleep?* I thought, not knowing and wishing that I had spent more time with the ducks and chickens in our village before laughing out loud at the ridiculousness of that thought.

"Yeah, well, at least I won't have to worry about the foxes with you..." I murmured to the egg.

"Psssst!" A sound came from outside. A *human* sound, and I woke from my reverie. Whoever it was, they were close. I did as Fan had taught me and kept very still and very quiet.

"Pssst – I can hear you, come out!" The voice came again, still outside, and with relief I realized that it was none other than Rahim, Fan's husband (second husband, as she would often point out).

"Rahim?" I whispered before there was a scrabbling sound on

the rocks and, drenched from the waterfall, there clambered into my hideaway the wild, black-haired and black-bearded second husband. He wore sandy colored robes tucked into his trousers, and the look of relief on his face was obvious.

"I could hear you singing all the way across the lake!" he said in an exasperated tone, but I could tell that he wasn't really angry. "Nas came back last night, and the whole Citadel is in uproar." His eyes fell upon Thump, and I saw them light up. "Aha! Nas said that something happened, but I'm glad that we didn't lose another one."

What about losing me? My heart panged a little. I had to remind myself that, as nice as Rahim was, he still followed and believed in all the same things that Fan did. Money. Dragon eggs. Making it rich one day.

"Yeah, I got one," I said, unable to keep the disappointment from my voice. I realized that I didn't *want* to give Thump up now. *Which is stupid.* I tried to remember what this meant. *This egg will knock off years from my debt to Fan. It might even clear it.*

But with my discovery by Rahim, I also had to consider the fact that I was no longer free. My dreams of making it all the way across the northern wilds, through the Kingdom of Torvald and to the far-off south had been just that; the dreams and fantasies of a young woman.

Think, Dayie, I told myself. Be smarter. I didn't survive this long by being fanciful.

"Right. Put more of this on." He held out more pots of Fan's foul-smelling dragon lotion, and proceeded to liberally douse himself with it, too. "And put some on that egg, too," he ordered me. "We don't want its mother sniffing it out and ruining all the good work you've done." At least he thinks I did some good work, I thought a little piteously before Rahim gestured for me to wrap the egg back up and follow him out of the cave.

CHAPTER 4
DAYIE, HUE AND CRY

I'll say this for Rahim – he seemed to know his way around Hammal, I thought as he led me by twisted, narrow badger trails and fox tracks, down gullies and up ravine walls over the spur of the mountain into more civilized lands.

"My people have been coming up here for generations, right under the dragon-head's noses," Rahim confided in me as he helped me over an old, moss-covered fence and onto an overgrown track that led down through a line of orchards, terraced onto the mountainside. "Good fishing, and good money to be made in Torvald," he cackled, rolling his shoulders as he set a fast pace.

By the time the orchards started giving away to the odd granary and manor house, the sun was already burning off the morning dew, and I could hear the city that we had stolen from waking. A great white wall appeared on our left, topped with small wooden-built guard huts and large wooden platforms. On our side of the walls, this land seemed given over to allotments and then the small, crooked streets of farmer's cottages, gradually becoming more and more respectable the further down we walked.

"Don't look," Rahim coughed into his cloak, pulling his hood up over his head and grabbing me by the shoulder like he was an old peddler and I his wayward child.

"Don't look at what?" I said, turning to see. A few platforms away, along the inner wall, was a dragon.

Holy stars and roots and sand. I stumbled, almost falling over except Rahim steadied me. The dragon must have been at least a few hundred meters away and another few hundred meters up, but it was perched on the wooden platform in the way that a cat sits and looks over the rocks, down at mice. She was a Blue (I knew it was a she, somehow, don't ask me how – something in the set of the face) and that meant that she was *long*. Her tail looped over her front claws and swept back around to drape over the battlements. Even from this distance, I could see the sharp barbs that erupted along its edge. The Sinuous Blue was thin, like a desert pony – you could clearly see the barrel of its lungs before the scales shrunk inward around its belly – but I didn't think it was unwell, and I hoped it was not hungry. I could tell that was just how those dragons were made.

There was sound in the air, a click and a clack like the hiss of steel, and the Sinuous Blue turned its long, graceful snout towards us, and delicately scented the air.

"Oh no oh no oh no..." Rahim's hand was shivering on my shoulder, but before the Sinuous Blue could take any greater interest in the two ant-like peddlers entering the outskirts of its city, the air was split once more by the Dragon Horn.

BWAAAARRM! The sound rolled down the mountain around us, and the guarding Blue raised its head like an alert guard dog, turning to quiver in excitement as it looked back up the terraced layers of streets and white buildings, far to the top of the dragon mountain. Its scales made the sound of sighing sand as it stood up, arching its back like a cat before snapping its long wings out like the thunderclap of sail cloth. It sprang lightly into the air, and I watched it catch the air, powering up towards the mountain in answer to the call.

"Look, there are others up there too," I pointed out to Rahim, as a small vortex of winged shapes spiraled out of the Dragon Enclosure far, far above us.

"And they're all probably about to start hunting what you have on your back, girl!" Rahim's hand tightened painfully on my shoulder, shoving me forward.

The streets became cobbled, and then they became busy. All of the normal errands of a city, I guessed: bread-boys with their barrels of loafs running back and forth, in between the shouts of wagons as the merchants and stockmen and women worked to get their goods to market. These Torvaldites weren't like the southerners, I thought. For one, they were far lighter skinned, and with hair that would crisp up in the fierce heat of the south. But Torvald was a cosmopolitan city, for all of that – I saw some traders with the fur wraps around their legs and the heavy cloaks and beards that Rahim told me where the Northlanders, as well as many who clearly travelled from the south – darker tanned skin, or ochre and mahogany-black. All of the travelers we had met on our way up here had claimed that the Citadel of Torvald was the 'center of the world' – a claim that I knew that Fan and Rahim scoffed at and found ridiculous, but walking through these busy streets, it was easy to see why they thought so.

"Just keep your head down and do as I tell you." Rahim's grip was still fierce as he chose the smaller alleys and lanes to guide us down. The city was worried, and it showed in the way the people we passed looked up at the dragons flying high in the sky and whispered questions to each other as they moved about their business.

But, luckily for us I guessed – it was still the morning of the last day of the Festival of Summer, and that meant that the city was filled with carts and wagons, visitors and entertainers. Outside every tavern we passed there was a lounging, coughing, and sometimes still sleeping crowd of revelers from the night before. Rahim guided us through the seedier parts of the city, I recognized. Even the center of the world had its shady areas, it seemed.

I heard the stamp and shriek of horses and we emerged into the large, open area before the outer city walls (thankfully with no dragons sitting on them this time). I recognized this place as where we were parked, and already Rahim was steering me past the other stalls and collections of traders towards where our two caravans were already packed and loaded. This place must usually be some kind of market site, I thought again, but now it had been given over to wagons and stalls, caravans and hastily-built paddocks for the entertainers and troupes that came for the Festival.

"I got her!" Rahim hissed to where Fan was dousing out the small cook fire in the stationary metal sconce rivetted to the floor.

"Good." Fan looked me over, and the glare that she gave me could've melted metal. "You and me are going to talk. *Later.* Now get that thing to the Egg Boxes before I really lose my temper," she muttered under her breathe, turning to start winding ropes from where we had hung our awning.

Hi. Nice to see you're alive, Dayie. Wow – you got an egg all by yourself, Dayie? I thought angrily as I hopped up to the rear caravan back board, opened the door, and stepped inside.

"You." It was Nas, already inside and tying down the storage boxes on their little shelves. This was the 'good's' caravan, which meant that it was home to all of the props and equipment as well as our supplies and us, the youngest members of the troupe. There was a narrow bunkbed fixed into the wall, and Nas had already thrown his dirty linens over my top bunk. I growled, ignoring him as I crouched to pull at the hidden latch under one of the storage boxes that released the trapdoor at the bottom of our caravan.

"Well, at least you managed to bring *one* out with you," Nas said, and in anyone else I guess that would be a compliment – but in him I could tell that it was an accusation.

"Nice to see you too, Nas," I said, before muttering, *"Coward."*

"What did you say?" He turned to stare at me, his few wisps of mustache hair quivering like an angered gerbil. He looked ridiculous, and I had almost been caught by dogs and dragons.

"You left me up there!" I spat at him as my hand pulled at the hidden trapdoor, perfectly matching the wooden floorboards. "I could have died."

"Shame," he grunted, moving to push past me, but suddenly he didn't, and he was leaning over me, his hot, smelly breath in my ear. *"You* almost got us caught. We still might get caught, thanks to you!" He poked me hard in the back.

"Ow! What do you mean? It was your idea to steal two eggs…" I said, my anger threatening to boil over. Me and Nas had many fights over the years, but I never quite knew how far I could take it. I would be rewarded with kicks and shoves by him, or if he went to his mother, a beating by Fan.

"You took too long. We could have been gone by now, leaving last night – but no. Fan had to send Rahim up to go get you, and now look out there – Torvald have sent out the bleeding dragons!!" He poked me again, hard, his eyes dark and full of rage. "If anything comes of this, and if you breathe a word what happened to Mother, I'll kill you."

He's lying. He would never do that, I thought. *Wouldn't he?*

With a bang of the door, he was gone, leaving me with Thump in my arms, shaking with fear and anger both, and I didn't know which emotion was the stronger.

"Great," I said, taking a deep breath until my heart calmed down a little.

Tock—tock.

"I know, I know, little Thump," I murmured as I lifted the trapdoor finally to see the recessed, long and low wooden box that was mounted to the underside of the caravan. There were several compartments there, each lined with fresh straw, and I could see that Nas's egg was already tucked away safe at the end. "It's going to be alright," I murmured to the egg, easing it into one of the boxes, before packing it with handfuls of straw from the empty containers. For some reason, I knew that even as discreet and as warm as this place was for it, I didn't want it to be here. I didn't want it to be in this place, hearing the foul language and snarls from Nas – but what could I do?

"Dayie! Hurry up in there and help us with the horses!" Fan

banged on the walls of the goods caravan and I sighed again, taking one last look at Thump.

And that was when I noticed the egg had one curving crack running from tip to halfway down its fat body.

"Hold her steady, girl." Fan snipped at me where I sat beside her on the lead caravan. It turned out that I was a better driver than any of the Hazim family, probably because I knew not to push our horses too much and to give them regular breaks. We clipped towards the outer gates of the Citadel, two open avenues already bustling with other carts and people and everything under the watchful eyes of the Torvald guards.

"Halt!" I heard a bark and whistled soothingly at the horses. The gates around us were a wide pointed oval of stone with the walls themselves many meters thick. There were shouts and a few raised voices as I realized what the guards were doing. "They're stopping everyone who's leaving the Citadel," I whispered to Fan at my side, dressed in her travelling cloaks and blankets (because it was *so damn cold up here in the North*).

"Of course, they are, stupid child. We wouldn't have had this trouble last night if you had come home at the right time." She pinched me hard on the forearm out of sight.

"Ow." Home. That was a joke. That one night of freedom, and

the morning with Thump was the best thing that had happened to me in years.

These Torvald gate guards were grim-faced men and women wearing breastplates tooled with a rampant dragon and deep red cloaks. On their heads they wore pointed helmets, and in their hands, they carried long spears with curving blades like lances – apart from the one guard without a helmet and without a spear who was walking towards us. She had blonde hair, tied back in a knot, and she was looking at us seriously.

"Inspection. Everyone leaving the Citadel is to be searched, Queen Nuria's orders," the guard captain said, and her tone brooked no argument.

But I was looking at the creature that was being brought to her by another sort of Torvald guard –one that didn't wear armor; well, not metal armor anyway, but thick padded leather jerkin and leg greaves, as well as over-large gauntlets. When I saw what this younger woman was urging towards us on a lead of fine silver links, I saw the reason for this extra padding – it was a dragon.

The Messenger Dragon was small, barely as large as a hound dog, and hovering in the air on wings that thrummed blister-quick. I flinched at it instinctively, as it looked like a young Orange Drake to me – only that it was white and speckled-blue, not orange.

"Your girl's nervy," the captain muttered up to Fan, who was doing her best to look nonchalant.

"Orange Drakes," I burst out. "Down south, we have dragons like that one, only a bit bigger. And they'll pluck your eyes out as soon as they look at you," I said, before realizing that I was gabbling and shut up, my face flushing crimson.

"Huh." The captain looked at me briefly. "Well, the Messenger Dragons aren't as bad as that. We train 'em ourselves." She nodded to the other woman, who tugged lightly on the hanging chain and the Messenger Dragon hummed over to alight on the caravan behind us, its head bobbing up and down as it sniffed for something.

The eggs. I wondered if I had put enough of that dragon salve on it as Rahim had told me too. I wondered if Nas had put enough of the same dragon salve on his...

"You're from the Southern Kingdom then?" The captain was leaning against the baseboard at my feet as she didn't take her eyes off the Messenger Dragon. It didn't seem to find what it was looking for, and hopped through the air to the rear caravan, piloted by Rahim. The goods caravan.

"You've come a long way," the captain growled.

This time it was Fan who cleared her throat. "We're Gypsies from ancient and long lost Shaar, my good woman," she said imperiously. "We're used to travelling a long way."

Her tone was too argumentative, too combative I knew, and as the captain looked up to regard the woman at my side I added quickly, "And that's why we wouldn't miss a chance to come up here to see the Festival of Summer I've been hearing so much about," I said.

The captain's look softened a little as she regarded me, before turning back to the Messenger Dragon on the goods caravan. I saw the guard nod at its handler, then she clapped a gauntleted hand on the side of our wagon and stepped back. "You're good to go. Have a pleasant journey through Torvald lands."

"Oh, we will, officer…" Fan said, smiling broadly as I clicked my tongue to tell our horses to start trotting forward, and, in a just a few heartbeats we were outside of the Citadel walls and joining in the rivers of traffic that led to the southern roads.

"And don't you *ever* dare to talk for me again!" Fan spat at me as she hopped lightly down from the caravan and into the wooded clearing that she had directed us too.

We had been heading south along the main roads for the best part of the day, until mid-afternoon when Fan had conversed with Rahim and he had directed us down a smaller branching track, and then off past fields and under the eaves of woods. We hadn't stopped for lunch or rest until now, when the sun was already lowering in the western sky. I don't know how far we had come, but I did know that the horses were stumbling and likely to trip and throw a shoe if we pushed them any further.

"Uh...?" I said in shocked astonishment at Fan as she stalked across the clearing, kicking drifts of leaves first one way and then another in her fury.

"You know what I mean. *Get* down here and come to me, right *now!*" the older woman screeched.

"But the horses need seeing to..." I said, before realizing how cowardly that sounded. This argument had been brewing the whole journey home, and now that we were far from other travelers and prying eyes and ears, Fan felt comfortable enough to release her rage.

"Are you disobeying me? Don't forget who paid for your life, girl!" She stamped her foot. "You can see to your blessed horses later, after I've let with you!"

"Well, at least she's not going to kill me just yet, then," I whispered soothingly to our nervous beasts as I slid from the drivers' bench and down from the baseboard to the clearing floor.

Whap! Her back-handed slap caught me by surprise, spinning me around and back to the caravan wall. Tears instantly blossomed in my eyes, but I had no time to wonder if she had split my lip or worse as I felt her claw-like hands seize my long hair, and she dragged me backwards into the center of the clearing.

"You *stupid,* ungrateful little girl!" Fan threw me to the floor, before matching her shouts with a sharp kick to my belly.

"*Ach!*" The pain rippled through me. "What did I do – I got you the egg!" I gasped in pain, flinching as Fan raised her foot again – but only kicked the drifts of leaves instead.

"You told that guard we were from the Southern Kingdom! How am I going to run this operation again?" Fan said. "You *do* realize what it is we're doing, don't you?"

I was wise enough to not say anything. I'd learnt that answering her – even helpfully – would only inflame Fan's anger when she was like this.

"*My* work with the Training Hall only lasts as long as the Training Hall doesn't get trouble from the Ruling Families in Dagfan. If Torvald starts breathing down their neck – then that's it. Our life as Dragon Traders is finished, and it'll be back to plying two-bit villages up and down the coast with fortunes while we try to not get killed by the Deadweed!"

I stayed huddled. It still wasn't safe to uncurl yet.

"And Nas told me how you left him up there on the mountain – even after he came in and rescued you!"

What!? It was hard to control my outrage, but I managed it. *Nas. You pig.*

This time, Fan knelt close over me, snarling in my ear. "*One* more piece of grief from you, my girl – and I'll throw you to

Deadweed myself. Let's see how good your 'way with animals' gets you then, huh!"

Animals. Wera always said I was good with animals. I mentally corrected her, as Fan stood up slowly, hissing out a long breath and straightening her hair.

"It's lucky for you that you still owe me a lot of money, Dayie. That means you get to live. And *work.* Now stop sniveling and get up – tend to the horses and dig out a toilet pit for us."

Lucky me.

🐉

"Dayie, come and get some food."

Rahim beckoned me to the fire. It was a lot later, and I had been hiding by the edge of the caravans with the tethered horses, out of the way of Fan's wrath and Nas's spiteful little looks. Fan had retired to her caravan and Nas was still sitting against the tree on the other side of the fire, but at least Rahim was there. He wasn't a *fair* man, I considered as I stepped into the circle of fire light, but at least he could be a nicer person than either of the others.

Nas's sucked his teeth as I hunched, grateful for the warmth at least, but I ignored him. He would be insufferable for a few days, but then Fan would start spreading her foul mood around the troupe and he'd catch some of it as well – or at least, I hoped.

"There." With a clang he ladled out a generous slop of lamb stew into a tin cup and handed it over to me, before throwing me a hunk of bread. His eyes were shadowed as he looked at me, and I wondered if it was with worry or regret – or maybe he was just calculating his costs as he looked at me. I didn't know. Either way, food was food, and I ate quickly. It tasted good.

"Esterbrigge," Rahim cleared his throat and said suddenly.

"What?" Nas said rudely, looking up from the bit of carving he was failing at.

"We're going to travel south to the Torvald town of Esterbrigge and then take the river boats south to Dagfan," Rahim declared. That wasn't our usual route, and I started to frown.

"But… why? Esterbrigge is right over near the eastern marches of Torvald, isn't it?" I asked.

"Because of *you*," Nas snorted in disgust, clearly priding himself on his display of knowledge. "We can't take the southern road straight to the Fury Mountains because Torvald will be searching for the eggs."

"That's right, son," Rahim grunted measuredly. "I have some family out in Esterbrigge, and they can pack us away on one of their transport barges and we'll be through the Fury Mountains in no time." He scratched at his beard. "It might even take us about the same time as the southern road as we'll be travelling by water. Which will make Fan happy, at least," he added in a slightly exaggerated whisper. I never understood why he stayed with her, but then again, I didn't understand much of anything about Fan at all. I knew that she and Rahim had been travelling all over the south for a long time before they arrived at the idea of becoming dragon traders – the dangerous profession that delivered wild dragon eggs to Dagfan's Training Hall in return for a lot of money.

The only problem was, that most Dragon Traders concentrated on the wild mountain dragons of the southlands, and thus had very short careers. And lives. If Fan actually managed to pull this off, to introduce two extra noble northern dragonstock into the southern breeding programs, then that would make Fan the most successful Dragon Trader of all time. I *thought* the Training Hall already had some northern dragons, but I wasn't certain. I knew that they didn't have many, for sure.

"We travel fast, and we travel quiet," Rahim stated to both of us. "So I want no more fighting between you two, you hear? Nothing to cause suspicion, or make my life any harder."

"Yes, Father," Nas said, and I mumbled my agreement. Not that I believed that Nas would keep his end of the bargain at all.

"I'm going to bed," I said, picking up all of the cups and plates to wash up on my way past. Rahim was already taking out his small bottle of brandy, and I knew that would keep both him and Nas occupied for several hours to come.

After doing their dishes for them (it had become almost second nature now, unfortunately) I retired to the goods caravan and closed the door lightly behind me. I waited in the darkness until I heard Rahim's gruff voice working its way through an old Shaar song. That was where he always said his people came from, 'Distant Shaar; long ago and far-away' as he claimed. I think he was making it up.

I knelt to the floor, released the trapdoor catch and eased it open to take a look at Thump. "Hey," I said, feeling a little surge of joy just at seeing it.

The egg had shifted in its seat, and now I could see that another curling crack had joined the first, making an almost spiral across its top.

"You've been busy!" I whispered in delight.

Tock-tock.

It was hard to not feel joy at this little life (not so little, to be honest) struggling to survive. I wished it the best. It was a fighter. But then, in the very next heartbeat I wondered what sort of life I was about to give it.

The Training Hall of Dagfan only had seven Riders, I knew. 'The Seven,' as they were called, were almost regarded as gods by the people of Dagfan. Tales of their training with their fierce and savage dragons were legendary.

"Is that what you want, little Thump?" I whispered, but this time got no response.

Acting on the same impulse that allowed me to know just when a horse was about to go lame, or was in foal before it showed, I reached down to pick up my egg and instead stuffed the wad of my cloak in the hole, before covering it with another thick layer of straw. Gingerly, I carried Thump up to my bunk and then curled myself around it, just as I had in the cave. Within moments, a radiating, soothing warmth spread from the egg into me and I fell into the sort of deep restful sleep that I had only rarely over the last few years.

It didn't occur to me then that by the time that morning came, everything would be different. Before first light, I was woken up by screams and shouts as we were attacked by Dragon Riders from Torvald.

CHAPTER 5
DAYIE, ON THE RUN

The smell of smoke and burning woke me.

"Flee! Get to the horses – run!" Rahim bellowed outside. I threw aside my scratchy blanket as I sat up in alarm and realizing I still had Thump cuddled against me, quickly wrapped the blanket over us again.

"What's going on?" I said, the air smelled of soot and my eyes were stinging.

"Get up! Your actions have doomed us all!" It was Nas, already rolling from his bunk, seizing his boots and his kitbag and kicking open the door – to be engulfed in a brief wave of smoke. He coughed and hacked, and jumped out of the goods caravan, leaving me and Thump behind.

Fear lent speed to my actions as I wrapped Thump in my spare cloak and threw my things on as the goods caravan started to fill with the bluish haze of smoke. What do I do? What do I do? I thought as my bare feet hit the floorboards and I seized my walking staff from the side. My mind was blurring and racing as I tried to think. What should I carry? What would I need?

I had the egg, that was all. I jumped out of the caravan and into the smoke after Nas.

"Skreyargh!" The sky split with the sound of Dragon Riders as I stumbled through the smoke, heading for the horses. I had to release them, give them a chance to live at least. The two caravans were as yet unharmed, but flames were shooting up the sides of the nearest trees. It was hard to tell if it was morning or still night as the smoke was so thick.

Whoosh. Something large and very dark moved overhead, and the fierce wind of its passage sent the flaming trees into a crescendo of noise, and the subsequent air-blast almost threw me off my feet. Looking up, I caught a glimpse of the shape as it swooped upward after its attack run. The powerful beat of its wings had shredded the smoke for a moment, and I saw the rear claws and the long tail arching across the sky of an adult Stocky Green dragon.

It was immense. It was also terrifying.

"Dayie!" Someone screeched. "Get those horses harnessed to

the goods caravan, now!" It was Fan, dragging bags and bundles of precious valuables from her own lead caravan, one hand moving to cover her mouth.

"There's no time!" I shouted, still stumbling to where the panicked horses were rearing and screaming. The fire was still on the other side of the clearing to them, but horses hate fire. They're sensible like that.

"You do as I tell y—" Fan screamed at me, before the world split open with a powerful crash.

One of the trees had fallen, crashing straight through the canopy of its brethren, burning as it fell, to land across the clearing, our camp, and the goods caravan that I had so recently been inside.

No! Nas's egg! I was shocked. Was it still okay? Had the tree smashed it? I almost rushed back, but the conflagration of tree and broken caravan was too fierce. Flames crackled and leapt into the air, and the heat scalded my face. I could no longer see Fan who was on the other side of the burning caravan and of Nas and Rahim there was no sign.

This was it. This was my chance. I slipped the horses' knots from the tree (thanking the sands that I had kept them on a hitch knot last night) before turning and running after their galloping hooves, into the woods.

I was going to survive. I was a fighter.

Thump. The egg on my back was agitated, and I didn't blame it as I blundered through the woods, my desperate scramble now turning into an exhausted lurch. How long had I been running for? Which direction was I going in? I had no idea. And why were there so many be-damned trees in the North? I thought, as I stubbed my bare feet for the umpteenth time on an exposed route.

Thump. The egg moved once more.

"Easy, I know. We'll stop soon…" I promised it, as I finally caught up with the horses. They had congregated on a wide sward of grass in the woods, beside where the ground fell down steeply, given over to shrubs and spindly trees, and they wouldn't go any further.

When I collapsed to my knees on the grass beside them, I realized just why they had stopped running. It wasn't just tiredness – it was that down the incline, revealed by a gap in the trees, there were Torvald dragons.

"Oh crap," I breathed, looking at the two shapes—still a long way away—that swooped downward and then back up, in obvious attacking runs. One was a Stocky Green, and the other was a much longer and much thinner Sinuous Blue. They seemed to be taking it in turns to swoop back and forth along – *what was that?* I set the egg down on the grass, and crept forward to get a better look.

The rise of land that we were on overlooked a wooded valley with a snaking river winding through the middle – and, creeping up the bottom of that valley was a lurid discoloration. It was bright, verdant green at the tips, hiding thick purple-brown vines that moved up the valley. When I say *moved,* I do actually mean *moving* as even from this height I could see the bright green tendrils flailing and writhing at the outer edges of the mass. The river further up was entirely choked by the stuff, and the Torvald dragons were swooping down to send plumes of flame after flame against it.

Deadweed. I knew it well. It was what had killed Obasi and Wera, after all. Deadweed had thorns that could puncture armor, and its reaching vines seemed to know where you were as they grabbed at you, lightning-quick. Its putrid yellow flowers also exuded a mist when they opened that could kill a grown man instantly if he breathed it. It was the bane of the south, and I'd heard that it had only recently started infecting the northlands, travelling along the coast and rivers like I was watching now.

"That means the Torvald Dragons weren't trying to attack us after all," I sighed in relief, crawling back to the horses and Thump behind me. That meant that these Torvald Dragons hadn't scented us yet, thanks to Fan's dragon ointment – *of which I had none left,* I realized.

My luck, at least, seemed to have changed though, as the distant Green and Blue fired their last few parting shots, setting fire not just to the river weed, but also to the surrounding tree lines as well. Deadweed was a strange conundrum, travelling along the coast and rivers in spores or seeds, to take route randomly wherever there was water and the right conditions. That was what made it so difficult to eradicate, as you might fight off a major outbreak at the river mouth, only for it to crop up several hundred leagues up and downstream the next season. This river appeared to just have one long mass that had been quietly growing in the middle of the valley, relatively contained from the rest of Torvald, thankfully.

"Skreych!" The dragons whistled and shrieked at each other as they climbed out of the valley, their destructive job done. We had just been camped in the wrong place, at the wrong time, and I was very grateful for that fact. I was now out here, free from Fan and the others.

Tock-tock...Crack! An unexpected sound from Thump made me turn around and look, in awe, as another crack appeared on the outer shell.

It was amazing.

It was also very, very bad news.

"Uh, Thump? If you *don't* hatch right now, that would be just great..." I whispered as I saw the crack reach all the way around to the other two, and then start to wobble and shake.

Tock. Tock-tock!

"No, Thump, please don't…" I said uselessly as the dragon acted on a millennia old impulse, and the shell cracked and burst.

It was beautiful.

It was the red squiggle of a dragon newt, its body easily already as big as a small dog, and as bright as a drop of crimson blood. Crimson. It was one of the rare Crimson Reds, famed for being stronger, braver, and more headstrong than any other.

The dragon newt already had long ears that it flexed slowly, opening them up in a fanning movement at the back of its long snout that lightened to the color of bone that I guessed must be its egg tooth. If they were anything like chickens, that would fall off in a matter of hours, if not days. It opened its maw to reveal two perfectly-formed rows of pinprick teeth, and a fleshy pink – and forked tongue.

And its eyes. My breath stopped. It had opened its eyelids to reveal two golden-green orbs, perfectly bright, sparkling, and slit down the middle like a cat's.

"*Peeep!*" the thing beeped, before burping and hissing at me. It moved its head back and forth, before the lower shell burst outwards as it pushed with its stocky little red-scaled legs. The folds of scale along them and its belly looked baggy as if the creature had been born with room to grow into. On its sides were two still tightly curled wings looking like folded sailcloth of a deep black-red, and raising behind it in wobbly gestures was a fat and long tail, already with little barbs apparent on its spine.

The dragon newt peeped at me again as it tottered forward before promptly falling over into the grass.

What do I do? I looked at the thing for a second, before my instincts kicked in. It was a baby. A new baby. It needed warmth, it needed its mother's scent, and it needed food.

Without thinking, I scooped up the newt into my arms (groaning at how heavy it was already), cuddling it to myself and folding the blanket over it. Now what? The newt needs food. Food that I haven't got to give it. "What do you eat, anyway?" I asked it, my heart breaking at how cute and fierce it was all at the same time. *Milk?* I haven't got any. *Don't birds feed their young their own food?* I wasn't about to do that.

"Scree-pip!" The newt made a little buzzing chirrup, pushing against my chest with its powerful legs as it adjusted itself in my arms and settled—like a cat. I watched as it folded its head back into its belly and closed its gold eyes. Within a few seconds it had huffed to sleep and was now burbling snottily against me.

"Mamma-la, mamma-la," I sang to it, daring to stroke it with one hand. Thump felt warm under my hand, and I could feel the strong kick of its heartbeat. It would be strong, and healthy – but only if I could find it some food.

I looked to the horses, and for once in my life cursed the fact that I was always thorough in my job, removing their paniers before tethering them up last night – so there was no chance of them having any supplies on them. Next, my gaze swept to the horizon, and the drifts of burning Deadweed that were rising and shredding on the wind. I couldn't see any sign of a settlement, and I had no idea how far we were from the nearest one.

Think, Dayie, I told myself. You have no food, no camping gear, no compass, and no clue where you're going. And the pain from my dirty feet reminded me that I also had no shoes.

"No," I whispered as my heart fell, realizing what it was I had to do next. Not for me, but for Thump. I made an awkward sling for the newt (which he burbled through, completely oblivious) before whistling and clicking to the horses until they started to pick their way towards me.

I would have to go back to the only place where I knew there would be food. The camp of Fan and Rahim.

CHAPTER 6
DAYIE, THE ROAD SOUTH

The clearing was a mess. The fire had burned its way through one entire side, stopped only by the damp of the earth and the fall of several of the trees against their fellows, but it still smoldered. The ground was scorched black in the places that it was visible, but everywhere else was a fine grey silt of ash. I didn't know much about woodlands, but I was sure that this wouldn't be a good place to hang around in. Didn't forest fires have a tendency to reignite?

"Scree-pip!" burbled Thump against me, moving its solid little claws awkwardly as if it wanted to get out.

"What's wrong, too tight?" I said as I shifted the sling, but Thump moved spastically and kicked his sharp back claws to get out. "You don't want to get out there, it's a mess!" I scolded, but the sharp jag of its claws showed me otherwise, and already he (I knew it was a he, somehow) was too big for me to control as he first flopped, then kicked out to land with a thud on the ground.

The horses behind us wouldn't go near the clearing, shying away, snorting, and then nervously picking their way through the good trees to the far side.

"Okay then, just don't roam too far, please," I murmured to them, my concentration taken with Thump's faltering steps. Or not so faltering, as he half hopped, half jumped forward into the mess of ash and dirt with some enthusiasm.

"Oh, for goodness sake!" I said as he instantly coated himself with the thick, sludgy ash and started nosing through the dirt as if seeking something. I had thought that he would be weaker than this, only being a few hours since he had hatched – but then again, he was a dragon. Maybe they had to grow up quick in their fierce world.

Keeping one eye on the newt, I picked gingerly through the ash, warm on my bare feet, until I approached the mound of wreckage that had been the goods caravan and the burning tree. Almost all of it was a charred mess, but there were still recognizable items in the destruction: a tattered and mostly burned bit of blanket, a few pots, cutlery, and a good hunting knife. All useful things, I thought – but not what I was looking for.

Chomp. Chomp. *Hack.* I straightened up to see that Thump had gleefully resorted to mouthing one of the burned and charred wheels of the wagon, breaking off bits of the charcoal-wood and was happily crunching it down into grits in its strong jaws.

"Oh, so you like burnt stuff, do you?" I thought. Maybe it shouldn't surprise me that fire-breathing dragons eat charcoal. Burn your meal before eating it, I suppose.

Well, that was one less problem to worry about, I thought. Using the tattered blanket as wrappings as I pushed and heaved at the branches to get at some of the less damaged contents of our caravan. Where was the other egg? I kicked around the burning mess – but I couldn't find it. It was gone.

In the end, and after much swearing and burnt hands, I came away with a mostly-intact half-bag of grain (I had to shovel out the burnt top layer), a very small bag of now roasted dried fruit, and, wonder of wonders, two empty water skins. I had enough to keep me and Thump alive for a few days at least.

"Screep!" The newt bounced up towards me, its belly now a round and distended fat globe, nosing happily at the fruit bag.

"Gotta have something healthy," I laughed as I doled out a generous handful and he eagerly snatched them from my hand hungrily, before rooting around in the sooty mulch for the ones that its snout had dislodged. It didn't seem to mind the state of its food as his hissed and its belly made burbling noises.

"Now, I guess we should get you some water, how about that?" I said to it.

"We've got the water," said a voice from the edge of the clearing, sending me to my feet and dislodging Thump to sprawl on the dirt with an outraged hiss.

It was Rahim, and he looked terrible. He stepped out of the greener side of the undergrowth, already leading one of the horses that I had brought back by a tether-rope, and he was coated with grey soot and ash. His beard was disheveled, and he had deep shadows under his eyes. Over his shoulder was slung a wide canvas pack that was clearly heavy with all of the things he had already salvaged from the fire.

"You survived," he stated, a ghost of a smile on his face that quickly turned into alarm when he saw the dragon newt at my feet. "By the sands…" he froze, his eyes looking wondrously to me, then back to the baby dragon, and then back to me. "Is that what I think it is…"

"If what you think it is happens to be a baby dragon," I replied. I don't know where I got my courage from. Just being around Thump changed everything. I no longer felt at Rahim's or Fan's mercy. I felt like I had a purpose beyond making them money. I had to look after this little creature until… *Until what?* I still had no idea what we were going to do.

"Oh hell," Rahim shook his head. "This has never happened before. The Training Hall hatches them, not the Dragon Traders." He pulled a face and his brows furrowed. I could tell he was calculating something.

"Maybe the Training Hall won't take him now…" I said lightly, steeling myself to run, to pick up Thump if I could, and run.

But where are you going to go? The worry battled my newfound courage. *Back to Torvald? And be tried as a dragon thief?* How long could me and Thump live in the wilds alone before we either starved, or were discovered?

"Oh, they'll take him alright," Rahim nodded. "But it might lower the price." Then a brighter look crossed his features. "Or it might raise it."

"Uh. I'm not sure that's a good idea…" I said, feeling the lump of my heart in my throat. Was I really daring to disagree with the Dragon Traders? Maybe I was only doing so because I hadn't seen Fan anywhere. Nor the lead caravan, as it happened. Sparing a look at the jittery horses, I realized that two had always been missing. *So Fan had managed to hitch her own caravan and high-tail it out of here?*

"It *is* the idea." Rahim broke my thoughts with a serious look, at me, and then over my shoulder to where, emerging behind me came Nas with his knife and his own bulging pack. They had me outnumbered, and, from the gleeful look on Nas's face, he had been waiting for the moment when he could beat me like his mother did.

Thump hissed at my side, first at Nas, then at Rahim.

"Come on," Rahim's tone was still grave, but he managed to

take a little of the threat out of it. "*We* have the water, and *we* have the horses that you found." A considered nod. "Thank you for that. We won't die out here, any of us. Now, I suggest you agree to come with us to Dagfan, as we originally planned, and take this little monster of yours to the Training Hall."

"Thump's not a monster!" I said vehemently, as the newt managed to hiss once again below me. He already stood nearly as tall as my knee.

"Thump? That's what you called it?" Nas taunted me. "Wow. What a noble and heroic name. That will go down in history as one of the dumbest names a dragon ever had…"

"*He*. Thump is a he," I spat back at him, but all of a sudden I could feel how parched my throat was. I needed water. Thump needed water.

"He'll give his Rider his own name before too long," Rahim said, nodding at Thump.

"What?" I was confused.

"Dragons have their own names. In their heads. Their name is what they are, and the old tales say that they share it with their Riders," Rahim said sagely. "Now, are we agreed? You come with us, with 'Thump' to the Training Hall? If you can keep it from flying off or eating us, then I promise that I'll call your debt to us settled afterwards."

Why is he doing that? I thought, before I saw in the man's eyes why. He didn't think any of us were going to make it. He had lost his wife – Fan had abandoned us all to die when she thought that the Torvald Dragon Riders had come for us – and now he was struggling to find a way to stay alive.

Which meant me, and this dragon here, I thought. I'm going to be free just as soon as we travel south. I looked again at the newt now leaning heavily against my calf with its eyes already drooping. It was tired, and probably dehydrated. Bending down, I scooped him back into the sling as he hissed sleepily. *Maybe we'll find another way to escape,* I thought as I looked at the newt, and Rahim and Nas relaxed, thinking they had won.

If I can steal enough food, money, and one of the horses... I thought, before realizing that I had no idea what I would do after that. Maybe the Training Hall really was the best place for him, I had to force myself to consider. At least the dragons had beds and food there, and he would be amongst his own kind.

"Aha!" Nas sounded victorious as he had started to kick aside the wreckage of the caravan, in his hands he was levering and pushing at 'his' Torvald egg, still stubbornly uncracked. "Looks like you're not going to be the only one with a dragon!" he crowed, making me feel sick.

"Come on." Rahim grumbled. "I don't want to waste any more time out here, with those damn Torvald Riders out there." He looked suspiciously up at the skies, then lead the way, which to my shame, I grudgingly follow. "We won't be going to Esterbrigge now," he called back over his shoulder. "Not with *that.*" He didn't have to explain what he meant by that, as I knew he meant Thump. "We're going as fast south as possible. Cross country until we hit the Fury Mountains."

I could have told him that the Dragon Riders of Torvald weren't searching for us at all, but were instead looking for the Deadweed, but I decided not to. At least if Rahim and Nas were busy worrying about what was up in the skies, that might give me and Thump a chance to escape.

That chance, however, did not come soon as it turned out, as Rahim led us south at a brutal pace. At least we had the horses; four in total after Fan had taken the other two, and enough room for all of us to ride. We had lost the saddles, but Rahim and I were comfortable using blankets instead. Nas, on the other hand, moaned almost the entire journey.

"When is it going to hatch, then?" he asked me once again, one hand straying to the large mound behind him in his sack.

"*I* don't know, do I?" I snipped back. I wasn't actually in a foul mood as it was spitting a refreshing rain of the sort we had so little of in the south. Actually, I *did* know when Nas's egg would hatch, thanks to my 'gift'. Call it intuition, or maybe the result of having just spent longer around living things than Nas had ever done – or probably ever would in his life – but I could look at his egg and just *know* that it was going to be a slow grower. The newt hadn't woken up inside there yet; it was still growing.

"You need to keep her warm," I told him. *Young dragon eggs need warmth,* again a piece of knowledge that popped into my head from nowhere.

"I thought *you* didn't know anything?" Nas said back to me, earning a sharp bark of reprimand to us both from Rahim up in front. We had been travelling south for what felt like weeks, but I knew that it couldn't have been. The days had become a weary, awkward, stressful – but also a sort of happy blur as we pushed ourselves up and down wooded valleys, picked around the sides of fields, tracked across high moors and followed river routes south once again. Every night we would stop only when it was truly dark, and Rahim would wake us up again in the greys before the dawn to resume our trek. Some days the older Gypsy would allow us to pause for lunch, if we found a particularly good stream or meadow to rest the horses – and twice he had bid us wait in the nearby woods as he had slipped into a nearby hamlet to return with heavy sacks of stolen food and wine.

"Before we were Dragon Traders, this was how we lived," Rahim confided in us late one night around our scratch of a fire. Thump had curled himself as close as he could to the burning coals and would usually eat the remnants of the fire in the morning. "Fan hated it, saying that we were made for better things," Rahim said sadly into the fire. "She said that we were from the ruling families of distant Shaar. We were made for palaces and warring with our neighbors on tall and fast ships. Not out here stealing chickens and some widow's penny pot."

I could see that Rahim loved his wife, in his own way, and although the idea disgusted and shocked me, I even started to feel a little sorry for him. Rahim appeared to be a man who was much *more* suited to this roving life, much more so than either me or his son Nas. But he was also a man who had been broken by the betrayal of his wife, and I guess that made him obsess about getting this one last 'job' done.

The land had started to change around us, the woodlands becoming a little sparser and giving themselves over to wide and long fields of rippling wheats. We were heading into the south, and the warmth of my home. But, rising every day in front of us were the jagged teeth of the Fury Mountains. Even in the morning they would gather the storm clouds that gave them their name and appear as a low black line across the southern horizon.

Now, however, we had stepped out of a stand of sparse and sun-bleached trees to see long grasslands and plains ahead of us, split by a large causeway.

"The Great Southern Road," I said, remembering it from the

journey up here. It was built high from the plains, its edges an easy ten feet up to the packed rock surface. Scrubby trees and ditches ran along the embanked edge, and it was into this wilding edge that Rahim directed us.

"We can't risk bringing that"—he nodded to where Thump was treading through the last of the trees to sniff at the grasslands air—"up onto the roadway with us."

The Crimson Red had grown in the few weeks that we had been travelling. So much so that even Rahim and Nas kept on sharing looks during the day and would suddenly fall quiet when I woke up in the morning.

They didn't know what to make of Thump's growth. I looked over at the young dragon. Thump was now almost as large as the horse that I rode, with strong, powerful limbs that were as thick as young trees. His chest had filled out, and he had only had a bit of that baggy of scaled skin left running along his undercarriage, telling me that he had much more to grow yet. His tail was the longest thing about him, however – it stretched out behind him to almost the same length again and ended in cruel barbs. As if sensing my gaze, he turned and blinked his large golden eyes at me slowly.

You're just about as handsome as they come, I thought toward him, smiling.

"Hss." He opened his maw and let his long, forked tongue loll out in a way that I somehow knew was his way of smiling or laughing. Sometimes it even seemed like he knew just what I was thinking!

I don't know why he had grown that fast in the few weeks that we had been travelling fast. Was it the charcoal that he was eating every morning and night? Was it the rabbits and voles that he hunted (a sudden, quick pounce and a terrified, final squeak from his prey)? *Maybe dragons just grow that fast,* I told myself, and wondered if that was a lie.

Wera had always said that animals responded to me. What if Rahim and Nas were right to look at me darkly like that – what if *I* was the one causing Thump's growth?

The thought made me shiver, despite the relative warmth of these grasslands that we were approaching. I had seen people look at me with that mixture of fear and hatred before. The villagers who had surrounded me after Obasi and Wera had been taken by the Deadweed. They had finally summoned their courage to challenge *me* about the devilish plant – as if *I* had created it, or caused it to grow so fast and attack our village!

And after that they had sold me to Fan, I remembered miserably. But at least if they hadn't done that, then they might have run me out of the village – or even killed me.

"He'll be fine." I cleared my throat as I looked back over to where Rahim and Nas were regarding me silently. "He knows how to be quiet," I assured them.

"He better had," Rahim murmured, earning a short hiss from Thump, before we moved, as one, out of the woods to join the thickets and rabbit-trails by the side of the Southern Roadway.

"Halt! In the name of the queen!" We were into our second day beside the Southern Roadway when we heard a commotion approaching us.

"Shh!" Rahim put a stubby finger to his lips and we all froze. We were deep in the thickets of goat willow and alder along the muddy creek that ran on this side of the embankment, and it was impossible to see what was happening on the road above us – but it didn't sound good.

Thud. The Crimson Red thumped his tail in annoyance on the dirt. It was too wet down here for him – not that he didn't like water – he loved the streams and rivers that we had crossed earlier, spending as much time as he would be allowed to dive in and out, catching the bright silver wriggles of fish before paddling to shore to enjoy his feasts – but in this glorified ditch, it was muddy and smelled faintly of fox.

"Easy," I whispered to him, setting a hand to his large back scales. They were large and polished, and warm to the touch.

"Nas – you go see what's happening up there. Keep out of sight," Rahim ordered his son, only for him to look at me with a glare.

"Why can't *she* go?" he hissed stubbornly.

Rahim groaned under his breath, rubbing his hand over his face. "Because if you really want to be left here without Dayie but with her dragon, then by all means, I'll send her!" Their suspicions over Thump had started to turn to fear over his size; his big claws, and the sharp bone-white of his teeth. I knew that was a bad sign from past experience. Fear leads to hatred. I saw Nas look between me and Thump, who proceeded to lick his lips very slowly as if he knew exactly just what we were talking about. Maybe he did.

"Fine." Nas turned to scrabble up out of the ditch, and within a moment had disappeared, leaving Rahim and me and Thump below.

We could hear the approaching jangle of harnesses and the thunder of hooves, before a short blast of a horn broke through the trees, making Thump startle and swish his tail in agitation.

"Stop! By Order of Queen Nuria!" We heard the thin, muffled voices call far above us, and then the sound of angry muttered voices.

"It's not us," I said to Rahim, keeping my voice low. "If it was – they would have sent dragons." I was sure of it. What we had done – what *I* had done – was to steal from the very dragon sanctuary what was most sacred to all of Torvald. I don't know how long a dragon holds a grudge for, but I rather think that it might be a very long time indeed.

"Hm. I'd still not want to be accidentally found out, thank you very much," Rahim shot back at me just before we heard a thrashing about in the trees, and the sliding form of Nas appeared through the bushes.

"What is it?" Rahim asked immediately.

"It's the Torvald guards. A whole contingent of them. They were telling the travelers that they can't go any further – that they have to leave the roadway and camp for the night."

"What?" Rahim's eyes went wide. "Why? We're almost at the Fury Mountains!" The older Gypsy was right, the Fury Mountains had been rising steadily hour after hour as we had proceeded south, and now they were a wall of black rock ahead of us, erupting from the sparse, grassy grounds almost without warning. The southern half of the sky was gloomy and dark as the Fury Mountains were always crowned with thunderclouds, it seemed.

And the Southern Gate – the pass that led straight through the mountains and to the Southern Kingdom— was straight ahead of us.

"The guards told the travelers up there that they're closing the southern roadway, and that their dragons are coming from Torvald." Nas's eyes were round with fear.

"Maybe they found out that it's the Southern Kingdom that's been taking their eggs," I said in what I now saw was a very unhelpful comment as Rahim's glance went dark with fury. *Or maybe it was the Deadweed that I saw them attack?* I thought, looking at Nas and Rahim calculatingly. They had thought that the Dragon Riders had attacked earlier in the forest because of *us,* and our theft. That had made them scared and had made them concentrate on getting us south. But now? It was *me* that wondered if the dragons above were searching for us.

"And whose fault is that?" he asked sarcastically. "If your actions have started a war between the realms…"

A war? I stumbled on my feet. But it hadn't even been my idea to steal the eggs – it was Fan's! I had never even considered the possibility that would be the outcome of our theft. But why not? I chided myself. Did I not realize I was stealing on behalf of Dagfan? No, I hadn't – I had just been trying to survive Fan's orders.

"They wouldn't. That won't happen, will it?" I said in a small voice as we heard the shouts and whistles as travelers above us started approaching. We'd passed an 'on-ramp' a little way back – a place for other travelers top get access to the road and for weary travelers to pull off for the night – and I guessed that it was to this place that they were turning their wagons and horses.

"Do we go forward or back?" I said. Everything was happening too fast. I didn't know what we should do. What I wanted to do.

"Can't go back, can't risk getting discovered, not with *that.*"

Rahim nodded at the Crimson Red at my side, and for his answer, he climbed onto his horse and started urging and kicking it onward, south, through the creek. "Our only hope is to out-ride the guards. Get to the Southern Gate before they do. Otherwise we have no hope of getting through to the South Kingdom." He was already picking up his pace, urging his horse on as fast as he dared.

"Get there before the Torvald dragons do?" I murmured, now talking to myself as Nas had leapt to his own horse and followed his father. Thump looked both north and south, before looking at me with clear irritation.

"I know, but what can I do?" I said, nodding for us to follow the others.

Rahim pushed his steed at a punishing pace, especially given the terrain. He couldn't give the steed her head, and she couldn't gallop in the confined avenue of this gully, with its snagged roots and overhanging branches, but he cantered as fast as he dared, forcing us to try and keep pace with him.

Bloody fool will have her trip, I thought, looking over to how Thump was doing, which, as it goes, was absolutely fine; the dragon was winnowing through the bushes and trees with agility and grace that belied his size, and if he was struck and scraped by any of the blackthorn branches, they just splintered, unable to penetrate his already tough hide.

I didn't have so tough a hide, however, and it wasn't long before my shoulders burned with the repeated scratches. I pitied the poor horses who stamped and threw their heads thanks to the annoying bramble scratches.

"This is madness!" I dared to call out to them, earning a snort of anger from Rahim ahead.

"No, what's madness is—"

He didn't get a chance to stop as there was a sudden loud screech from above us, and a flicker of shadow over our thicket. Rahim snatched at the reins of his horse- too fast – I thought, and the horse skidded through the mud, then reared, and Rahim tumbled backwards into the bushes with a groan.

"Father!" Nas rushed to his side as I finally, and thankfully, slowed my own worried horse down to join them. The trees and shrubs were getting sparse, and I could see the darkened thunderclouds overhead and open ground ahead of us. The Southern Roadway had started to drop in height as it had swept towards the mountain range, and I could see up ahead the pass through the Fury Mountains, and, in front of it and still far above us in the airs, circled two Torvald dragons – Stocky Greens.

"Ger' off me." Rahim was waving his son away even though

he clearly had a cut across his forehead. "Get my bag. Find that dragon lotion, now!"

Nas scrambled to do his father's bidding, rifling through the panicked steed's saddlebags (not caring how nervy the horse was, I noted in disgust) before drawing out the last two pots of the dragon lotion Rahim had managed to save.

"Get that stuff all over you – and all over that damned dragon, now!" he said tersely, easing himself into a sitting position and holding his bleeding head.

I could hardly pay either of my companions any heed as I slid from my own horse to watch the events unfold up ahead of me.

They were still a long way off – a few hundred meters perhaps – but the clarity of the air here picked out every detail of the rocks and the dragons as they swirled and swooped nearer to the pass and the Southern Roadway that joined it. The twin walls of the mountains ended in large jags of broken boulders, gullies and scree slopes as if great spoil piles had been left all around here by some ancient, gigantic race. The Southern Roadway was a causeway that ran down to the floor of the pass, with the rock walls of the mountains sheer around it. It was a wide pass, with easily enough room for several wagons and several more to travel abreast.

But the pass was also partially obscured, and there were great mounds of something purple, brown and green reaching up to the causeway, threatening to start eking its way across the great road.

Deadweed, I saw. Somehow, a patch of Deadweed had spread via the mountain streams and rivulets and found its purchase here, right on the tip of the boulder field and was about to clamber over the pass, sealing off the northern realm from the south.

"Uh, guys? We have to move," I said, looking at the Torvald Dragons as they swirled lower and lower, preparing their attack runs.

"Don't be an idiot!" Rahim hissed, directing Nas to press one of the pots of the foul-smelling lotion into my hands. "Get that stuff on you and that dragon of yours, now – do as I say, girl!" he barked, and I doled out great handfuls of the stuff to smear on my face before slapping it onto Thump.

"Skrech!" Thump sniffed at my hands and pulled back in disgust.

"I know, but those dragons might recognize you…" I said, earning a heavy tail thump against my legs, but he acquiesced all the same to having me smear the substance over his scales. It was white and gloopy, like goose grease – and I don't think that it even came close to covering him, but it might confuse the Torvald Dragons above us, at least. Although I thought they likely had other things on their mind about now. I finished up the pot and looked up as the first Stocky Green started swooping down towards the Deadweed.

Before they could get there, though, there was a sudden, indignant shriek as other shapes fell from the slopes of the Southern Gate, large shapes, their wings snapping around them as they whirled around and under and over each other to meet the intruders.

Dragons? Wild dragons? They had the orange and yellow colors of the Vicious Oranges of the south and were smaller than the Stocky Greens, but there were more of them than the Torvald dragons—*Eight? Nine?* I hastily counted.

And on their backs were other Dragon Riders who seemed intent on attacking the Torvald Riders.

CHAPTER 7
AKEEM, BY RIGHT OF BLOOD AND BIRTH

These Torvald Dragons were large, *much* larger than the Vicious Oranges we rode – but that would also be their weakness. They would be like elephants, and we would be the tigers.

"Rise!" I shouted to Heydar, my lieutenant and most trusted companion. He rode his own Savage Orange, Nanda, and at my command, Aida – my own dragon – thrummed with eagerness at the fight ahead.

This would be the first time that we had ever fought other Dragon Riders, not that I wanted to. To me, they were comrades, or brothers in a strange way—but because of who they were, and why they were here, that made us enemies. The Torvald Dragon Riders were pushing into our sovereign southern territory, and I had come to stop them.

"Ssss!" Aida lashed her heavily barbed and pronged tail in the air behind me, frustrated at my reticence. Despite everything that we had been through, despite her saving me from my father's enemies and me saving her from the wild dragons that roamed these mountains, she still had a fiery hot temper.

"Easy, girl." I settled on my saddle, one of fine leathers I had ordered made myself, by my father the Prince J'ahalid Mudin Dar Awil's best leather workers. My father was a prince of this realm, *the* prince of one of the ancient ruling houses, one for the far north, one for Torvald in the middle, and us in the south. But that was many centuries ago now, and the Binshee Tribe that we belonged to have taken to the high Fury Mountains, living near the dragons we love. It was our sacred task to defend the southern realms, even if the three current ruling lords of the 'civilized south' – Lord Ehsan, Lord Kasim, and Lord Qadir—tried to portray us as dangerous revolutionaries.

"I don't want to spill dragon blood today, but be assured if we have to – I will."

Aida growled warmly in her throat and I knew that she would be ready to attack given the slightest nod from me. The thought filled me with a fierce, feral sort of joy that I had to force myself to keep in check as I drew my saber and held it aloft towards our foe.

The wind caught us, and the other dragons and riders of my company performed just as they had trained to (which was a bit of a blessing as it was a maneuver I wasn't fully confident in); swirling in wider, darting sweeps and circles to give the impression of a storm of wings and scales, teeth and claws. It was all I could do to hold on to the saddle pommel and my sword as the wind pushed and pulled at me first from one angle, and then another, before Aida levelled out and we flew straight towards the Stocky Greens. 'The Storm' was a maneuver I had copied from the wild mountain black dragons – the way that they seemed to 'boil' over and around each other, to give the impression of wild ferocity and speed.

And it appeared to work as the Stocky Greens flared their wings and clumsily fell back from our onslaught.

Phwip! Phwip! My Riders levelled out of their own swallow-quick turns and shot around the two much larger dragons, not attacking, but forcing the dragons to turn and change direction as they tried to track us.

"Don't hit them, don't *actually* hit them…" I murmured under my breath as Heydar screamed past the larger of the two Greens, narrowly avoiding a swipe from one of its massive claws.

Idiot, I thought at him, even as I was impressed at how well he rode.

It had been only a handful of years since we had gone up into the Fury Mountains, in a desperate attempt to bond with some of the Savage Oranges.

The bond I had built with Aida wasn't one that was based on

fear or enforced loyalty. This was a bond of shared struggles, of respect and, dare I say it – friendship.

"Sss!" Aida hissed her agreement with me as I used my knees to gesture her forwards and down, towards the larger Stocky Green. She read my intentions perfectly, intuitively, and flared her bat-like wings out to slow her fight as I confronted the Torvald Riders. *They need to know that they cannot pass these mountains,* I thought. It was a gamble, and I didn't want it to come to bloodshed, but a stand had to be made. The south is defended by the south. No one else.

There were two of them, as was their wont. Two men this time, in those absurd horned hats that I was sure were dangers to each other as much as they were to their dragon's wings. The one in front was riding low, his eyes bright as he watched my movements, and in his hands, I could see the reins that led to the dragon's mouth, and at his feet the complicated, double-stirrups that I knew the riders would press and kick to tell their dragon to turn or bank, dive or rise. No such machinery for us wild dragon riders of the Fury Mountains. I felt a moment of superiority (which was quickly consumed, I had to admit, by the fact that their Stocky Green was almost twice the size of my Aida).

The rider behind the first was already half-risen from his own saddle just in front of the wings of the Green, with one of their short Torvald spears already in hand, and ready to throw.

"State your business!" I shouted over the airs at the dragon, as Aida screamed her own challenge to the Stocky Green.

The Torvald spear-thrower halted, looking at first confused, and then angered at my challenge.

Play it cool, Akeem, play it cool... I counselled myself, my sword still in one hand.

"Our business is at the command of Queen Nuria, Empress of Torvald and the northern lands, and Defender of the Western Archipelago!" the Rider called.

I nudged my knees forward, and in response Aida flew slowly forward and around the Stocky Green, forcing them to turn in their flight. "I thought the Western Isles already had their own Protector? The Council of Roskilde, wasn't it?" I called back, allowing a sneer into my voice. "Is Queen Nuria used to taking titles to herself?"

There were muttered gasps from the Torvald Dragon Riders ahead of me. What? I thought. I hadn't insulted her, not yet. If they believed *that* was an insult then they should hear what Heydar had to say about Torvald.

"It's been a long time since Torvald called itself an empire," I shouted again. Two generations at least, I knew. Not since Queen Saffron and Bower had defeated the old Dark King and had effectively been the only power in the world west of the World's Edge Mountains. But that had been before the distant Western Isles had seceded to the Council of Roskilde, under

Protector Lila, and before the Binshee Tribe—my family—had fled to the Fury Mountains.

A long time in anyone's history, and Torvald had to be taught that it could no longer think of itself as the center of the world anymore.

"Who are you? Who is your lord? I see no flag you fly under!" the Torvald Dragon Rider demanded.

"The Wild Company needs no flag," I called back as Aida swooped around the Torvald dragon once again, faster than it could follow us, before hovering with her powerful wing beats and waiting for the Green to catch up. "The Southern Kingdom has always claimed this pass, and I claim the right to refuse your passage by right of blood and birth!" I shouted, letting some of my anger seep into my voice. "The blood of me and my kinsmen and women, of my countryfolk and of my neighbors and friends who have long labored here. No more will Torvald have free access to the South!"

Their Stocky Green shrieked in consternation, and their Riders appeared equally as agitated by my words. *Good,* I thought. They were harsh words, too strong for what I had intended as a show of force perhaps – but I also knew that the Southern Kingdom would never be able to stand on its own two feet if it was constantly overshadowed by Torvald.

We had Dragon Riders, now. And not just the Seven of Dagfan; I curled my lip when I thought of the Seven Dragon

Riders who had passed the Training Hall of Dagfan's barbaric challenges. They were regarded as the only 'true' dragon riders of the South, even though I knew that their bonds were made from fear and hatred, not the shared friendship as ours were. My Wild Company would protect the Southern Kingdom from all enemies, and we would not bow and scrape and beg and pander to a foreign queen in the North for our survival.

Times had changed, and what had once only been one empire of the mainland, was now two kingdoms.

"You fool!" The 'navigator' of the Stocky Green shouted to me, the one with the reins and stirrups at the front. "We're not here to challenge Prince J'ahalid, we're here to stop the Deadweed!"

What arrogance these Torvald Riders had, I thought. Just because they have that Sacred Mountain of theirs, they think they have the right to lord it over the rest of the world. "Let the South see to its own problems!" I bellowed, raising my saber up into the air and then bringing it down to point at the patch of Deadweed already making its way across the causeway. I could see the forward tendrils flailing and reaching below me, grasping at rocks, digging into the soil as it put on new growth in horrible, ugly waves.

"Fire!" I shouted.

CHAPTER 8
DAYIE AND THE WILD COMPANY

I watched as the storm of southern Orange dragons broke around the two Stocky Greens of Torvald.

Were they attacking each other? My hand shook against my chest as I wondered if *I* had caused this by daring to steal Thump.

"Skree-pip?" Thump chittered at my side. He (apart from smelling foul) appeared excited and tense as his head moved and darted to try and follow all of the movements of the dragons above. He half-raised his leathery, darker-crimson wings and I wondered if this was it, if this was the moment that he would fly off and leave me.

But Thump hadn't shown any inclination to fly yet, apart from a few awkward wingbeats, after which he hastily refolded his wings close to his body. I had been starting to wonder if he *could* fly at all, and whether being raised by me, or having been taken out of the Dragon Enclosure had stunted his growth. Now, however, I saw what the real reason was – he had just never seen that was what a real dragon did.

"Please, Thump, wait, just wait with me…" I begged him, but my eyes were caught up on the drama happening in the skies ahead of us.

The southern dragons had stormed out of the pass, surrounding and swooping out of reach of the Stocky Greens, and each, I saw, had a Dragon Rider on their backs - singular riders, however, not the double saddles that the Torvald Dragon Academy used. I heard roars and shrieks of fury and indignation as there appeared to be some kind of argument going on between the two groups, before suddenly the Orange dragons turned in mid-air, and, like a storm of crows, they swept down one after another to spit their dragonflame down at the flailing and writhing Deadweed below them.

It was like watching a scene out of one Rahim's songs; the dark thunderhead clouds above, the brilliant blaze of light from below as the Orange dragons wheeled and whirled, their undersides illuminated by the flames as if they, too, were creatures made of fire. The two much larger Stocky Greens gave great beats of their wings to rise out of the way of the onslaught as I looked at the effect of this conflagration.

The Deadweed burned – but that did not mean that it was an easy destruction. As soon as the Savage Oranges started their attack, the weed reacted in a way that I had only ever seen once before, when I had lost Obasi and Wera.

The vines curled in and raised themselves, reminding me of the striking arms of the Praying Mantis – and, even as fire engulfed them and withered their limbs, I saw them shoot out, smoked and scorching, to attack the dragons that dared to attack it.

"No – look out!" I gasped, caught in the moment as the vines darted upward and struck like whips. There was an outraged shriek as one of the Savage Oranges had its leg caught – the vines wrapping around it fast and tight, and started to pull the desperately struggling dragon back down towards its poisonous heart.

"*Aiiii!*" There was a shout as the Orange's Rider tumbled backwards from the dragon's back, falling into the burning mess of vegetation as little puffs of yellow spore – the deadly flowers of the Deadweed – were expelled. I knew only too well what that meant.

Thump started forward, opening his mouth in a hiss but we were way too far away, there was nothing we could do, and when the little Crimson Red realized that, he dropped into a halting trot, eyes wide at his fellow reptilian's agony.

"*Hoi!*" There came a shout from one of the black-clad riders, and a Savage Orange swooped from the skies – the same one that had been flying the closest to the Torvald Dragons. There was a flash of flame on bared steel as he soared *through* the billowing flames, raising his saber to slash at the vine dragging the other Orange down. It was just enough to weaken the vine, and the Orange shook itself free, holding its leg awkwardly and hooting in despair as it rose above the smokes and fires.

"Oh no, it's lost its rider…" I said, my heart breaking, before there was the heavy thud of Thump leaning against my leg and almost bowling me over. When I looked down, he was looking up at me with large eyes.

"No, you're never going to lose me," I promised him, the words startling me for their intensity even as I spoke them.

"Stop jabbering and get back on your horse!" Rahim was now on his own mount once again, his head hastily bandaged in a scrap of linen already dyed red from his fall. "Now's our chance to make a break for it. While they're busy, we can skirt through the boulder field and get up to the Fury gullies over there." He pointed to near the pass, where there appeared to be ravines and ridges leading into the Fury Mountains.

"Are you mad?" I said to him. "There could be more Deadweed out there!"

"And we have a dragon." Rahim was already urging his skittish horse forward, with Nas following suit behind him. "I'm not waiting around for this to play out, and for either those

Torvald Greens or whomever that other lot are find us out here!"

For a moment my heart hammered. Did I *dare* disobey him?

But Rahim was right. The pass would be a mess for hours if not days to come. On this side were the Stocky Greens which would sense Thump sooner or later, and on the other side were these strange, *other* dragon riders. I had no idea how they would take to Thump.

But at least we'd be in the south, I thought, watching the Crimson Red, who appeared only too happy to get a better look at the display of might and speed that its brethren were performing. I saw Thump checking the aerial battle off to our side often and watched as his eyes eagerly drank in all the details. The dragon appeared to be studying, and learning.

"I promised you your freedom, girl," Rahim reminded me, pausing behind a boulder the size of a barn.

And with that I clicked my tongue at Thump and both he and my horse trotted forward, towards the mountains.

The sun seemed to set early in the mountains, and by the time we had put the plains behind us, it was already full dark. The burning conflagration of the pass was still a dull orange glow on the western horizon behind us, but the smell of soot and smoke had long since faded. I didn't know how long the Orange dragons kept up their assault of the Deadweed – or how often they had to fire it before it finally died – but I couldn't imagine anything surviving the firestorm we had skirted. The Orange dragons of the South did not appear to have as much fire as the dragons of the North did, maybe thanks to their smaller size, but what they did appear to have were numbers.

Rahim had led us into the rocky gullies of the Fury Mountains, then forced our stubborn mounts and feet to start tracking up as fast and as far as we could, often following dizzying switch-back trails that led to more higher ravines. By the time that the final sounds of the firestorm were lost to us (not the glow, however) I was certain that it was getting too dark to travel any more without fear of ending up falling *into* one of these ravines. I was about to mention this to Rahim when he finally held up a hand and called for a halt.

"No campfires," he murmured instead pointing at Nas's pack which still had some old bread and dried bits of rabbit inside. "Any light will stand out like a sore thumb in this dark, and we don't need any attention now, do we?"

"No Father," Nas, now the dutiful son, said. Something had changed in him in the last few days of our travel. He still hated me, I could see that easily enough, but I think the rapid growth of Thump – and then seeing the confrontation of the two groups of Dragon Riders firsthand had scared him. His hands shook a little as he threw me a hunk of bread and an even stingier strip of cured rabbit as if he were loath to let our hands accidentally touch.

What, you think you'll catch the magic off me? I thought, even though I didn't think that what I had *was* magic. Just a way with animals.

"Those Dragon Riders," I said as I sat down against Thump, who kept pawing at me insistently, confused why we weren't lighting a fire, from what I could tell. "They were angry. They were about to fight…"

"Torvald's always protected its borders…" Rahim muttered from his roll of blanket.

"Not those, the *others,*" I said, remembering how they had appeared as fast as thought, storming out of the pass like that, like a surge of monsoon-water, white water and chaos and noise. "I think they were *wild* Dragon Riders. One of the merchants mentioned them to me on the way up here," I said, unable to keep the awe from my voice. There was a story going about the south, that a troupe of adventurers and wanderers had managed to do what no other person in the south had ever managed to do outside of the Training Hall – to form their own natural bonds with some of the wild Savage Orange dragons, just like the Dragon Academy Riders of Torvald. They weren't like the Seven Riders of Dagfan, the aging and embattled heroes that were all the south had 'officially' to show for their years of trying to capture and train dragons.

"Ridiculous," Rahim scoffed. "Those were the Seven of Dagfan, clearly."

"I only counted five or six," I said, keeping my voice small even as I dared to contradict Rahim.

"Well, maybe one of them was sick today!" Rahim turned over to scowl at me. "Everyone knows that the wild Dragon Riders are a myth, and I'll tell you a bit of free advice – there are a lot of things that people *say* to be true in this world, but *aren't,* but people believe it because it makes them sleep at night."

"Yeah!" Nas added his agreement, although I think that his father's wisdom was lost on him.

"If you were to ask me what we saw, we saw the Seven Riders of Dagfan riding to protect their homeland from the Dead-weed, and Torvald." Rahim nodded. "And I will bet you, Dayie, that any talk of wild mountain Riders is a myth made up by the prince to give his people something to believe in." Rahim, having set the world to rights, settled into his blankets. "Now I'm going to sleep, and I suggest you do the same."

But I couldn't sleep, and neither could Thump. For some reason, I couldn't bring myself to believe that we had seen the Seven. That would have been pretty amazing in its own right, of course – but the Seven were supposed to fly dragons hatched from the northern dragon bloodlines from eggs stolen, bartered, or found. Blues, Greens and the like. These dragons that we had seen had definitely been the Savage Oranges, one of the two types of native mountain dragons of the south – the other being the Midnight dragons who rumored to be impossible to control.

"But what do I know, huh?" I said sadly to Thump, pulling my cloak a little wider around us both. Thump made a whistling, whining sort of a noise. The thought flitted through my mind that it was cold up here, and it would be a miracle if it didn't rain and flood us out before too long.

But all the same, we were in the south, and I had seen what Riders and their dragons *could* do, if they worked together. Those thought of daring and adventure filled my mind as I managed to drift into a fitful sleep, cocooned by the warmth of my dragon.

"Dayie," said a voice, waking me from my slumber. I was cold and uncomfortable on the stony floor, and since Rahim hadn't allowed us to set a fire, there was no remedy. Not that anyone would have noticed, I thought – as I could smell the smokes of the burning Deadweed far below us.

"What?" I grumbled, worming my way out of the coarse blankets to see that the night was still dark around us, and there was no one talking to me. Rahim was still fast asleep, laid out like a log in his own blankets (which were thicker than mine, I noted), and Nas was curled up a little way away, snoring loudly.

I must have been dreaming, I decided, settling back down.

"Dayie," the voice said again, and this time I jolted upright from my makeshift bed.

"What!?" I said again, earning a low, sleepy grumble from Rahim, as he turned over and ignored me. Thinking Nas was playing tricks on me, I turned to scowl at him, but the youth and my nemesis only kept on snoring. I had spent long enough sharing the same cramped cabin to know what Nas's snores were like.

I couldn't sleep now. My body felt tired and heavy, but my mind was jittery and awake. I hated these moments and figured that it had to do with the cold mountain air, and all the stress and excitement of the last few days. Looking up, I saw that the sky was alive with stars. Even despite the cold, it was quite beautiful, in a way.

"Dayie," that voice said again, but now that I was (mostly) awake, I noticed something very strange. It wasn't like I had heard it with my ears. Or maybe I *had,* but, as shivers ran up and down my arm, I realized that the words made more sense inside my head than outside of it.

It didn't make sense. "I guess half of me is still asleep," I muttered, shaking my head. I had heard of that happening--

when you were so dog-tired that you started to dream with your eyes open.

Thump. There was the heavy thud of a reptilian tail, and I looked over to where Thump was standing at the edge of the rocks and looking at me. Once again, he swished his tail and it hit the floor heavily. The way that he was looking at me was almost *too* intense, and I felt that eerie sensation once again, that maybe, just maybe…

"Thump? Was that you?" I whispered. There had always been tales that Dragon Riders had a way to talk to their dragons, but I had thought it a romantic notion – just a way of explaining how close their bond was.

The people who sold me to the Gypsies thought that I could talk to plants and animals, I reminded myself. Which was ridiculous. I had never heard an animal speak words to me in my life, and neither did I expect to. But what I did do was just listen to what *they* were saying, with their bodies and their eyes and their movements. Was that so hard?

"Some don't listen. Can't hear," the voice said, and this time Thump pawed at the ground as if he wanted to go out hunting. Or attract my attention.

It was then that I felt, in the core of my being, the unavoidable truth: I was hearing Thump. And Thump was talking to me, using only his thoughts.

I couldn't believe it. All those old legends were true! Of dragons talking to kings and queens, advising and warning the heroes of the history books.

"You, you can talk?" I was on my feet, the blanket still wrapped around my shoulders as I took a hesitant step towards Thump.

The Crimson Red even *looked* different to me, now – and it wasn't just the starlight. *He doesn't look like a lizard,* I thought, noticing the way that his eyes moved and flickered to mine, and the way that his nostrils flared as he thought and mulled over my own words. *He looks like a person.* As if the scaled, reptilian skin that he was wearing was just that, but there was a vibrant, intelligent person just like me or Rahim or Nas inside there, looking out at me.

There was a change of pressure in the air between us, like a heat haze or a light wind – although I could feel no heat, cold, and there was no breeze. Was Thump trying to talk to me again?

Another thump of the tail, followed by a soft "Skrech!" of annoyance, as if Thump couldn't quite form his words to me. Maybe I *had* been imagining it all...

With a light bound, Thump pounced forward and snapped out

his long neck (he was getting bigger by the day) and very lightly nipped me on the hand. All it took was a moment.

"Ow!" I said, "What did you do that for?"

"Stupid." That voice again, and as I looked up in wonder, Thump bounded off behind the rocks, his claws scrabbling over the gravel and sandy ground of the mountainside gorges beyond.

"Hey – where are you going?" I hissed, casting a hurried look back at the others, before I seized up my pack and hurried off after my dragon. Maybe this was it, I thought. Maybe this was the night that we make our escape.

Thump was leading me somewhere, that much was obvious as he stopped up ahead of me, sniffed the air delicately and then seemed to choose another direction – through the rock fields and cutting across a slope of bare rock.

"Wait up, Thump!" I allowed myself to say a bit louder, wishing that I had thought – or had time to seize some of the group's supplies before we had made our escape. I didn't feel bad at all about stealing from Rahim and Nas. Even if Rahim was the far better of the Hazim family, he was still the one who had worked to keep me as a captive for Fan for all these years. They would have been able to hunt for more food, I reasoned. Not that it mattered. All that mattered now was putting as many leagues between us as I could.

"Here! Here." That voice crept into the back of my mind, with the cold mountain air waking up my limbs and the sharp stones digging through the soles of my shoes, it was impossible to deny where it came from.

"How are you doing this?" I whispered. Did all dragons do this? Why hadn't Thump spoken to me before? Maybe he'd been too young? I knew about animals, and I had hand reared more than enough in my time to know that their first noises weren't the same as when they were all grown up. Just like human babies, they were working out how to use their voices. And now that Thump had his– did that mean that we would talk like this from now on?

"Skreyagh." As if to disprove my theory, Thump made an excited chirrup as he sat on a rock and craned his body, intent like a cat, around to where the path entered a gorge.

"What have you found, boy?" I whispered, something in the lines of his body telling me that I should be quiet. *He had said 'here' – he had found something—*

And that was when I smelled it too, the rich scent of roasting meat and fresh woodsmoke. My stomach grumbled, and I wondered just who it was that had attracted Thumps' attention.

CHAPTER 9
AKEEM, SUSPICIOUS

"Sss!" Aida woke me up by making her long, rattling warning call beside me, which vibrated down the long avenues of her throat. The Oranges could sound like the worst, most dangerous rattlesnake if they wanted to – and the biggest, too.

"What is it?" I rolled into a crouch, one hand reaching for my saber. The rest of the Company was asleep – something that made me annoyed, as there was no one on guard – but I wouldn't berate them for it. Not yet, anyway. The Company had fought hard and they had fought well, but we had still lost Munir to the Deadweed and the flames. His dragon, Scarlet, had left after the battle. I didn't blame her. She needed time to be alone, and to think whether she still wanted to hang around with us humans.

But losing Munir and his dragon to the Company was a hard

blow, especially now that the North seemed to be pressing against our borders, and we could be surrounded by enemies... I raised my eyes to where Aida was rattling at the darkness, to see where the rocky ledge narrowed and the walls rose on either side to form a natural corridor of rock.

"What is it, girl, mountain goat? Wolf? Big cat?" I whispered, easing myself out of the blanket and bringing my saber with me. It was just wishful thinking on my part that it could be one of the other denizens of the Fury Mountains though. The other animals usually sensed the dragons and stayed away.

Which means it has to be a person...

"Scrh!" a sound like a soft croak came—a guttural cough—and I knew instantly that it was a dragon.

"Up!" I whispered to Aida, rising to my feet. It couldn't be Scarlet come back for why would Aida hiss so territorially? It could only be either one of the Vicious Oranges or the smaller Orange Drakes, and that would mean trouble. The larger Vicious Oranges – which all of these dragons of the Company were – could inflict serious damage if they thought we had wandered into their territory, and the smaller Drakes could be just as dangerous if they swarmed us.

We'll scare it off, I thought, putting a hand out to touch Aida's quivering neck. "Ready?" I patted the top of my chest, my special command that she should prepare her dragon fire, ready to spew it at the rocky opening. It might not be enough to kill a dragon, but a serious scalding would make it think twice about attacking us!

"Wait, *wait…"* I held up my hand as Aida started to breath in, her neck swelling with fire—

"Ooof!" The next sound that came from the shadows was one that I was not expecting at all. It was a woman's small call of surprise, as if she had tripped over something. I heard a skittering of rocks. Did the wild dragon out there have a captive? Was it about to eat someone?

"Show yourself!" I shouted, eliciting garbled mumbles and groans around me from the rest of the company. "Drop her!" I shouted again, starting forward, Aida hunting low at my side. I didn't know if a wild dragon would even be able to understand me, but I had dealt with them a lot over the last few years. Usually a forward display of strength was the best, as dragons didn't fight if they didn't have to. They were like mountain goats, or prides of wildcats in that regard. If members of different hatches met in the wild, then there would be a display of aggression – and usually the largest dragon won without shedding so much as a drop of ichor. If I and Aida could prove we were bigger and badder than it was, then there was every chance that it would drop its possible meal and flee.

"I said *show yourself!"* I bellowed louder, advancing as forcefully as I dared.

There was a startled human yelp—not a draconian one— and

out of the shadows crept a girl, and at her side was a young northern Red dragon.

What the....?

"You're bonded," I repeated to the girl, who looked at me strangely under her half-closed eyes.

"What?" she said – a slight frown. She was wary, frightened a little maybe, but she stood her ground in front of us as the Wild Company stood up around me, and our dragons unrolled from their sleeping curls to regard the new interloper.

The girl was young – late teens, early twenties maybe – but the way she stood; back straight, one hand hovering over her belt knife, and not to mention the simple, sturdy tunic and breeches that she wore told me that she was no pushover. Her hair was a shocking platinum white, and her skin was pale – definitely not what I was expecting. She was a northerner, like the Dragon Riders – but she wasn't dressed like one of the Torvald Riders. No armor. No silly horned helmet.

I relaxed my sword a little, not that I trusted her, but because I wanted to give her the *impression* that I trusted her. She could be a scout, after all. An Academy recruit, sent to find our camp.

"I'm what?" she said again, her eyes darting from me to Aida at my side.

"You're bonded. To your dragon there." I nodded. I could see it in the way that they moved together without even sharing looks. If she took a step forward, her dragon was at her side almost as if they had shared thoughts.

"Bonded," she repeated, her eyes narrowing a little.

How can she not know? I thought. It had to be a ruse. She must be a Torvald Academy spy, I nodded to Tahnoon, making a circling gesture above our heads, and the bald man nodded gravely in return, turning to hurry back to his own Vicious Orange and take to the skies.

The girl was skittish, taking a step back at the sudden clatter of the Orange Drake's wings. She *appeared* as though she didn't know what she was doing here, but I doubted that very much.

"What's your name?" I asked, ignoring her earlier question.

The girl was quiet for a moment, then she muttered, "Dayie."

That's a southern name, I thought. *What lengths these Torvaldites will go to conceal their treachery!* I took a breath, ready to order her capture when suddenly Aida turned and hissed, but not at the younger northern Red, but at me!

"Aida!" I said, surprised.

"Shh!" my dragon said, her voice rippling into my mind with

images of soot and fire in my imagination. It had been like this ever since I had first met her – we had bonded and shared our minds easily – as had some of the others of the Company, but not all. She was annoyed at me. And, I watched her start to carefully saunter forward between me and the girl, stretching out her nose to sniff carefully at the nose of the Red.

"Aida? What are you doing!" I hissed in alarm.

Aida was an older female dragon. Not old enough to have any fade on her scales, but she was the first of our Company and had become the unofficial Matriarch of our band of dragons. She seemed to be taking a motherly, protective interest in the younger Red. She chirruped softly at him, and, surprisingly, he returned the call with his own soft whistle.

"Thump – is that wise?" Dayie the spy appeared just as shocked as I was.

"Thump?" I muttered. "Who calls their dragon Thump?"

The girl scowled at me and then startled as if poked in the back. "Who ignores their own dragon?" she shot back at me over the still smoldering fire.

"What do you mean, I'm not—" I stuttered, before Aida lashed her tail against the sand.

"You are, Akeem. These people are not Academy Riders, although this one comes from the Sacred Mountain. They are young. They need our help." Aida looked at me with her

golden eyes before she turned to nudge at the coals of our cookfire with her snout, rolling some of the charcoal and sooty embers towards the younger Red who paused warily then ate them hungrily.

"My dragon tells me that you're not Academy," I said, feeling a little embarrassed at Aida showing me up like that. "But that doesn't explain who you are, and what you are doing out here with your Crimson Red."

"I…" the girl opened and closed her mouth. She was trying to hide something. Why? The dragon?

"I come from the South. A small village by the coast," she said to me. Was it a lie? I couldn't tell, until the next words that fell from her mouth. "Deadweed destroyed my home. Killed my foster parents." She raised her eyes to look at me. "I want to do what you do. I want to fight Deadweed."

"No," I said quickly, and firmly. As much as I always wanted another dragon to add to our force, and another rider too – how could I trust someone I knew nothing of? How could I be sure that she could fight? That she would defend the South with us, when she was so obviously not a southerner by heritage? There was just no way that I could trust an unknown outsider well enough.

And besides which… I looked at the fey white-haired girl once again, and the clear glint in her eyes. There was something a little unsettling in the way that she looked at us. Like she was wiser than all of us, or that those eyes contained hidden depths…

"But…?" She looked from to the others desperately.

"Akeem," Aida lashed her tail. *"They need guidance. They have only just bonded – but she is unlike anything that I have smelled. Magic lies thick about her."*

That was it. I knew that there was something strange about her besides just her looks, something that I couldn't put my finger on – only now I could. There was an air of the strange about her, and Aida had explained it. It was magic.

Unfortunately for the girl, my dragon's opinion did nothing to change my decision. If anything, it was another reason why I couldn't take her on with us. I needed people I could trust, soldiers I could trust in order to defend the realm – and magic was too unpredictable. And, on top of that – she was young.

"So are you," Aida pointed out.

Maybe, but I grew up fighting.

"Maybe she did as well." The dragon swished her tail. I sighed. One of the many problems of being a dragon rider – of any nation-- was the fact that if your dragon disagreed with you, then you had to work twice as hard just to get your way. Dragons sure could be stubborn!

"Can you ride?" I asked the girl.

"A horse? Of course..." Dayie said. She had relaxed a little from the fight or flight posture of her original stance but had since seemed to take on a sullen air.

"No, not a horse – I mean a dragon. Can you ride, uh, *Thump* over there?" I said. *And she calls her dragon Thump. Just what sort of name was that?*

"Ride? Uhm, no – I mean, I'm sure I could, but I haven't tried yet—"

"Well, if you can't ride your dragon, then you are a long way from learning how to fly in formation and to fight on the back of a dragon," I said. "So, no, the answer is still a no. The Wild Company cannot train you."

"Akeem – you're being cruel," Aida whipped her tail at me, making me jump back. *That* earned a few chuckles from the others of the Wild Company, which only made me more adamant.

"The answer is no," I said once more.

"Then I will find someone else to train me!" she said defiantly. "Or I'll just have to train myself!"

"Like you did," Aida chided me.

But that was different, I shot back, feeling the heat flush into my face.

"How?"

I had to. I'm a son of the rightful prince. I have the entire South to think of. I had a duty to...

"And do you not think this girl has a duty? A fate just as you do?" Aida's voice in the back of my mind was mocking. Of course, I thought this girl had a fate. We all had our fates. But *I* was trying to save the Southern Kingdom. I wasn't playing at being a Dragon Rider!

"Then you'd better be heading north," I said grimly. There was no way that I would advise anyone to go to the Training Hall of Dagfan. Not after I had heard of the ways they tried to force bonding with their dragons.

"I come from the South," Dayie said, but there was something else in the flicker of her eyes. Something that she wasn't telling us about. Something more than the magic that seemed to shimmer around her. *Why couldn't she go north? Why did she have a young dragon in the first place?* Had she been kicked out of the Torvald Academy for some reason? But then what of her story of her foster parents and her life in the South? It was so vague, anyone could have cobbled together such a story in an instant.

"Ssss!" There was a sudden thunder in the sky as Tahnoon and his dragon swooped down, the Orange dragon beating its wings ferociously in a storm clatter to avoid crashing into the rocks.

"Tahnoon – what is it?" I called up sharply.

"Wild mountain dragons. Attacking travelers on the other side of the ridge," he said, already signaling his dragon to rise once again into the air.

I looked over at the girl. "Stay here," I said on an impulse I didn't quite understand, even though I had already told her we would not train her. "I have more questions for you," and whistled to Aida to prepare for a fight. Aida chirruped warningly once at the younger Red as I climbed onto her back, and we jumped into the air.

CHAPTER 10
DAYIE, MAKING FRIENDS

"**W**ell, that was fun, wasn't it?" I said miserably to Thump as soon as the other dragons had leapt into the air.

"Friends," Thump said, his voice appearing once again in my mind as it had done before. It felt weird to hear the dragon in my thoughts. *Was this what it was like for these Riders?* I looked up at the swirling shapes of the Wild Company as they flew toward the mountains. "Did they all hear their dragons too?"

I was still annoyed that the one – the leader, clearly, had denied me the chance to train with them. What was wrong with him? He didn't look any older than me, and yet *he* had a dragon and I had heard him proudly announcing his right to defend the South to the Torvald Riders just earlier. What gave him that right and not me? Aside from the fact that he knew how to fly on a dragon's back and I did not.

"Wild dragons. Feral," Thump said, lashing his tail back and forth in agitation as he watched the disappearing silhouettes of the Wild Company as they swept over the ridge.

"Yeah, I know…" I said. I had heard about them – dragons with dark midnight-blue scales that were even more savage than the Vicious Oranges, and who hunted in boiling, chaotic packs through the wild places of the world. Hadn't there been a story of some Torvald king learning how to ride them once? I thought, before shaking my head.

"Oh." I realized then just who the wild dragons must be attacking. "That Rider said just over the ridge, didn't they?" I whispered to the night air. Which was precisely where I had come from.

Rahim and Nas, and the horses. *They* were the ones being attacked by the wild mountain dragons.

"Ghrrr!" I kicked the dirt in frustration. I don't know if I would have cared if it had just been Fan back there, on her own. Even though her son Nas was a total creep and a bully – that didn't mean that I wanted him and his stepfather torn limb from limb and eaten alive.

"Or the horses," I thought in annoyance. Especially the horses. I had managed to nurse those horses through all exhaustion and all sorts of injuries caused by being overworked over the years – they were like friends to me. No, they *were* my friends. It was mostly for their benefit rather than Nas and Rahim that I turned back to the path and beckoned to Thump. "Come on, we should help."

"No," Thump said, not following me at all. I turned to argue with him but he stretched out with his two forepaws and, with a sound like snapping cloth, unfolded his wings.

Thump's wings were darker than the rest of him, a deeper Crimson that was almost black on top, but brightening to a much lighter orange color underneath. As I watched him open and close them experimentally, it was like watching sudden flashes of color, like a warning system.

"Are you sure you can fly?" I asked. He had shown no inclination to yet, and in response he just pawed at the dirt and pointed his snout up at the night sky.

"Okay then – if you're sure…" I walked up to his front right leg and tried to copy what I saw the captain and the others of the Wild Company do, reaching out to hold onto the tines of his neck and shoulders that were getting bigger and stronger all the time and pulling myself up awkwardly.

"Oouff!" I failed, clearly, as I ended up crossways, lying on my belly just behind the dragons' shoulders.

"Screch!" Thump hissed impatiently as I readjusted.

It's just like riding a horse, just like a horse, I kept telling myself even though a dragon was nothing like a horse. Still, it gave me the confidence to sit down behind his shoulders, at the natural 'saddle' that existed there between spine ridges, before leaning forward.

With a jubilant hiss, Thump turned— "Woah!" I cried as I almost fell off—and trotted across the flatter part of the hill, gaining speed and momentum.

"Just, you know, make sure that you can do this…" I said worriedly as his trot turned into a gallop, and I was bouncing painfully up and down on his back. *Nothing like a horse, nothing like a horse-*

With an eagle's shriek, Thump jumped into the night airs and stretched out his wings. They made another almighty cracking noise as they extended – and we were heading back down towards the dirt.

"Wooah-!" I shouted as Thump hit the earth and pounced again like it had been just a large hop – and once again he snapped out his wings and this time my stomach lurched as the wind started to take us. But it wasn't enough, we were going down once more, until Thump furiously started to flap his wings so fast that I thought he might damage them.

WOOOSH. In a split instant, we were being thrown forward by his efforts, heading straight for a wall of rock.

"Up, up, up!" I screamed, but instead he turned, showing his belly to the cliff face as we glided in a rising circle around the

Wild Company's campsite, before he started beating his wings once more, again and again-

And suddenly we were up. The campsite fell beneath us in a slightly lighter mosaic of dirt and boulders and the blackened scorch mark of the fire – and we were swooping over the ridge and heading northwards. We were flying!

I barely had any time to even think about what we were doing – what *Thump* was doing— before the sounds of fighting came from up ahead of us. The rocks, gorges, ravines and fast-flowing mountain rivers flashed past underneath us and I drank every detail in. I had never seen the world like this – and it made me feel stronger, braver than I had ever felt before.

Whoosh! The night lit up below us in a stream of orange dragon fire, illuminating the barren side of a hillside where I had left Rahim and Nas, and with the dark silhouettes of shapes trying to rush down the hill towards them.

It was the wild mountain dragons. My stomach turned over. I had never seen them before, though I had heard about how they moved – but no words could do what I saw now justice. They were dark as a scribe's ink, and long, like a snake. Their wings were small and they appeared to have two larger near their 'shoulders' and another two smaller near their 'hips'.

They did not have the long snouts of the other dragons, but instead had stubby, snub-like maws that were forested with wetly gleaming teeth, and thick manes of tines around their heads. They shrieked like screech owls as they flowed down the mountainside, intertwining in pairs over and under each other like a nest of adders as they approached the Gypsies.

Another dragon call echoed, and another blast of orange dragon fire scorched the mountainsides in front of Nas and Rahim, driving them back but not even slowing them down. I could see why they called these sort 'wild' dragons as it appeared that they only had one thing on their mind – dinner! The Wild Company were flapping and hovering over the Gypsies and the terrified ponies, trying to drive back their wilder cousins.

"Scrarp! Scrah!" Thump was making a strange, coughing sort of sound as we flew ungainly towards the scene, until I realized that he, too, was trying to spit fire at them.

"Easy, one step at a time, please…" I gasped in fear. I didn't even know if Thump *could* breathe fire yet, and it was too dangerous for him to do it wrong somehow.

Another screech, and one of the wild mountain dragons twisted in the air in a sudden leap that was far quicker and higher than I had thought them capable of, and I heard an accompanying scream from one of the Wild Company Orange dragons as the wild dragon's teeth met flesh.

"No!" I heard a shout – and I recognized it as the young man who had been so rude to me earlier. One of the larger of the Orange dragons swept down to harry at the jumping wilder one.

Thump was eager to get involved in the fight, but I didn't know how much use he would have been. He was still smaller than the Orange dragons – and the captain had been right, he had no fighting experience, *yet.* "Please, Thump – Rahim and Nas, the horses…" I said instead, pointing over his shoulder to where the Gypsies were huddled in terror.

Thump screamed in joy and flipped his wings, angling our clumsy flight into an arrow straight towards them, forward claws outstretched-

When he did not slow down upon our approach, a terrible thought crashed through me. Did Thump think I wanted him to attack them?

Whumpf! We hit the knot that was Rahim and Nas and the horses as fast as a storm wave, and then Thump was rising once again into the air on the other side, with my clinging on top, and with something else attached to us. We were heavier than we had been before, and I looked past the rushing wind and the blurring rocks to see that Thump had seized Nas in his front claws.

"Argh!!" my tormentor was shrieking, kicking and wriggling his legs as he screamed in terror.

"Nas! Nas – it's me!" I shouted at him as Thump dipped and slowed, wheeling in the night airs.

"Dayie!?" I saw Nas's face look up at me in incredulity, before he flushed pale as Thump dropped him.

Thump! I gasped.

SPLASH! The mountain river exploded in a plume of white water as Nas hit it. Then we were turning back to the scene of the battle. It seemed that Thump, the months-old dragon had a plan, as he once again tried to level out his flight, failed, and instead threw himself forward into a barreling dive that swept under the larger Orange dragons, in front of the wilder mountain dragons and snatched Rahim in his front claws.

"AGH! AGH!" Rahim was yelping like a stuck pig, holding onto Thump's talons as they skewered his jerkin before he, too, was dumped into the river along with his stepson.

But what about the horses? I thought as Thump laboriously tried to flap his wings – he was getting tired – to turn back to the fight. I didn't know if this was a part of Thump's plan, but it appeared that sudden explosion of Thump just nearby them had broken their petrified state, and they had bolted away from the swooping Thump – which was also (thankfully) away from the wild mountain dragons as well. Thump appeared to know precisely what I wanted to do, as he tried to follow them, performing pigeon like dips and rises to get ahead of them in their stampede.

"Good boy – who's the best? Who's the bravest!" I breath-lessly congratulated him as he turned towards the bare patch of hillside a little ahead of the fight behind us.

Thump's entire body vibrated with tension as he tried to 'leap' onto the ground, resulting in a sharp, painful clack from Thump, and me being thrown from his back to roll over the dirt.

When I finally stopped tumbling, I lay on my back, coughing up at the stars as the horses skidded from their gallop and instead stamped nervously, snorting at us; a girl and her dragon in heaps on the hillside in front of them.

"E-easy there," I coughed at the horses, holding out a scraped hand towards them, my head still spinning in circles, thankful that I didn't have anything broken – at least, not that I could tell.

"Mamma-la, Mamma-la," I coughed in a sing-song voice at them, and slowly our horses' rolling eyes gentled as they accepted that yes, it was me, their friend. I had to lead them further across the hillside, until the sounds of the battle were just muted echoes before they started to calm down properly however. Behind us stumbled Thump, one wing folded up and the other partly folded as if he wasn't sure how it went back together again.

"You know what, Thump?" I groaned as I found a patch of

scrubby mountain grass for the horses to eat. "We're *really* going to have to work on your landings."

By the time that the Wild Company had turned back the wild mountain dragons and found us, the sun was already cresting the eastern horizon, and I was leaning with my back against Thump. We sat and watched, the horses pulling at their tethers as the Orange dragons approached. I wasn't surprised, because even *I* felt a little sense of trepidation as first one, then another and then another of the Orange dragons fell to the ground with a loud thump that shook the ground around us.

"Please don't scare them," I groaned, my body still aching. "They haven't had the best night so far…"

"*They* haven't?" barked their arrogant captain, jumping from Aida and stalking across the hillside towards me. The sun highlighted the dirt and soot across his face, and the *very* annoying fact that he was actually pretty handsome – or he would be, if he didn't have that look of thunder on his face. "One of my dragons is injured, thanks to you!" he snapped.

"Me?" I stood up. "What on earth do you think I've done?" I said, as the man gestured behind him. Two of the other Wild Company riders pushed Nas and Rahim out into the dawn light towards me.

"These two have explained that you're with them. So there

you go. How about you look after each other a bit better, instead of making my job more difficult?"

Rahim and Nas hurried sheepishly over towards me, looking owlish and worried between me, Thump, and the other dragons. "*Your* job?" I said, annoyed. "And would you care to explain what that is? So far, all I have seen is a bunch of bandits living in the mountains who are very, *very* rude!" I spluttered, and to my surprise that earned a few chuckles from the other Riders as they shook their heads and stepped back to their dragons, leaving their leader to argue with me on his own.

"We are the Wild Company, the defenders of the South!" the man practically shouted. "And I am Captain Akeem..." He stopped suddenly and took a deep breath.

He said it like I should bow or something, but I was not about to. What did I care? It looked to me as if I had managed to do exactly the same thing he and the others had done. I had befriended a dragon—bonded with it, he'd said—and now I'd flown into battle. He didn't seem so special as to warrant that I scrape before him

Or maybe I was still smarting because he didn't want me to join them. I would be stuck here, with Nas and Rahim unless I wanted them to get eaten...

"Nice to meet you, Captain Akeem," I said tightly. "You already know my name, so I won't give it again." I bit my tongue, forcing myself to say the next words. *Don't let him see that he has annoyed you. Don't stoop to his level,* I tried to retain the upper ground. "I thank you for helping my travelling companions out of a spot of bother, but I don't think we will be needing your services again."

"My services?" the young man spluttered, his eyes flaring as his mouth opened, closed, then opened again. He looked like a fish. "Good luck to you!" He turned on his heel and stalked back to his dragon – and the chuckles of his men, which appeared to be the only gender he flew with. *Was that it?* I thought with a flare of annoyance. I'd met plenty of bigots in my time, but this was the first that I had met one flying a dragon. Within moments they had lifted up into the skies and were flying high and fast to the south.

There was a moment of silence before Rahim's voice broke it. "You might be good with animals, Dayie, but you are bleeding awful at making friends with people."

What was that supposed to mean? I thought in a huff, barking at them to get their stuff together, because if I was to guard them on the route through the wild Fury Mountains, I wanted to get it done quickly. *And now I'm responsible for them,* I thought, in wonder. What did I ever do to deserve that?

And then what? I wondered, my eyes once again returning to the specks that were the Wild Company. *What do I do with Thump in the south then?*

ACT 2: THE RIDER-IN-TRAINING

CHAPTER 11
DAYIE, AND DAGFAN

"**A**nd there she is," Rahim said at last, pointing down the last rise of land towards where the sprawling, terraced down collapsed over a wide bend in the Taval River that flows on this side of the distant Fury Mountains. We'd been travelling now for almost ten days, and had made it through the high passes thanks to Rahim's knowledge of the winding Gypsy tracks there. Luckily, we hadn't encountered any more of the wild mountain dragons, which I thought was owing to Thump being much more active now, confident and flying every day.

Either that, or the wild dragons had well and truly got the message that we weren't to be messed with. But it wasn't just Thump who had changed over our journey, it was also Nas and Rahim.

"Or maybe it's you," Thump pronounced above us, swooping high over the thermals.

"Thump! You have to come down now!" I whispered up to him, earning a quick whip of the tail in mid-air in response as he ignored my command. I grinned. How could I be angry at a creature so spirited and handsome?

But maybe that was one of the reasons why Rahim and Nas had changed their attitude to me, ever since we had saved them from the attacking dragons. Thump had certainly gotten big, and he was almost consuming his weight in river fish every day now. As we had kept on pushing through the wilderness, Rahim had even started asking me – *me* – my opinions on things, on which route to take, and whether I was going to deliver Thump to the Training Hall as the Dragon Traders had originally planned.

Of course I was, I had said, only I added silently that I was also going to go with him. If Captain Akeem and his Wild Company wouldn't take me on to help fight for the South, then that only left the Training Hall of Dagfan. I was terrible at flying, and Thump needed a place where we could learn together.

"But they never asked to have a fully hatched dragon and a girl," Rahim said again, his voice low. I knew he was trying to be gentle, he was trying to tell me that my dreams might not amount to anything. I bit my lip to keep from telling him that until recently I had never *had* any dreams – and had fully expected to work for Fan for the rest of my short life!

"I get it, Rahim," I said. "We are not what the Training Hall is

looking for – *I* am not what the Training Hall is looking for."
What was it that they always said about that place? That the
Seven were 'older' Dragon Riders – in the sense that they
were all under thirty-- because every other Rider that had been
recruited since had been eaten or trampled by the dragons?
And that each of those Seven left were only there by dint of
being the nastiest, meanest, and most stubborn.

And I was just a teenaged girl, I thought with a frown. But
there was a lot that the Training Hall – and the city of Dagfan
hadn't figured on when they'd sent us to steal dragon eggs. I
was so impressed with this new thought that I felt compelled
to share it with Rahim.

"Look up there at him, Rahim. Look at how he flies. He's
allowed me to ride him three times now – what other Rider
can say that down at the Training Hall? They are used to
receiving an egg, and I am going to come to them with a
young bull dragon who already can take a rider, and *me* who
already knows how to ride him."

"Don't push it..." Nas looked at me skeptically, and *yeah,* I
knew that my arch nemesis was right. I had ridden Thump
three times over the last week, out of a total of about six or
eight attempts. But that was better than none, right?

Nas had changed too – he had lost some of his spikier edges
around me and was instead *almost* polite. Almost. Not that I
could forget his little cruelties to me back when he thought
that I was just a good-for-nothing servant of his mothers'. Or

maybe Thump was right, and that it was *me* who had changed the greater. Every time that I looked at Nas or Rahim now, I didn't feel the instinctive flinch that I used to have, as I expected the next harsh word or command.

Now, instead, I felt confident, even felt a little pity towards them. They didn't have dragons (Nas's egg still hadn't hatched) and the mastermind of this whole plan – Fan – had left her son and her husband to save their own skins. Without her poisonous influence, it appeared that the other two were almost nice human beings.

Almost, like I say.

"Well, *I* think that I'm going to impress them," I said proudly, whistling once more to Thump to come back before he got spotted. The Holy Sands alone would know what they would do if they saw what they thought was a rogue bull dragon flying towards them.

"Well, maybe *you would* think that you're the best thing to happen to them," Nas muttered snidely. Like I said, he was *almost* a nice human being. I just shook my head and said nothing as I went to greet Thump before we initiated the next part of our plan.

Dagfan was a river city, which meant that it was in constant threat by Deadweed travelling along its banks and taking root.

Luckily for Dagfan, though, it had two major things going for it – one was that it was home to the Council of the three Southern Lords, making it the place where they held their trade negotiations and discussed matters that pertained to the whole Southern Kingdom. That meant that Dagfan was also one of most highly protected cities in the South, with towers and walls and secondary ditches and patrol boats going up and down the river, in search for fast-rooting infections of the Deadweed.

The other thing that it had going for it was the Training Hall, which was built in the site of one of the ancient coliseums that could be found throughout the southern lands, on the other side of the city from where the palace rose on the high bluffs. According to legend, Dagfan was once a cruel place, with many gladiatorial deathmatches held in its coliseum, but some believed that was just a rumor spread by Torvaldian agents.

From where we stood, we could see the Training Hall clearly from this vantage point: a wide fortified circle whose walls were built high and thick. It had been repaired and rebuilt so many times, Rahim had told me, that it was almost impossible to judge now which of its stones were original or which were fresh.

"It might not be such a great home for a girl and her dragon," Rahim said to me in a quieter tone, which I ignored. What did he want me to do, continue to travel with them, the Dragon Traders? And do what – be content as his wife's servant until such time as she determined my debt to her was paid? Become a travelling carnival sideshow and hope to settle my debt faster? *'Pay 2 coins to see the girl and the dragon?'* No thanks. I had seen what Deadweed could do, I had seen Deadweed kill my foster parents – and just recently I had seen how dragons could be used to fight it. Now fate had given me, not a dragon with which to buy my freedom, but a dragon. There was no other way for me. I just had to get to the Training Hall before Rahim found Fan again.

Nas returned in the blazing hot afternoon with a wagon large enough to hide Thump. I say *hide* – he was getting so big now that the axles groaned as the horses pulled it towards the outer markets around Dagfan, and he had to curl his neck, wings and tail in on himself or else he would break the canvas covers and spill out of the sides.

But the Dragon Traders were a well-known bunch, and we didn't get stopped by the guards of Dagfan as Rahim had feared we might. He didn't want anyone to see Thump – and neither did I – before we got to the Training Hall. There, I had an inkling of hope that they respected or understood dragons somewhat – and wouldn't run around in a blind panic at seeing a rogue, unridden dragon in the streets, or call for the guards to attack Thump.

Luckily for us too, Dagfan was a merchant and trader's paradise. The guards were more concerned with armed arrivals than they were with merchants, and we naturally joined the river of other carts as they swept through the cobbled streets, underneath the watchful eyes of the white-stoned palace itself, and out to the shanty warehouses and market streets that led to the Training Hall itself.

"Rahim!? Nas!" A nightmarish screech broke through my thoughts as I sat at the head of the wagon, driving the horses and dreaming about when *I,* Dayie, would be one of the Seven (*they would have to change their name to the Eight,* I had been thinking very proudly).

"Rahim – it's you!" Screeched the voice as a figure broke through the crowds to stalk towards us.

Oh no, please no, I thought.

It was Fan.

"Fan – my heart!" Rahim called excitedly from his side of the bench, jumping down to hold out his hands to her.

"Mother!" Nas emerged from the side of the wagon, where he had been on duty making certain that no bits of the dragon started to show. My stomach cramped in anxiety. It was a visceral feeling, like my body remembered her stinging blows more than my mind did.

"She harms you?" Thump said in the back of my mind.

"No," I muttered, sensing his anger like a heat wave through my mind. "Not anymore, anyway." My resolve hardened. *I have nothing to fear from her anymore. There is nothing that she can do to me now...* I was set on my plan to make the Training Hall take me on.

"What have you got there?" Fan ignored her second husband's outstretched arms, and even ignored her son as she strode straight past them to the wagon and reached to pull at the canvas.

"Don't," I said warningly, and surprisingly, she listened, pulling up short as she looked up at me.

"Excuse me?" she said, her features screwed up and tight as she glared up at me. "I see that you're still alive – more's the pity-- and that you haven't lost any of your bad manners!"

I had to grit my teeth to stop myself from shouting at her.

"Fan—" Rahim said warningly, reaching her side. "Never mind the girl. You are back with us now, we are together again…"

"Fan?" said another voice, and I looked over to see a very large southern man dressed in black loose pants and a simple, armless leather jerkin. He had braided black hair, and a large scimitar at his side. "Who are these people? Are they bothering you?"

The leader of the Dragon Traders squinted between them,

clearly calculating. "No, Liev, they are not. These are my family."

"I thought *I* was your family?" the large man – Liev – grunted, pushing his shoulders back to look down at Rahim, who was merely looking between Fan and the new man in confusion.

"Wife? What is the meaning of this…?" Rahim said.

"I took another husband, Rahim. Liev here is a mercenary from the Inner Sea, he helped me take the river road to the south," Fan said, without a hint of shame or embarrassment.

"Wife – I'm not even dead yet!" Rahim burst out.

"And how was I supposed to know that, Rahim! I thought that this brat up here—" another scowl in my direction, "—almost had both my husband and my son killed! I was alone! You know as head of the family I have the duty to keep the family name alive!"

"But – uh…?" Rahim looked from Nas to Liev, his gaze darkening.

"I had to find some way to rebuild the Dragon Traders, you old fool!" Fan scolded him. "Now that we have Liev with us, we are sure to do well on the next run."

"The next run…" Rahim echoed, clearly perturbed. I wondered if he was now seeing his wife as I saw her—as a self-serving, greedy bully—and I wondered if he would be strong enough to do anything about it.

"Yes. But I am glad that at least you managed to bring my property back from that uncivilized, freezing tip that is Torvald!" Fan snapped, turning back to the wagon. "Now – let's see what we have to sell…"

"I said don't touch it," I growled, one hand moving to the long-knife at my belt.

The look on Fan's face was one of pure hatred as she hissed. "Liev – stop standing there like a loaf of bread and make yourself useful: Get this brat off my wagon and give her a sound beating while I take a look…" Behind her, Liev grinned as he cracked his knuckles and started walking towards me, and Fan seized at the leather straps securing the wagon's canvas to its bed, and pulled—

"Sssss!" There was a sound like a boiling kettle as the canvas was ripped from her hands, and Fan was thrown back by the slap of a long, Crimson Red tail. Liev, walking up to my side of the wagon shouted in alarm and jumped back – and the rest of the market street started to panic as Thump shoved his snout from the wagon bed and roared.

"Leave us alone!" I heard him shout in my mind, although my ears heard the deafening challenge of the young bull dragon. He arched his neck, and his wings snapped out like the crack of a whip, scaring the horses and scattering traders and customers alike.

"Dragon! Wild dragon!" the cries spread around the street.

"What the—what did you do?" Fan gibbered from the floor of a broken stall, its fruit smashed and mushed all around her.

I stood up quickly, mounting the back board so that I was standing directly under the rearing dragon, and put my hand up to his swelling chest.

"We aren't yours anymore, Fan. And if you attempt to stop us, I won't need a dragon – I'll kill you myself," I spat at her. It felt good, after all of these years to say that to her at last.

"We hunt?" Thump lashed his tail behind us, scattering the wooden railings of the wagon and taking out a stack of barrels that stood by the side of one of the market stalls. Our wagon horses whinnied and stamped, trying to get away.

"Not yet, Thump, not yet..." I whispered, looking over the street. This wasn't quite how I wanted my introduction to Dagfan to go – but then again – how else were you to introduce a dragon?

"Call the guards!" someone was shouting.

"Call out the Seven!" Another added their terrified voice.

"No – wait, I mean yes..." I said, confused. I *wanted* to meet the Seven of course, but that didn't mean that I wanted them to try and attack Thump! "You don't understand..." I called out to them, and neither did the Crimson Red behind me, as he reared up again and pawed at the air, bellowing his challenge to this strange world of buildings and running people.

145

He's scared, I thought. The dragon had never been in a city amongst humans before – as an egg he was surrounded by caves and other dragons, and now…

"Now you've really gone and done it, silly girl!" Fan spat from her mattress of squashed fruit. "The Seven will come and put an end to you and your dragon – and good riddance!"

"Skreyargh!" Fury rippled through Thump at Fan's words as he pounced down onto the floor, making the wagons along the street shake, horses spook, and causing more people to flee for their lives. He lowered his head towards Fan, stalking forward like an angry cat. I realized then just how much he *had* grown. He was almost two or three horse lengths now, and I smelled burning as well. It was Thump, ribbons of thin black smoke curling up from his jaw as he pulled back his scaled lips to reveal long white teeth.

I wanted to shout no to him. I wanted to tell him not to eat Fan – but another part of me silenced that voice. *Why?* I thought. She was cruel to me. She had never been anything but nasty to me-

The street had gone deadly quiet, and there was no noise apart from Fan the Dragon Trader's terrified panting, and the crunch of the Crimson Red's claws as he trod closer, and closer.

"No – please no. I don't want to die, Dayie…" Fan gibbered, and I think it was hearing those words from her that unfroze my heart.

"Thump, no," I said, and the dragon paused to turn his head, still smoking to look at me.

"Why? She's our enemy," the dragon said. *"She hurt you."*

"It's not that simple, Thump. I wish it was," I said with a sigh. "But we have to show mercy sometimes, to show our enemies that we are not like them. That we are better than them..." I held the dragon's eyes seriously as I spoke the words.

The Crimson Dragon just looked at me, and I could tell that he was trying to figure the sense in my words.

Clash-Clash-Clash-Clash! Before Thump could decide, there came a sudden ringing sound of a gong, along with angry shouts. I turned, just as large shadows fell over the street, flashing past us and overhead.

It was the Seven. They had come.

CHAPTER 12
DAYIE, & HOW MUCH AN EGG IS WORTH?

"*C hallengers.*" Thump beside me bounced onto his hind legs, raising his neck to follow the much larger forms of the dragons as they swooped and flapped around our sector of the market street. My heart tripped over itself – this wasn't like last time, seeing the Wild Company and the Torvald Academy Riders face off against each other. I felt no rush of awe and admiration at the sight. It was something in the way that these Greens and Blues flew, the way that they angled their great heads to search the ground for us. They were ready to fight, and we were their target.

As I watched, a Green convulsed in the sky, its long neck reaching up as it bellowed a great ball of flame up into the airs, and another Sinuous Blue –far longer and thinner than the Green, flared the scales and tines around the back of its head and along its neck. I knew enough about animals to know that these beasts were leering for a battle, and, turning back to look at Thump I saw how small he was compared to them. He might be able to scare a street full of merchants and traders, but I did not think that he would last a moment against these larger, battle-hardened dragons.

They bore the marks of their battles with nonchalance, great white scars that threaded across the underside of their wings, as well as puncture marks where impacted scales had long since healed, but oddly. Several had ragged wings as if giant bites had been nipped from them, and one even had a stubbed tail where it should have ended in a wide barbed fork. As I watched, two of the dragons almost collided, and turned to rear and spit at each other. These dragons had none of the cool authority and solidarity of the Torvald Enclosure dragons. Nor did they fly in formation as Akeem's Wild Company had. They flew like a storm of crows, sometimes flaring at each other as much as they circled to find the best attacking angle to take against us.

"No, no… this is all wrong." I stood in front of Thump, holding my arms out as if I could protect him from their dragon flame. "Wait!" I cried. "He's not wild! He's to be trained at the Hall!"

"Am I, now?" Thump hissed his own challenge back at them. He was nervous, but either too foolish or too brave to back down even an inch from the circling dragons above. Behind

me, Nas and Rahim had edged to the side of the plaza, while Fan still lay in the smashed stalls.

Whump! A shadow turned into the loud thunder of a landing dragon as a Stocky Green landed on the nearest flat roof of a warehouse. This one appeared to be larger and older than the others, and one of its eyes was a milky white, and on its back there sat a thin rider.

"Calm your beast!" the Rider called arrogantly, pointing a small hand spear down at us, with a short blade and long black handle. *A prod,* I thought distastefully.

As the rider dismounted, I noted that he was also tall, wearing black, loose-fitting robes and with rough black hair tied back with a headband. The other encircling Seven seemed to afford him with some sort of respect as they raised their flights and circle a little wider, giving this one the first chance at an attack.

"He's no beast!" I called back, some of Thump's defiant fire seeping into my words. "He is a Crimson Red, straight from the North!"

"Hsss, fool!" Fan hissed at me (she had managed to crawl away from her fruit and vegetable puree to the side of one of the nearest alleys). "The South *doesn't* steal dragon eggs, girl!" she muttered to me, in clear contradiction of what she had done, but I saw what she meant. It was an open secret that the Southern Princedom hired Dragon Traders to find and

poach Dragon Eggs – but they would never admit to condoning such theft from the Academy of Torvald.

"I don't need your help," I spat back, as Thump's tail lashed the mouth of the alley as Fan yelped and jumped back.

"I said *calm* that dragon, now!" the man barked, reaching the edge of the building and casually climbing down the single story, to land with a heavy groan on the cobbles below.

"That's Talal, Head Trainer at the Training Hall!" Fan hissed once more, despite my rebuke. She had returned to the mouth of the alley and even dared to call out to the man approaching us. "Sir! Sir – it is me, the Dragon Trader, look what I have brought you…" she simpered.

It was just like Fan to always try to make some money out of a bad situation, I thought darkly.

"A young male bull?" this 'Head Trainer' said incredulously. "What were you thinking? How did you get it here?"

"He'll not harm you," I said quickly, hoping that what I said was true. "We have come to train with you, to learn how to defend the South. To defeat the Deadweed…"

"We…?" Talal was only a young man, perhaps into his thirties, but he had the shrewd look and the tight watchfulness of a battle-hardened soldier. "The Training Hall takes eggs, trader. Grown dragons are useless to us." He cast a look heavenwards, towards the other dragons. Did that mean that their only response would now be to drive out the 'rogue dragon' so close to the palace? I thought in horror. Drive out, or....?

"He's already fought," I burst out. It wasn't technically true, as he had only swooped in to save Rahim and Nas from the wild mountain dragons, but it was still flying under duress, right?

"What?" the man called Talal said.

"He fought wild mountain dragons, and I did. I was on his back," I said, scanning the hushed crowd until I saw my witnesses. "Ask them, there." I pointed to Rahim and Nas.

Talal didn't bother to ask them--their nods of assent were proof enough.

"Dayie? What is happening?" Thump was still hissing behind me, pawing at the air.

I made a choice. They might not ever accept us if he didn't calm down. *"Mamma-la, Mamma-la,"* I sang the song that always calmed scared and anxious animals. It had worked with him since he had been just a hatchling newt, and now it worked once again. At first his eyelids lowered, and the grumble in the back of his throat subsided to a low buzz, before he started to lower his head a little, and even his over-active tail stopped its wild swishing.

"What did you just do?" Talal looked at me intently as I stroked Thumps' snout and whispered into the Crimson Red's ears. But the Training Hall might be my only hope, but I wasn't willing to give up all my secrets to it yet.

"I have a way with animals," I said, which was the truth. If I told him about the song—a song I didn't even know the origin of—then just like all the villagers of my childhood, he might think that I was just another witch and have us driven out of the capital anyway. The thought that maybe I *was* a witch, creeped into my mind, but I shoved that idea aside.

"I'm good with horses, chickens, goats, dogs…" I shrugged. "And I guess dragons, too."

"Hmm." Talal nodded to himself. "You say this dragon of yours has already taken a Rider? With no saddle?" he said in a measured way.

"No saddle." I nodded. "And the rider was me."

Talal gave another piercing look around us as he stroked his thin and scratchy beard. "Fine. If you are as good with *our* dragons as you are with this one, then you might become useful. Consider yourself, and your dragon, recruited."

I couldn't believe it. "Thank you! Thank you, thank you!" I said again, hugging Thump's neck hard.

"This is good? We hunt?" Thump's voice murmured at me.

"No, we're not hunting yet. We have a home, dragon. We have a home," I said to him, patting his scales that still felt cool despite the heat of the sun.

"How much?" Fan's voice broke through my reverie, her greed managing to overcome her fear as she rose from the alley-

"*Sss...*" Despite his soporific stage, Thump still managed to hiss at Fan, making her squeak and skitter around us in a wide circle.

"Excuse me?" Talal turned to look at her.

"I'm the Dragon Trader who brought you this dragon. It was *my* caravan that did all the hard work. How much are you going to offer for it?" Fan said.

"You know the usual price," Talal muttered, as my confusion warred with my outrage. *I* had done all the hard work! I thought. *I* was the one who had brought Thump all the way south – and she ran off at the first sign of trouble!

"Usual price? Pfagh! You heard the girl. A grown dragon that already can take a Rider and orders. I want double. No, triple!" Fan said.

The man called Talal was silent for a moment, before nodding. "Fine. A thousand and five hundred gold crowns to be paid to the Dragon Traders of Fan Hazim," he said loudly, pulling out a small bronze token from his jerkin. "That is my sign, when you present that to the palace, they'll make the payment," he said. "I'll send a messenger as soon as we're done here."

"Good." Fan's face broke open into a victorious smile. She

turned, grinning to me (the token disappearing in the many folds of her own attire) "Come on then, girl. Let the man have his product."

"What?" I said, astonished. "I'm not going with you. You heard the Head Trainer. I'm useful to the Training Hall."

Fan snorted. "I paid good coin for you, Dayie, and if you think I'm going to let you go when you still have to make up for all of the losses of my expedition, then you really are stupider than you look. You owe me, girl. And Fan Hazim never lets a debt go."

"No—" I said, astonished, to be echoed by none other than the head trainer Talal.

"No, Trader Hazim, our bargain clearly states…"

"You know the rule of debt, Dragon Trainer," Fan scolded him. "I bought this servant fair and square, and she is indebted to me until the debt is paid. Not even the prince himself can break that law."

The Head Trainer opened and closed his mouth at her audacity, and for just a moment I thought he was going to acquiesce to the Dragon Trader.

"One servant girl?" he finally asked. "How much? The Training Hall will buy her."

Fan went silent, clearly wondering whether she should argue her case or not. "She's clearly special. She has a way with animals, and she has to make up for all the goods and cargo I lost on the way down here…"

"Not the Training Hall's problem," Talal said fiercely. "I'm buying the girl, and the dragon, not what happened on the road down here."

"Pfagh!" Fan said again, but I had no doubt that she would simply add on the cost of her losses to my price. I felt suddenly cheap and belittled by this, before catching myself. *Is this how you feel, Thump?* I asked, reaching out to put a hand on his side.

"Human blabber," Thump reassured me. *"They can talk all they want about coins and owning things. No coin or bit of paper owns me."*

I guess you had a different perspective on everything if you could just open up your wings and fly away at any moment, I thought.

"And me," a voice broke into the negotiation. To my surprise, it was Nas, struggling from the mess of the wagon and canvas with his own, very heavy egg. "I got an egg too. I want to be a Dragon Rider, just like Dayie," he said stubbornly.

"Nas? Put that down before you break it!" Fan said. "And get back to the horses!" she said, before turning to Talal and, without skipping a beat said. "One trained dragon, one *egg, and* the girl? Four thousand gold crowns."

Talal laughed. "Five hundred an egg, you know the price. A thousand and five for the dragon, and, because I think she might have some potential, *thirty* for the girl. Two thousand and thirty gold crowns."

I staggered. That was a fortune for the likes of us. I couldn't imagine that Fan would ever consider turning it down.

"*I'm* not going back to trading with you, Ma," Nas said defiantly, not turning back as she had ordered to the horses. "I want to ride dragons, and that is what I'm going to do. See," he turned to Talal. "I have my own egg and everything…"

"Nas – what nonsense are you talking about?" Fan hissed at him.

"You left us for dead, and found yourself a new family," her son responded, shooting an angry look at Liev. "I don't care what you say or do, I'm not a servant. I've come into my maturity now. I can do what I want." He turned to Talal. "Will you accept me?"

All eyes turned to the Head Dragon trainer who had a smirk on his face. "*We're* the ones who usually select warriors to become Riders, kid," Talal said. "They're usually soldiers, or horse racers, or mercenaries, or show some aptitude for it."

Fan burst out, "He's not allowed!" Both Talal and Nas ignored her.

"You're young. And you don't come to us able to ride your

own dragon, as this girl does," Talal reasoned. "So, I'll tell you what. For the price of that egg, we'll take you on and we'll feed you, train you, teach you to fight with swords, bows, spears. How to fight in a battle, how to ride horses—"

"I can ride horses, already," Nas interrupted, earning him a sharp look from Talal before he went on as if he hadn't heard.

"—as well as dragons. *And* we'll teach you how to look after a dragon – but there's still no guarantee that either of you two will survive the training, and it will cost you that egg you have in your hands," Talal said.

"That's outrageous!" Fan said, but she wasn't talking about the loss of her son, she was talking about the loss of the five hundred gold crowns. "We almost died over that egg! Two thousand and thirty gold coins we agreed on, not one thousand and five-thirty!"

"That's the offer, kid, take it or leave it." Talal spoke only to Nas, not to Fan Hazim, and, just like me, it seemed that Nas had no intention of going back. Seeing his mother abandon them for another husband must have changed things for him.

"Agreed." Nas was ecstatic, walking forward with egg as Fan hissed and growled with rage.

"You'll both rue this day, idiots!" Fan spat at both of us, her natural son and her ex-slave.

"Hey, watch it," Talal growled. "You're talking to Trainees of

Dagfan, now!" But the man's warnings only made Fan concentrate her ire on me, as I guess that old habits have always been hard to break.

"This isn't over, *slave.*" She spat at me, turning and fleeing back into her alleyway, her dress still caked with mushed vegetables and fruit. Her last words gave me a shiver of apprehension, but it was easy to push that out of my mind as I looked over to Nas to give him a slightly uncomfortable nod.

"You made the right choice," I said.

I know," he responded back to me, looking just as awkward and uncomfortable, as neither of us knew how far we could trust each other now that everything was about to change completely and forever for us.

CHAPTER 13
DAYIE'S EXPECTATIONS

"Welcome to your new home," Talal called over his shoulder, as he led us into the renovated coliseum that was the Training Hall. Not that I could see much of it beyond him, as 'Green', his unimaginatively-named Green dragon was lumbering ahead of us, and blocking the arched corridor that we had to walk through. Green was an older dragon, older than all of the others here and had become a sort of unofficial patriarch for the Seven--Nine now, I thought.

The Training Hall was set at the back of the market and ware-house district, where the cobbles ended and the earth broke into slabs of bed rock that cut through the ground and made any other buildings impossible.

"In centuries past they used to march here, before it was a Dragon Hall," Talal had explained, indicating how the broad path swept up to the high walls of the large round building and into one of the many archways that led inside.

"Why isn't anyone at the gates!" Talal snarled as soon as they were thrown open, revealing a long corridor into the central space on the far side. Much smaller wooden doors branched off this hallway, leading under the terraces of stone galleries that I saw when we walked out into the light.

"Krawk!" Green gave a mighty croaking roar and sauntered across the large circular arena of sand towards where a low cave-like archway sat on the far side. Smoke pooled out from its opening, and when Talal pointed over to the dragons, I guessed that was where the dragons slept.

"The dragons have caves under the bluff of rocks through there," he said. "They pretty much roam freely if they have completed training."

If? I thought a little suspiciously. How on earth would anyone stop them?

The coliseum itself was given over to the arena, which was baked sand and divided into separate areas. One area had lots of stone pillars standing at close proximity to each other, whilst another had a series of hoops and hurdles set out, whilst a larger area appeared bare, save for casks of water against the walls.

"This is where we train, and not just with the dragons – but we also train how to fight, how to ride, shoot. I wasn't lying about what I told your mother back there," Talal informed Nas, who appeared embarrassed at the mention of Fan's memory.

"Up there, we have the dormitories and the halls." He pointed to the galleries that terraced up along the inside walls, some with windows that would look down over the arena. "It's bigger than the Academy they've got up in the North, actually," Talal said proudly.

"But they have the Dragon Enclosure as well," I pointed out. An entire crater given over to their dragons, and not just a set of caves.

"Easy there, Trainee… Whose side are you on?" Talal said with another smirk.

Thump's, I thought instinctively. "I didn't realize we were at war?" I said, thinking about the confrontation that I had seen between the Wild Company and the Torvald dragons.

"War? Who said anything about war?" the Head Trainer frowned at me, turning to pause in the center of the arena. "But be sure of this – the *Kingdom* of Torvald has been pushing at our borders for generations now, and she's never taken much interest in the welfare of the people of the South."

Funny, that was almost exactly what Akeem had said, too, I thought. It was one thing to hear an opinion from one person, but now I was starting to think that maybe it was true. Not that I had heard or seen any particular ill will from the actual Torvald citizens to the south. In fact, the merchants and travelers I had met on the road up to the citadel of Torvald had appeared to be only too pleased that we had travelled from so far to visit 'the center of the world'.

"The worst enemy that we've got right now, mark my words – is the Deadweed." Talal's voice grew grave. "That is what this place is for, although the prince will try to tell us that we need it against Torvald…" the man said. "But the real enemy is the Deadweed. If we don't do anything, we'll be overrun before next summer."

"We saw some on the way down here," I agreed. But of course he knew that, right? He must be working with the Wild Company after all.

"Where?" he snapped, his eyes suddenly sharp.

"Right by the Southern Gate," I said.

"The Southern Gate? But that'll choke our main access to the North!" Talal abruptly turned and whistled up to the terraces. After a moment, there was the bang of a shutter as a round faced and round-shouldered man leaned out from three stories up.

"Nefed! Get a message to the Palace. Deadweed spotted at the Southern Gate!" he called.

A look of alarm spread over the man's face. "I'll get the others called in, Talal!" he bellowed down, before slamming the shutters back.

How could they not know about the Deadweed? I thought, but I had no time to ask as one of the larger gates banged open on the ground floor of the arena, letting out a small tide of people.

"The Seven?" I gasped in awe.

"Ah, no." Talal's shoulders shook as he laughed. "Those are the other trainees. Like you."

"Trainees?" I said, confused. "I thought you were training us up to join the Seven?"

"I am," Talal said. "But the Seven are the only ones who have passed the training yet. Well, actually they are the only ones who have *survived* the training. We actually have twenty or so trainees willing to become Southern Riders."

"Oh," I said, watching the raucous bunch parade and rough-house on their way over to us. For some reason, I'd had the impression that the Training Hall was an elite place, where the Seven wise and noble warriors would see my value immediately. *'The girl who hatched a dragon!'* they would have said to me, or *'you flew him yourself – without any training?'*

But there was no sage respect from my peers. In fact, it appeared that they were just another bunch of teenagers like myself and Nas, and that none of them appeared to be very polite or very respectful. They were untidy, for one thing – wearing shirts and pantaloons, some with leather jerkins and some of the boys just shirtless in the high heat.

"Ladies and gentlemen!" Talal shouted at the approaching crowd. "Please welcome…" he suddenly turned to look at me. "What are your names again?"

"Dayie," I said, and as Talal paused for me to continue, I added. "Nothing else. Just Dayie."

"Outstanding," the Head Trainer muttered, nodding at Nas besides me.

"Nas Hazim."

The other trainees looked at us blankly, not a friendly face among them. I don't know what I had been expecting, but whatever it was, these young men and women weren't providing any clues as to how they would take to a Dragon Trader Gypsy and an orphan girl joining their ranks.

"They'll be joining us, and one of them even already has a dragon!" Talal said, waving a hand to where Thump was still carefully snuffing the back of the arena. He raised his head as I looked over at him, and I swear that he blinked at me.

"He's big." I heard a gasp from the others, one of the taller young men said that, already with a scar splitting his face long since turned white. I wondered if the shirtless youth had earned that here in the arena, or whether he was one of Talal's 'hardened soldiers' that he said that they recruited from.

"He is," I said proudly. Looking at him now, he seemed to have grown even since the confrontation at the market, though, to be honest, he was still far smaller than Talal's Green. Thump was well proportioned, and anyone could see his vitality and vigor in the bright shine of his scales and the shining black of his talons.

"Screch!" Thump called defiantly, showing off. He even earned a worried shuffle from the other trainees behind us.

"I bet I could ride him," the scar-faced trainee said. He was one of the shirtless ones, with short-cropped fuzzy hair and a large scimitar hanging at his belt.

What? "No." I turned in the sand. "*I* ride him."

There was a moment of silence, and I noticed that all eyes were not on me or Thump – but on Talal, who appeared to be watching our exchange closely. What was going on here?

"Dayie – we have to keep to a strict training schedule here," Talal said gravely to me. *Why was he telling me this? He knows that I came here to work, after all!* "We have to train not just to be a dragon rider, but we also have to work with you as a soldier and with your Crimson Red separately too. You might not get to spend as much time as you want with him."

"I brought him here," I said defiantly. "I raised him from an egg."

"Horse crap…" came a mutter from the trainees behind me. "That dragon is six years old if he's a day, that would make her what, **twelve** when she stole the egg?" A snigger of laughter bubbled from the assembled youths, and I felt shame and indignation wash through me. But it was true. I had cared for Thump, and he had thrived. I couldn't explain why things grew well around me. All I knew was it wasn't my fault!

"It's true!" I kicked the sand.

"Here we go, she's throwing a tantrum…" someone said, just loud enough for me to hear it.

"Who said that!" I stamped, glaring at the crowd of twenty-something trainees that was even now dissolving into fits of giggles.

"Dayie…" Nas hissed at my side, his eyes going wide. He was embarrassed by my anger. *Why?* Was he so eager to fit in with these new people? On the other side of us, Talal seemed to be allowing the teasing to run its course, not getting involved even when I glared at him.

"He's *my* dragon," I said to the Head Trainer – *that* seemed to have some effect, as his face hardened into a glare.

"If he's to train here, Dayie— if *you're* to train here– then both of you will need to learn how to keep your temper and to take orders. I haven't got the time or patience to try and get some sense into you if you don't want to learn."

It was like getting slapped in the face. I was still angry with him, and a part of me was thinking *why didn't he take my side?* But it was also different getting reprimanded by this man than it was by Nas's mother. Fan would slap me and blame for anything that didn't go according to her plan in the camp – even if I had nothing to do with it at all. But Talal was making a point, and even – dare I say it – offering me a sort of choice. I felt oddly humiliated by the fact that I hadn't lived up to this man's expectations already.

"I want to learn how to fight," I said, my voice sounding small to my ears.

"Right, good." Talal nodded. "Now. I'm afraid that you won't get as much time with your Crimson Red as you would like. But it's for the best. I'm making Dragon Riders here, not pets."

"I understand." I nodded as Talal whistled for two men to step forward – these weren't dragon riders I don't think – but they were big and burly, and they had long iron goads in their hand – each tipped with blunted horns at the end like a fork.

"Get the dragon a cave, fresh straw, meat and water," Talal called, and I watched as the men started warily walking around Thump who hissed at them and lashed his tail.

"What is this, Dayie? Who are these people?" he said in my mind.

"Just follow them, it's going to be okay," I said, nodding slowly at him. "This is where the other dragon went, the Green one."

"Who's she talking to?" one of the other trainee's muttered in front of me, and Talal gave me a sharp look, but I didn't flinch as I kept my eyes straight on Thump.

Thump made it clear he didn't like it as he hissed and thumped his tail loudly on the sands, but this was the only option that we had. I couldn't release him to the mountains, where he'd be picked off by the wild mountain dragons, or the Vicious Oranges, or Deadweed. At least here he would get a safe den, and food, and we could train together. I just hoped I was doing the right thing.

"And the same for you two," Talal nodded at one of the other trainee recruits. "Latifa. Show them to the dorms and find a bed for them, then show them around."

A young woman stepped forward, dark skin and with long braids tied and knotted down her back. She nodded seriously at Talal and gave me a small, serious smile. "Come on, dinner isn't far off," she said to us both, waiting for us to join her as she led the way towards the terraced galleries.

I was here at the Dragon Training Hall of Dagfan, I thought. I had done it, I was finally free – but I didn't feel as safe and as secure as I'd thought I would. The other trainees were mean, and I didn't like to be apart from Thump. I just prayed that I could make a home here.

CHAPTER 14
DAYIE, NOT ENOUGH &
TOO MUCH

L atifa was older than both me and Nas, a fact that seemed to have a very strange effect on the boy who had been my oppressor. Instead of being surly and bossy with Latifa, as he would have done with me, he nodded enthusiastically as she pointed out the trophies and mementos to the Seven that adorned the alcoves in this hall.

"Wild dragon skull, Sea Reaver battle-banner," she said with a bored monotone as if she'd given this tour a hundred times. This hall appeared to be a common room of sorts, with scarred and scored benches next to equally as battered tables, and from one of the doors I could smell the cooking of fragrant spices.

"Cinnamon and lychee curry, I think tonight." Latifa smiled, when she caught me sniffing. The interior of the Training Hall had an austere, workmanlike mood. We had walked pasts buckets of sand and water in equal measure – *'for burns and dragon fire'* – we were told, and other than the trophies of war, there were no pennants or tapestries that might indicate the high regard this place held in the South. If anything, it appeared more like a barracks than it did a noble place of training dragons.

"Deadweed seedpod." Latifa gestured to the last item sitting on its own plinth, making me shudder.

"What? You keep one of those things in here, this close to the capital!?" I burst out, earning an agreeing grumble from the girl. I think I liked her. She didn't appear as cruel or mocking as her fellow trainees.

"I know, right? But everyone's under orders not to go near it with water." Latifa paused, pointing to the strange, tapered, desiccated and brown octagon. It was almost as large as my head and looked very dead – but I still didn't trust it. "I know – none of us like it, but Talal says that we have to understand the enemy."

And you've had a lot of them, I thought, looking back along the common room alcoves at the evidence of battles with the desert tribes, the wild dragons, the Orange dragons, and the Sea Reavers of the coast.

"The South has been hard pressed of late, and even worse with Deadweed at our shores," Latifa responded as she led us to the first bank of stairs up to the next terraced hall. "Lord Kasim has started calling out the Seven for everything, and Talal thinks it's because he's losing too many troops on the ground."

"Which is why we're here," I said, earning a nod from Latifa.

"You're getting it."

The next hall was a sort of changing room, with the rear wall given over to multiple suits of leathers, stands of buckler shields, and light tunics. "Here is where we suit up for the day's practice, which begins at dawn," the girl said. "An hour of physical exercise, and then we split up into teams to either work on swordcraft, strategy, or with the dragons, stopping for lunch, and then swapping over in the afternoon."

As the Training Halls were built into the old terrace stairs of the coliseum, each level was narrow and the rooms curving, meaning you had to walk through each one to get to another. We walked past smaller chambers that appeared to be given over to healers (these places smelled the nicest, as they had herbs growing in the windows) which were occupied by white-robed men and women who nodded a greeting to Latifa as she passed by. There was another changing room, and then an abrupt doorway to the side of a set of stairs.

"That's the Seven's area. In there they have their meetings and their own training and common rooms. Sometimes they come down to eat with us, but more often than not they keep themselves apart,"

"You've met them?" I couldn't help but ask. The Seven were

legendary throughout the peoples of the South: the defenders of the nation against the horrors of the world. Our answer to the Dragon Riders of Torvald.

"Yeah." Latifa made a shrug of disgust. "I warn you though – none of that starry eyes nonsense here. They're not what you think they are."

"What about Akeem's Wild Company? Where are they?" I asked as we walked up the stairs to another level, which if we turned right was given over to dormitories and wash rooms, and left was once again met by a sealed door.

"Shush!" Latifa scowled suddenly, pausing before the door. "*Never* talk about them here."

"What?" I said, but Latifa's dark glance was enough to let me know that I shouldn't ask any more questions. Yet.

"Behind that door are the workrooms and libraries. That's where Talal studies Deadweed and tries to work out better dragon technologies; harnesses, stirrups, that kind of thing," Latifa said, her frown deepening. "We're really playing catch-up with Torvald, so, every time we manage to get a bit of Torvald harness or something, it goes straight to there." The girl turned left, however, taking us instead past lines of bunk beds, past doors leading to washrooms, and another hall of bunkbeds.

"You're in the first with the boys." She pointed to Nas before looking us both up and down. "Are these the only clothes you have?"

Another wave of shame spread over me. Being an orphan, and an indentured slave at that, I had never belongings to call my own. Fan wouldn't let me. "Just what we have," I said.

"Fine. Tomorrow, when you go down to the changing rooms, talk to one of the servants there and they should be able to find you spares," Latifa said, before shooing Nas away. "Go on and pick a bunk. Dinner will be in a minute, so after you're done, you can head back down to the common room at the bottom." Then she led me through the door into the girl's dormitory room, which was smaller, and not as smelly or as untidy as the boys.

Most of the bunks were unoccupied, so I had my pick – and I settled for one by the side of a window at the back of the room. It was instinctive to me to try and find a place by myself after I had spent so long living cheek-to-jowl with Nas and his family. At least I could see the dragon caves, I thought as I opened the shutters of the window and heaped the blankets on my chosen (top) bunk.

Latifa sat on the bottom of another unoccupied bunk opposite mine and cleared her throat. "Another thing you should know," she whispered, although I didn't know why as there was no one else in here with us. All of the trainees appeared to be downstairs in a 'free time, where they were wrestling or lounging in the shade of the arena.

"You asked about the Wild Company," she said. "Don't."

"What?" I looked at her oddly. Her tone had been flat and adamant. "Why not? I met them. Up in the mountains."

Latifa's eyes went wide, before her tone hardened. "No, you didn't."

What? I felt a little like I was having an out-of-body experience. "No, I really did. I watched them defend the Southern Gate, and then later, they helped Nas and his stepfather against some wild mountain dragons…"

"No, *you didn't,*" Latifa insisted. "Because the Wild Company *doesn't exist,* got it? Not around here, anyway. As far as the Training Hall is concerned – the idea of people befriending dragons naturally is a dangerous myth."

"But…" I was stunned. "I've done it myself. And I saw them. I talked with them."

Latifa sighed. "Listen, you're new, so you probably don't understand yet. But the Training Hall is run by the Palace, and the Palace is throwing all of their money and hopes at it to try and make it work. The Seven are like the flagships of that. If anyone starts talking about another bunch of dragon riders, ones who managed to do their bonding and training without the help of the Palace, then that basically puts a lot of noses out of joint. The Palace is scared that the Seven will leave this place and join the Wild Company, or that the generals and the public will start asking for the Wild Company's help rather than the Seven. It's a big no-no."

"But why can't they all just work together?" I said. After all – we're all on the same side, right?

"Just think about it like this," Latifa said. "It's pretty sand's-damn amazing that *you* got let in with your dragon," she pointed out. "The Palace wants people to think that *they* are the only ones who can train Dragon Riders, and they need to show that they can because they want to prove to Torvald that they aren't the only ones with dragons, see?" I nodded. "And besides which, the Palace provides everything for us, every-thing for this place. That is a good thing, right?"

Clash-Clash-Clash! There was a clanging of a bell from some-where below us, and Latifa stood up. "Just don't rock the boat, new girl," she said, before she led the way to dinner.

Great, I thought. The Wild Company didn't want me because I didn't know enough, but now it seemed I knew too much for the Training Hall!

CHAPTER 15
DAYIE, DAY 1

The meal that night was, as it turned out, cinnamon and lychee curry. With rice and fresh-baked bread. And spicy green leaves. It was delicious.

It was a shame that I had to eat it in the Common Room, though, as it meant being watched and questioned by every other trainee here. There was Roja, the larger shirtless young man with the scar who had made fun of me earlier – he appeared to hold court with his own band of larger and older trainee riders. It was clear to everyone that they thought they would be picked to join the Seven in the near future and were already acting as if the entire south owed them a favor.

Then there was Latifa, who was clearly well-respected by the few other women there, but who held herself apart and didn't spare any time to chat with either her female or male colleagues. I wondered at what sort of life she must have had before this.

"Oh, she's a mystery alright," said another dragon trainee – Abir, one of the younger ones, which put him of an age with me. He was thin and sharp-featured, with the fairer complexion and straight black hair of the southern city folk and not the desert tribes. He seemed to be equally liked by most of the trainees, if a little mocked for his smaller stature. "They say Latifa was a desert princess, but she ran away to join the Training Hall, more fool her." Abir laughed as he stuffed another hunk of bread into his mouth.

"On the contrary," I said. "I think learning about dragons is the most exciting thing in the world."

"Well, I can see why they let you in." Abir laughed. "That and you have a dragon. How did you get it?"

"Uh…" I opened and closed my mouth, unsure of whether to admit to my felony. Everyone must know that a lot of the eggs the Training Hall procured were stolen from Torvald and the North in some shape or another, but, like the talk of the Wild Company, I didn't want to get into trouble. As it happens, that choice was taken from me anyway.

"She stole it, of course," called out Roja from his court at the heart of the table. He stabbed a fork in my direction, as the talk and laughter of the rest of the room settled into wary whispers.

"She came with the Dragon Trader." Roja waved his fork at Nas a few seats up from me, whose face went dark. "And everyone knows that Dragon Traders are thieves, right?"

Nas's eyes squinted, and his hand tightened on his fork as he rose from the bench.

"And let's say we did steal that dragon," I burst out, before Nas could say anything that would start a fight. He might have changed recently, but I didn't think he had changed *that* much. "Don't you think it's unwise to make fun of the only two people in this room who have managed to do that?" I pointed out as I stood up. "Think about it. You saw my Crimson Red. Look how big he is. How strong he is. Do you really want to pick a fight with the people who could tame him?"

Roja's eyes flickered from me to Nas uncertainly, and I could tell that I had made my point. The funny thing was, that everything I was saying was completely true. We *had* snuck into the Torvald Enclosure. We *had* survived the burning of the road by Torvald Academy Riders, and an attack by wild mountain dragons. As far as I could see, Nas and I had more survival and dragon experience than any in this room.

"*Tame.*" Roja settled for a laugh, shaking his head as if it were all a joke. I kept on glaring at him before I sat down on my bench, earning a worried cough from Abir to one side of me.

"Don't get me wrong, Dayie, I agree with everything you've

just said," Abir said, eager to clarify, "but you called the Crimson Red *your* dragon. You should be careful about that."

"What?" I blurted out. The idea that me and Thump weren't one unit was unthinkable.

"All the dragons belong to the Training Hall now. They belong to the South," he said.

We'll see about that, I shook my head irritably.

The rest of the dinner passed in a muted fashion until the brass bell was rung from the arena, signaling that it was time for us to retire upstairs. Given the hot southern sun, we ate late, and Latifa told me that we were expected to continue our studies, stretches, or repairs to our equipment into the evening. Looking out the windows, after the sun had already gone down, I had to say that I was exhausted already. It had been quite a day for me and Nas, and I made sure that I caught him on the way up the stairs to the dormitory rooms.

"You alright?" I hissed at him.

"Yeah – why do you care?" he said defensively. There was shame and anger in his eyes, and the way that he held his shoulders back from me. Maybe he thought I was tainted goods, thanks to my time as his mother's slave. Or because I was an orphan, cast out by her own village.

Why do I care? I thought. A good question. "Because as much as I have always hated your guts, Nas – we're both new here, and we're in this together," I whispered to him. "Because your mother did you wrong. And because I don't want to see either of us flunk out or get hurt. I just want to ride my dragon."

"Hm." Nas nodded, then awkwardly extended his hand. "Truce?"

"Truce." I shook his hand, just as awkwardly. "If that bully Roja gives you any more trouble…" I started to say.

"I can handle myself," Nas said firmly. "I was always the stronger one, remember?"

I did. He had shoved me more than once. Fine, I thought. I had done my best, and I wasn't going to lose any more sleep over it.

As it turned out, it wasn't worrying about Nas that made me lose sleep, however, it was Thump.

Thump? I thought as I lay in the dark, trying to 'think' at the Crimson Red in the same way that he could 'think' at me. I still didn't have a name for whatever it was that we did. Or what it was that *he* did, maybe. Did all dragons talk to people using their minds? I didn't know the answer to that question. Was it only me that could hear dragons, or only Thump that could talk to me? Why? All were more questions that I had no answer for.

And neither did I have an answer for the growing sense of anxiety in my belly as I stared at the dark stone of the ceiling and tried to sleep. It was impossible. The rest of the girl's dormitory was already lost to their soft snores, and it was well past midnight and I was still lying here, worrying.

Thump had been taken down there to the dragon caves somewhere, I thought. And I didn't know where. I had no reason to think that he was being mistreated, or that they wouldn't treat all of their dragons with the utmost respect, but after the evening that I had – with the mocking and teasing of Roja and his fellows, and the heavy warnings of Latifa – I felt uneasy about leaving Thump down there all on his own.

Had I made the wrong choice by coming here? I thought. Could we have a life out there in the deserts, just me and Thump?

I tried to imagine what it might be like, just me and him. Would we be happy? I knew that I would get to spend more time with him, and I would probably learn how to fly – but then what? It was hard to describe what I felt now, but it was a sort of pride at being here at the Training Hall, even for its obvious faults and its politics. I had spent years as a slave, with nothing to call my own and always being the lowest of the group. I had spent my life before that as an orphan, taken in by Obasi and Wera, my father and mother, but even then, the other villagers had hated me for my 'way with animals.'

Worse still, I had grown up travelling all over, where I had seen how many peoples of the world treated the Dragon Traders, not because of their profession (which was very dangerous!) but because of the color of their skin. The Gypsies of distant Shaar were regarded just as Roja had said – wandering criminals, beggars and thieves. I didn't want to flee to the deserts or the wilds and be like that.

I had done what no one had done before, I had made the Training Hall take on a volunteer student with her own dragon. Maybe, even, this was what I was good at. After being told by everyone that I was useless or tainted with evil magic – maybe being a Dragon Rider was actually what I could excel at!

But still, it was too disappointing to say how my expectations of this place were far removed from the reality.

Talal had said we were to train separately from now on, but I just wanted to check on Thump tonight, I thought, as I snuck out of bed to slip my sturdier clothes on. After all, Thump had spent every day of his shell-less life with me, and every night, too. He might be worried, scared – especially this first night, I told myself.

And I guess I wanted to say sorry for him being led off to the caves and me not going with him, I admitted as I reached up to the shuttered window, carefully lifting it off the wooden latch and opening it wide. I was instantly rewarded with a thin stream of fresh night air, and the distant sound of lizards or insects.

Well, at least Fan taught me how to sneak, I thought, as I climbed out of the window, turned around and judged the distance to the roof of the lower level terrace below. Three of me in height, I reckoned. I was sure that I could do it if I rolled upon impact, but it would be a heavy landing and I didn't want to risk spraining an ankle. Instead, I lowered myself to the windowsill, my soft sandals finding the cracks in the masonry as I crab-climbed down the first few blocks of the dormitory walls until the jump was much safer, and then I sprang.

"Ooff!" I landed with a heavy thud, and rolled over my shoulder as I had intended, but still managed to scrape my hand and bang my knee. "Dammit!" I hissed in pain, holding my knee and praying that it wasn't too badly hurt.

I took a deep breath and looked and was glad to see that it wasn't bad. I'll have to steal some rope from somewhere if this is going to become a habit, I thought, before reminding myself I had promised just this once I'd check on Thump. Well. We'd have to see about that, I told myself as I scurried over to the next ledge of the building. This time I found the runnel of a gutter to help me descend – and I also had the soft sands of the arena to cushion my leap.

Now for the dragon caves. I raced first across the practice areas so that the columns of bricks and stone could hide my passage, before crossing the final part to the wide and low archway through which both Green and Thump had vanished.

To find the heavy iron gate across it.

"What?" For some reason, the idea of keeping the dragons behind bars felt strange and faintly horrible to me. *But they're large and dangerous animals,* I tried to tell myself. *They could fly away. They could get themselves hurt.*

But after travelling all the way down here with Thump free to roam at my side, and after seeing how the Torvald Academy enclosure left them free to come and go, it was hard to justify this gate being here. Thump had never expressed an interest in leaving me.

But what was more important right now was that I had no way of getting past this gate. There was a large metal lock, but I didn't have anything to act as a lock pick – and, judging from the size of the lock, no mere knife and metal pin would do the job (more tricks that Fan had taught me). No – this would be a serious operation, and I didn't have the skills to crack a lock of that size and complexity.

Beyond the gate, I could see the wide tunnel sloping down into the rocks, illuminated by guttering torches before levelling out some way ahead. I could once again smell smoke and soot, tinged with the acrid scent of charcoal, and a slight tang of roasted meat.

"Thump?" I held the bars and whispered in to the darkness. Would he hear me?

"Still a damn stupid name for a dragon," hissed a voice right behind me, and as I spun in shock, a hand fell over my mouth, and another clasped my other wrist. I tried to drive an elbow backward into my assailant, but he merely moved with my attack, neutralizing the force of my blow. It was a man's voice, and one I was sure I recognized.

"Calm down, I'm not going to hurt you!" he hissed into my ear. "In fact, I'm going to let you g—"

I bit his hand, and at the same time scraped my heel down his shins.

"Ach! You little-!" my assailant fell backward as I spun in the sand and readied myself for a swift kick to where any man wouldn't want it.

"You?" I stopped just in time when I realized who he was.

He was wearing a large, dark cloak, but the angered (and pained) face that poked out from under the hood was just the same. It was Akeem, the Captain of the Wild Company.

"Yeah, hi. It's me," he muttered miserably, holding his hand. "I was about to tell you and let you go, but now I think I should have just left you to the wild dragons instead!" he said angrily.

"What are you doing here?" I demanded. "You do know they don't like you here, don't you?" Not that I cared – he was too arrogant for me to like him either – but I didn't want to get into any trouble with my new home for talking to one of their sworn enemies.

"I *work* here." Akeem gestured to his robes and the heavy leather straps wound around his forearms. The same sorts of straps that I had seen on the Handlers who had the goads.

"You're a dragon handler? A servant?" I said.

"Well, only when I'm not busy saving the country." Akeem shook his head as he stood up, paused as he stepped around me, showing me his empty hands. "I'm not here for you. But it's lucky that I've got a set of dragon keys, isn't it?" He drew a large ring of heavy iron keys from under his cloak and, with a wrench and a twist opened the gate. "Now c'mon, get in. I can be seen doing this – but you can't." He beckoned to me to go past him, into the tunnel, before closing and locking the gate behind us.

"Right," I said, my hands on my hips. "I think you need to explain just what is going on around here, don't you?"

CHAPTER 16
AKEEM & THE DAGFAN DRAGONS

This girl had guts, I'd give her that. I had watched the northern-looking girl scale down the terraced walls of the Training Hall before jumping to the arena floor, intent on coming here. She had moved like she knew what she was doing – pausing at the stone plinths, breaking her movement into both fast and slow.

Maybe I had been wrong about her before, I thought, as I looked at her under the glow of the torches. She was pretty, for sure – and maybe her pale hair and her looks had allowed me to underestimate her. But now, I couldn't help but be impressed. It wasn't her height or her skill that made me question my earlier assessment—it was her steely stare of determination. And the way she had unmanned a potential attacker, I thought, as I rubbed my still-aching palm.

But she needed to see what this place was. If she had chosen to come here, despite my warning, if she was adamant on riding her dragon into battle, then she needed to see why I ran the Wild Company like I did.

"It's like this," I said, gesturing for her to follow as I walked quickly down the passageway. It was carved into the soft rocks of the bluff and was many times wider than I could stretch out my hands, big enough to fit a dragon, one at a time. After we descended a little while, it levelled out into a broad and long cavern, with gated openings all around it, with more 'dragon avenues' heading deeper into the rocks. The hiss and rustle of the creatures came from behind the gates, and the smell of soot was thick in the air.

"Dagfan doesn't know horse muck about dragons, but they think they do," I told her, earning a look of surprise from the girl.

"Then why are they training at all?" she whispered, shadowing me as I took her on a tour of the dragon caves.

I grimaced. There were as many answers to that as there were grains of sand, but only two that stuck out. "Torvald," I said, before adding, "Deadweed."

"Torvald has the monopoly on dragons." She nodded. She got it.

"Yes, and the three Lords of the South want to change all of that." I gritted my teeth, not at the idea of southerners having their own dragon-training (as that is what we Binshee taught our young men to do, after all) but at the ignorance and arrogance of Lord Ehsan, Lord Kasim and Lord Qadir to think that they could just force dragons and soldiers together and make it work! But there was one thing that the three Lords of the South (*usurper Lords,* I mentally added) were correct about. "Torvald will always have the upper hand over everything: trade, transport, communications, warfare, so long as they have the Dragon Academy," I said, earning another silent nod from the girl as I looked over to her.

"But what the South doesn't understand is that you have to befriend the dragons. Or better yet – you have to let the dragons befriend *you.* " I sighed.

"But anything different is crazy." She almost laughed, before catching herself under my serious gaze. "I mean, how could you get a dragon to do anything if it didn't like you?"

"Well…" I walked closer to the gated cave that I knew would prove my point.

There was a hiss in the darkness, and a sudden rush of air as I stepped back quickly. These dragons shouldn't be able to use their dragon fire, but still… There was a *clang!* as a large blue tail smacked against the sides of the gates, spilling straw and sand over the cavern before being replaced by the Sinuous Blue's scarred and fanged maw. It was clearly annoyed at us for disturbing its rest, and even more annoyed at the gate being there.

"Talal doesn't understand dragons, although he should – as he is closer to his Green than anyone here," I said wearily. *If only Talal had been trained by the Binshee,* I thought – a desperate illusion, as there was no way that the committed Dagfan Chief would have travelled all the way into the mountains to seek us 'radicals' out.

"Talal tells the Handlers here to regulate their food and their charcoal intake very carefully. The dragons here, like this one"—I led the girl away so as to not disturb the dragon any more--"they're not tame. If anything, they almost feral, but they will obey orders for food and attention."

"But – that's horrible!" the girl gasped as I took her down one of the wide corridor avenues to the next cavern of gated caves.

"Yes." I nodded. "It is. Talal picks the trainees and the Riders who he thinks will work best with each dragon, instead of letting the dragons themselves choose. He isn't letting them bond naturally, and as such – the bond is never strong. If a bond develops at all."

"But then, how do they fight the Deadweed?" Dayie said from behind me, her voice echoing in the chamber.

"Mutual aggression, I think." I almost laughed, but it was a sad laugh. "Have you seen the Seven yet?" I turned to ask her.

Dayie shook her head.

"No? Well, then, when you do, you will understand. Do you

know why there are only Seven official Riders of Dagfan?" I asked.

Dayie was certainly smart, as she said, "I am guessing it's not because they were the best at what they do?"

"Ha. If only. But, no. There are only Seven who have made it through the training because all of the others, the tens and tens and tens of others who have been put through the training as you are about to be, have been killed, maimed, blinded, burned, or eaten by the dragons they're supposed to bond with," I explained. "The Seven have a host of broken limbs and injuries – whilst my Wild Company have none caused by their dragons." I was very proud of that fact.

We neared the cave that I particularly wanted her to see, and I paused her, holding up my hand before we went any further. She had to know the truth. "That is why I am here, to try and change the training if I can, in any way that I can."

Dayie frowned as she looked at me. "Then why don't you announce yourself to Talal? Just go up and tell him that he's doing it wrong?" She appeared annoyed – at me, for some reason.

"How can I do that?" I hissed, keeping my voice low. "The Wild Company are half regarded as a myth, and by people like Talal, they are thought of as nothing better than dragon bandits. He'll have me thrown in jail, or executed, and besides which, I couldn't let it be known that the Binshee

Tribe, the true-born inheritors of the Southern Kingdom, was trying to interfere with the Training Hall. It could lead to a civil war.

"I'm sure Talal won't. He needs to know the truth how to work with dragons," she said stubbornly.

"Why are you defending him? Talal is a fool!" I snapped back.

"Maybe he is, but at least he *saw* I was going to be good at this. At Riding Dragons," the girl called Dayie said sharply. *Ouch. Did the girl have a point? Had I been unfair to deny her membership of the Wild Company? But no woman—certainly no girl—flew for the Wild Company. It wasn't done.*

But the girl just kept talking. "My life before this was horrible. I was little better than a slave. No, actually, I *was* a slave. Talal looked beyond that."

I let her words hang in the air, before replying. "Then you should be careful what you wish for, especially if you bring your friends to share your fate with you." I nodded to the gate ahead of us and gestured her forward.

This one smelled sweeter than any of the others, especially as it was the one with the newest and freshest hay and straw. Something passed through the air, almost like a heatwave but in reverse – a cool breeze that didn't disturb any of the sand on the floor – and it moved between the girl Dayie at my side and the resident of this cave.

"Screch?" came a soft call, and the change in the girl was alchemical.

"Thump!?" She rushed to the bars, hitting them bodily as if she thought that she could squeeze through them just with the sheer force of will alone, and, looking at her screwed up face, I could have almost believed that she would.

"Thump – what have they done to you?" she said, reaching her arms through the bars as far as they would go, trying to get to her dragon. I heard another scrape and then the head of the Crimson Red came into the light, drooped and low. I watched in admiration and awe as the girl didn't flinch at all as the creature carefully nudged its snout at her hands, before rolling its nose over them as if it wanted to be scratched.

She's bonded. She really has bonded, I thought. I felt suddenly as if I were intruding upon something private as I looked away. Behind me, the girl murmured to her dragon softly, barely more than a whisper.

"She is with him again?" My worry was interrupted by the thoughts of none other than Aida, my own dragon – currently hiding under a bluff by the Taval River some leagues away.

Aye, I nodded – to anyone else it would have looked like I was just murmuring and muttering to myself. *I did as you asked,* I said. It had been Aida's plan to bring the two together. To make the girl see what they were doing to the dragons here. To my shame, I had to admit that I actually wanted to forget about the girl and get on with my investigations of the Training Hall, but Aida seemed to think that there was something special about this Dayie.

"Can you not feel it?" my dragon scolded me. *"She has the breath of magic on her, just like the old dragon friends."*

"Don't say that!" I whispered, half in horror, half in hope. Everyone knew that since the evil tyrant King Enric Maddox of Torvald – and then the evil Witches of the West and their Undead Army, magic had become a dirty word. The oldest of books – *The Way of Dragons* included – seemed to suggest that it wasn't always thus, and that magic could even be a good thing, but most people (my father included) didn't agree. 'No witch like a dead witch' as he had told me on many occasions.

But Aida was right, I *could* feel something special around the girl. Or maybe it was something between her and her dragon. That pressure to the air, that lifting of the spirits. Was it the same for me and Aida?

"It would be, if you could listen to the magic in your veins, you great clod!" Aida was hissing her laughter at me.

I have magic? I thought, the very notion making my stomach turn over just a little bit. I didn't want to have magic. A childhood of seeing witches being dragged off by the southern Lords' guards didn't enamor me to the possibility of being one myself.

"Every creature has magic!" Aida's voice was a rush of warm wind against my thoughts. *"How do you think I am talking to you? Or that you have the sense to hear me?"*

I had thought that was just because we were bonded…

"Bonding is magic. Friendship is magic. How do birds fly? Magic? How do fish swim? Or mothers know when their babes are near?" Aida laughed at me, and I quailed a little. A dragon's mirth is quite a disconcerting thing.

"She will change things. This human and the dragon Zarr," Aida said proudly, always glad to be the first, whether it is the first to the kill, or the first to the water, or the first to decipher a puzzle.

"Zarr?" I muttered. She had called her dragon Thump. Did that mean Aida had got it wrong?

"Phee-pip?" As soon as I had said the creature's name, the Crimson Red made a strange chirruping noise at me, an invitation to turn and face it that I couldn't ignore. It was like a bird's call, but hopeful and questioning at the same time.

"Ah… I think he recognizes you…" Dayie said.

"It's his name. He recognizes his true name," Aida said. *"Only dragons can name other dragons, but this one was too young to remember the name his mother gave him. I could read it on his scales, but Zarr did not know where to start looking for it."*

"No, uh…" I scratched my jaw, suddenly abashed at the fact that I had to be the one to tell this girl what her dragon's true name was. "It's Aida, my dragon," I said.

"Not Your dragon, human. YOU are my human…" she insisted, which was something else I couldn't argue with.

"What about Aida?" Dayie looked at me defiantly. I wondered if she was jealous that her dragon appeared to be taking an intense interest in me.

"She says that Thump isn't your dragon's true name," I said.

"What?" Dayie crossed her arms across her chest.

"All dragons have a true name, given to them by their mother before they hatch. They are born knowing it, but uh…" I suddenly realized what this said about the dragon and the girl. That this girl had got her dragon as an egg, and that it was a northern dragon. That meant that she had to be one of the Dragon Traders – a bunch of criminal poachers and bootleggers who stole from dragon nests. I stammered, suddenly awash with emotions. She was a Dragon Trader – and they were a scourge on the land, ripping young dragons from their natural families.

But she also said that she had been a slave, I remembered. *Maybe this girl hadn't wanted to steal Zarr.*

"Well? Out with it!" Dayie said indignantly.

"Your dragon's name is Zarr. Aida could read it on him," I said in a rush.

"Phee-pip!" The name certainly seemed to have an effect on the Crimson Red, as he raised his head to look at me expectantly.

"Zarr…" Dayie whispered, and the Crimson Red turned its head to look at her, eyes wide. "Is that your name? Zarr?" I watched as she murmured to him, and the joy in both the dragon and the girl was undeniable. It was then that I realized, looking at the great head and neck of the creature compared to the girl, just how much he had grown in the last few weeks since I had first seen the girl.

"He's grown. A lot," I pointed out.

Dayie struggled to raise her head from looking in awe at her dragon, but a shadow passed over her features at my assertion. "Yes. It's his breed. From the North. They grow up quick."

I scoffed. "Lady – I may not know everything about dragons, but I know that there's no breed under the sky that grows that quickly."

Dayie flinched as if stung, and she looked at me from under heavy eyelids as she muttered. "Like I said, I have a way with animals."

"It's the magic. I told you." Aida returned to my mind, and I knew then that she had to be right.

Oh hell, I thought. What had I done, refusing to help her in the mountains? That meant she'd come here. A witch at the heart of Dagfan? But it was a question I knew that I couldn't answer, and I felt torn by. I couldn't have accepted her into the Wild Company. We were too new, and we barely knew enough about our own dragons to be able to teach anyone else. Plus, the rest of the South regarded the Binshee as bandits and savages. I couldn't offer her that future! It was bad enough that I'd dragged my own best friends into the position of being outlaws.

The Training Hall was the best place for her, I tried to convince myself. As bad as it is, her dragon will be safe, in a way… But would she accept that?

"Humans." Aida was once again chuckling her fire-soaked mirth into my anxieties. *"You have no idea of fate, do you? No way of sensing it?"*

Fate? I wondered.

"The girl and Zarr came to the Training Hall not because of anything you said or didn't do. It was their fate. They are here for a reason. And there is nothing you can do to stop that," Aida said. I didn't know much at all about dragon philosophy, but I figured that this was as close as they came to mysticism.

"What is she saying about me then?" Dayie was looking up at me shrewdly. "I know who she is, you stand there with your mouth open as if you've drunk too much wine."

"Well, ah…" I hastily coughed, closing my mouth and tried to take command of the situation once more. "Aida thinks there is a reason why you are here. And that it might help us."

"Yeah, I'm here to learn how to fight Deadweed." Dayie stood up, before frowning and looking back at Zarr. "But first I have to figure out a way to get this handsome fella out from behind bars."

"Good," I said, as I was starting to see that maybe Aida was right. Maybe it wasn't a bad thing to have this strange girl and her fast-growing dragon on the inside of the Training Hall. "Because then, I think that you and I can work together." I gave her a grin and extended my hand.

She didn't shake it. "What did you have in mind?" She looked at the hand, and me, coolly. "I seem to remember that I offered to help you defend the South before, and you turned me down."

"This time it's different," I said, though really nothing had changed except my opinion of her. "The South is being swamped by Deadweed, and every season it creeps closer and closer to Dagfan itself. The Wild Company doesn't have enough dragons to fight it all off, *and* we have to try and defend the borders from all the normal sorts of threats – wild dragons, rogue sorcerers, bandits…" I said.

"The Training Hall *needs* you to graduate as Dragon Riders to fight off the Deadweed – but to do that, it *needs* to change its training program. We can't afford any more trainees to lose their legs, or arms, eyesight or lives," I insisted emphatically.

Dayie bit her lip, looking at the sand of the cavern floor, and I could tell that she was thinking intently. "But you still think that they'll throw you in chains if you talk to Talal?"

"I am certain of it." I nodded. *And the scandal of the Binshee Tribe coming here to interfere with the Training Hall might start a war,* I shuddered.

"Then I'll try to show him that there's another way," I heard her say, before she added in a smaller voice, "somehow."

"*We'll* find a way," I insisted seriously. "We have to."

CHAPTER 17
DAYIE, DRAGON BLINDNESS

My first week at the Training Hall went by in a blur of exhaustion, owing to the grueling sessions of physical exercise that Talal gave us. Up before first light for a jog around the arena until dawn, and then to the washing rooms before breakfast, which was a delicious selection of fresh-baked pan breads, cold meats and fruit. It seemed that the Palace was very eager to give the Training Hall the best in the way of food at least. I had never eaten so well in my life!

After breakfast (during which I usually shared a bench with Abir, as we both avoided Roja and his gang of larger young men; Latifa always sat on the end, on her own, and refused to get involved with either the mockery or the conversation around the breakfast table), we would be back to the arena where the heat was already rising though the sun hadn't yet crested the high amphitheater walls.

"Wrestling!" Talal would shout at us, dressed in his loose-fitting sand-colored robes in the center of the arena. "This arena used to house one of the biggest displays of fighting that the South has ever seen! Let's make the walls ring with the sound again!"

It was hard to not feel a little excited – even proud of what I was taking a part of. Despite my misgivings, at some point during that week I started to feel part of something larger than myself. A story that would end in my being acclaimed a Dragon Rider, and Holy Protector of the South.

"Hyagh!" Jeona, one of the other girls lunged towards me across the sand, her hands raised and wrapped as mine were in simple linen straps. Even though I was the taller of the two, I guess I had more experience of ducking out of the way of Fan's common swipes, and I skittered to one side to avoid her grab, spinning on the sand as Jeona turned, our identical wrapped tunics and pantaloons flaring, Jeona's long black braid flapping against her back.

"Attack her, Dayie!" Talal barked, making me jump, and almost move too late when Jeona charged at me again across the arena. Of the five or so pairs of wrestlers in the open patch of ground, Jeona and I were one of two couples who were still standing. We were both already running with sweat in the rising sun, and neither of us had managed to best the other.

The other half of the trainees had been told to watch and observe the matches, and Roja and the others sniggered from the shade by the wall as they pointed out various flaws and mistakes.

"Footwork, Bogdan!" Talal shouted at the other pair still standing beside us.

Oh yeah, footwork. I tried to remember the wide and low crouch that Talal had shown us. It was supposed to be the best stance for fighting – but why?

"Ooof!" Jeona's weight hit me across my midriff – I had taken my mind off my opponent for a moment, and she had charged. We staggered backward, my feet kicking out underneath me.

Don't fall over, don't fall over! I gripped onto Jeona's shoulders as much to hold myself up as to actually wrestle.

"Go down!" the young woman hissed into my face as I scrambled, one knee hitting the sand and the other leg bending as she pushed her weight on me. But I was stubborn. I wriggled and squirmed, thankful for the sweat on Jeona's palms that meant her grip slipped, and I was springing up, free of her as she fell over behind me.

"Yes!" I punched the air. Jeona had been the first to go down. That meant I won the bout, didn't it?

"Foul!" Talal called out harshly.

"What?" I said as Jeona stood back up, wiping the sand from her shins and glowering at me.

"You were supposed to *wrestle*, Dayie, not dash around like a sand lizard!" Talal waved off all of the other competitors from the arena as the other trainees stood up to take their place. "Jeona? You can go rest. You did good today, but Dayie – you stay put," I heard Talal say. *Why was he favoring her? She lost!*

"If you want to be a Dragon Rider, you have to be prepared to *fight,* girl," Talal said contemptuously. "Otherwise, what's the point of anything that we're doing here? I'm not asking you to kill each other, but you have to be able to perform throws, barges, charges, locks, trips, shoves."

I didn't see how any of that would help me fight the Dead-weed, I was about to say, but the Head Trainer drowned me out.

"Right – which of the rest of you think you can teach this new girl how to fight?" Talal asked, and immediately my eyes went to Nas who was pairing off with the much smaller Abir. We'd had our share of fights before, the stars and sands knew, and he would surely be the one to take up Talal's offer – but to my surprise, he kept his mouth shut and looked away. *I guess he didn't want to be seen with me anymore,* I thought, a realization that oddly hurt even given our history.

"Easy," sneered a voice. It was Roja, of course, and the young twenty-something man rolled his shoulders to a cheer of his cronies as he stripped off his shirt to join me.

What the hell? I thought, settling my weight down into the crouch that we had been taught. Roja wasn't as tall as me, but he was broader by far. His shoulders were rounded, and his upper arms were thick with a certain flabby sort of bulk. He probably wouldn't have any qualms about giving me a black eye or breaking my nose. Instantly, my senses sharpened as fear spiked through me. This was just like how it was with Fan after she had a bad day—which took only the slightest mishap or provocation. I would catapult into this sense of wary nervousness, watching, waiting for the strike.

"Dayie? What is wrong?" Thump – *no, Zarr's* – voice slid into my mind. He was worried for me as if he had been able to sense my own fear.

"It's fine," I murmured, as Talal clapped his hands for us to begin.

"No, it isn't." Roja grinned like a desert wolf, clearly thinking that I had been muttering at him. He stamped forward, clearing the distance between us in a flash, and making me jump back in alarm. But it had been a ruse, I realized, as he didn't follow up his charge. He was grinning at me, victoriously.

"Come on and fight me, Dayie – I thought you said you were brave enough to tame a dragon?" He started to circle me, his shoulders high and his chin low. This did not feel like wrestling to me.

"So that's what this is about?" I managed to gasp as I circled counter-clockwise to him. "You want to prove that you can beat the only girl to bring in a dragon, is that it?" I wasn't taunting him—I just wanted to show him I wasn't scared.

"Dayie! You are fighting?" I could feel Zarr's rising sense of alarm.

"It's fine!" I hissed again.

"You say that a lot, little girl—" He jump-stamped forward, an easy attack to avoid, but I hadn't been betting on him spinning on one foot, bringing his rear leg out and around to connect solidly with my shin in a loud, slapping *crack!*

"Argh!" I staggered, managing to skip back but now limping. How bad was I hurt? I looked down to see the beginnings of a red welt forming just below my knee. I was lucky that he hadn't hit my kneecap.

"Rargh!" Roja charged as I looked up. He was filling my vision. There was nothing I could do—

"Dayie!" The roar was both in my mind and in my ears as the Crimson Red bellowed from below ground, incensed by what he was reading through my emotions. Some of the dragon's outrage must have bled into me, as I found myself lashing out, partly in terror to stop this brute from coming at me, and partly in shared Crimson anger.

I managed to forearm slap him across his square chin as I

ducked and sprang away. It was a petty blow-- one that hurt me more than it hurt him, but he coughed and shook his head as he turned quickly.

"So you *do* fight." Roja was grinning and panting as he brought his arms up high in front of his chest and head like a boxer, protecting himself.

"Roja...?" I backed away from the murderous look in his eyes. "Roja – we're wrestling, not fighting..."

"I was told to teach you to fight. So let's see what you got." The boy tensed. "Or are you full of lies, just like your thieving Gypsy boyfriend?"

"He's not my—" I managed to say, but Roja had no intention of actually talking to me. It was all a ploy for him to jump forward, this time swinging a left straight towards me as I ducked to one side, and he was already following it with a powerful lead right hook.

"Block! Use your wings!" Zarr was bellowing both in my mind and in the air. In a split second though I had no wings, my body was already reacting to the dragon's wishes – almost like his outrage and mine had become one. Instead of ducking or jumping away once again, I merely tucked my head and turned my shoulder *into* the blow.

THWACK! His punch was solid enough to feel like being kicked by a horse, well, a pony maybe, winding me for a moment.

"Claw! Bite!" Zarr urged me, and my hands lashed out forward to the sides of Roja's face, awkwardly seizing him. One hand snatched tufts of hair, and the other clawed at the side of his neck as I lunged forward, certain that I had a snout filled with a double layer of fangs as I closed my teeth on the unprotected flesh of his cheek.

"Aiii! Get her off me!" Roja was slapping me on the shoulders and the side of the head as his legs spun from underneath him just as mine had done in the earlier fight against Jeona. But Roja was bigger and heavier than me, and my weight was full on his chest as he overbalanced and fell to the floor with a hard thud.

"Go for the throat! Kill!" Zarr rejoiced in my victory as I released Roja's cheek, tasting something warm and salty in my mouth as I saw, in crystal clarity his shrieking throat with its pumping artery-

"DAYIE!"

Hands grabbed me by the shoulders, lifting me bodily from Roja and flinging me to the sandy floor. The impact rattled my teeth and made me see stars, breaking my connection to Zarr.

"What is she doing?" someone shouted.

"She's gone mad – she *bit* me!" Roja howled from somewhere nearby as I blinked and coughed the sand from my mouth. I tried to get up but I couldn't move. There was a heavy weight across my chest and another across my legs.

"Get off me!" I said, rather feebly, as the bright sun in my eyes was suddenly eclipsed by none other than Akeem, wearing the dun robes of a Dragon Handler.

"Get yourself together!" he hissed into my face at the sound of feet running towards us.

"You there, Handler – is she still fighting?" It was Talal, looming over us. Two Handlers held me down, one on my legs and Akeem across my chest and arms. They must have run to break up the fight as soon as it was clear that Roja was screaming in *real* agony, I thought. Not that it made me grateful to them.

"Get off me!" I sputtered angrily, feeling oddly hollow and sick, wondering where all of that fiery rage had disappeared to.

"No, sir, she's not." Akeem bowed his head and said thickly, his voice sounding rougher— not his real voice. "Dragon Blindness, sir," he added, carefully levering himself off me as the other one did my legs, allowing me to at least scramble to a crouch.

Dragon Blindness? What's that? I thought, looking around. All of the wrestling matches had stopped, and now there was a wide circle of Dragon Handlers, the Chief Talal and the trainees in a wide circle, staring straight down at me as if I were a phoenix or some other mythical creature.

"Dragon Blindness? Already?" Talal squinted at me with a mixture of horror and alarm.

"Sir? I don't understand…" I said, as Talal sighed and nodded to Akeem and the other.

"Get her out of here. Up to the Reading Room, and keep an eye on her," Talal said.

"Talal—sir? Chief?" I shook my head, feeling a bit headachy and jittery from the fight, but not *ill* like he seemed to be suggesting. "I'm sorry. I didn't mean to draw blood…" I said, knowing that it was a lie. Drawing blood was exactly what I had intended to do.

"I'm sure you didn't, Dayie. Just do as I say. Go with the Handlers for now, and try to relax. Breathe. Drink water," he said, and his disappointment was even worse than when he had been angry with me.

But he was the one who wanted me to fight! I thought in alarm, as Akeem roughly pulled me to my feet. With the other Handler on the other side, I was marched into the halls, while behind me, I could hear the mournful howl of a Crimson Red dragon, trapped below ground.

CHAPTER 18
DAYIE THE OUTCAST

"I'll take over from here," Akeem said as I was shoved through an open door into a large square chamber lined with scroll shelves. There was even one barred skylight in the ceiling which let in bright desert sun, illuminating the two spike-leaved Yukka plants in earthenware pots.

Akeem and his fellow Dragon Handler had led me up the stairs and through the semicircular halls and gallery corridors until he had come to this place, called 'the Reading Room.' It was aptly named, owing to all of the materials around, but the scrolls shared the space with a selection of divan chairs, stools, and a couple of tables at which were laid parchment and stoppered ink wells.

The wooden door banged shut behind me, and I heard the slap of bare feet on cool stone flagstones and then silence, before the door opened once again and Akeem appeared with a heavy skin of water in one hand, and a waxed-paper packet in the other.

"Here. Drink," Akeem said in his normal voice, handing me the water. I hadn't realized how thirsty I was until I was gulping great mouthfuls of the cool well water. Within moments, my body shakes, like a tremor, suddenly grew worse, forcing me to sit down on one of the divans.

"Ow," I said, rubbing my shin, and remembering the strong kick that had almost crippled me earlier.

"Can you hear me?" Akeem said, looking at me a little warily. "Are you in your own head again?"

"What are you talking about?" I said. Roja hadn't hit me that hard; my hearing was fine!

"Eat. You need the sweet." He offered me the contents of the wax-paper, which held some kind of sticky candied chopped mixture; apricot halves and nectarine pieces, figs and almonds. As soon as I had tentatively tried some, I found that Akeem was right, the taste of honey and sugarcane made me feel alive, and the orangey zest killed my headache in moments. "Food helps with Dragon Blindness. Not as good as rest, but food brings you back to your body, and the spicier or sweeter the food, the better," he said, leaning against the table with a look of relief on his face.

"You keep saying that—what are you talking about?" I said, helping myself to another handful of the candied mixture.

"It's what happens to the newly bonded, and especially if both dragon and human are young," Akeem said quickly. "Neither of you know how to keep your own emotions in your heads, and instead you freely take on that of your bond-partner." He shook his head at my look of confusion.

"I did something wrong?" I frowned. "But I was defending myself, just as I've done all my life…"

"No, not wrong exactly." Akeem shook his head. "Here, let me show you…" He turned to scan the shelves of scrolls. "I don't know if they even have it in here, this place isn't the Library – more of a place to study…" He took out a few scrolls, stuffed them back in frustration, before finally uttering a pleased exclamation as he drew out a much thinner one, and unrolled it on the table.

"Can you read?" he asked.

"Of course I can read," I said, but I didn't add the truth--*not well*. But Fan had wanted me to be able to quote prices and relay information that I had seen on any forays to town that I had been allowed.

"Then take a look at this passage, and you'll get a flavor of what Dragon Blindness can turn into." He folded the scroll over to the section he wanted me to read and brought it over to where I sat on the divan.

The parchment was old but still had that thick, flexible quality that made me think it must have been treated with preservatives, and the black-ink writing was handwritten, but thankfully written large and elaborate.

14th of Seven Moon, the Chief of the Maha Tribe reports,

The goats of the eastern pastures were being attacked, at night, and for many moons we thought it the work of lions or lynxes, until we came across great charcoal patches of burnt ground. We sent word to the Lord of the Eastern Deserts of course, but before he sent his riders, we conducted night patrols of the area. For several nights nothing was reported, until one patrol reported seeing a Vicious Orange Dragon swoop upon the pastures with great fire and fury. Which was not a completely unknown thing, but what was stranger was that they then told us that there had been a young boy atop its back as you or I might ride a horse. The boy flung himself to the ground and appeared garbed in the barest of rags, and after the Vicious Orange had fired the poor goats, the boy pulled and tore at them, in the manner of a beast!

The Case of the Haqq Oasis Witch,

The Merchant families of the southern sands relate a story in which a young woman wandered into their camp at the Haqq Oasis, unwilling to speak or make any noise except growl and snarl at them. She seemed intent only on getting water, and the merchants believed her to be a runaway. Knowing that crossing the desert is perilous for anyone, let alone someone on their own, the Merchants followed her to try and persuade her to join their caravan, at least until the next town. The woman reacted as though they were seeking to attack her and hissed at them.

When the Merchants did try to seize her – for her own benefit, they later claimed she howled in rage and was answered by none other than a Vicious Orange, flying out of the deep sands to set fire to their camp and eat their horses. The merchant families fled, but for the long moon that it took them to reach habitation, they would later claim to have heard the angry cries of a dragon, and the mocking laughter of a woman in the dead of night...

"Those are examples of Dragon Blindness," Akeem said heavily. "And also, as it happens, why the few people who even believe that my Wild Company exist, usually also think that we're monsters!" He shook his head. "Most see us Wild Company Riders as those who have given themselves over completely to the dragon; that we've become subhuman..."

"I, I don't understand..." I said, feeling sick. "Are you saying that I am going to become this? A mad woman?" I shook my head. "But the Torvald Riders don't go feral, do they?"

"The Torvald Riders have a stable community of both dragons and of humans, living side by side," Akeem said sadly. "If a young dragon or a young Rider bonds early, then there are other, older bonded dragons and humans around to help them to learn how to navigate this new relationship." Akeem paused, looking at me. "Bonding isn't just being friends with a dragon. It's something deeper than that."

"I know," I said, although I didn't. I knew that what was happening between me and Zarr was *something else,* but I couldn't describe what. I could sometimes hear his thoughts, and very rarely I could just feel his emotions, as if I were listening into the insides of his head. *Was it the same way for him, too?* I wondered.

"Have you been having dragon dreams?" Akeem asked seriously.

"Um, what do you mean?" I asked. I was a girl who had befriended a dragon and walked out of the North to go to the prestigious Training Hall – wasn't dreaming about riding and fighting on dragons a natural thing for anyone in my position?

"Dreams that feel not just like you are flying or fighting or *with* Zarr, but dreams that are like you *are* Zarr?" Akeem asked. "Opening your eyes to see what he sees, feel what he feels?"

"Um." *Yes.* But I had thought that they were *my* dreams. Just last night I had dreamed of being asleep in a dark and cool cave, surrounded by slightly charred straw, and my body big and radiating warmth...

"I'll take that as a yes." Akeem groaned. "Look, no one in the South really understands it yet. We think the North understands it, but whatever the secret is, they're not telling us. But some people who bond get lost in that bond. They forget the person they were and cannot do anything but be like a dragon."

"And the dragon. Does it become more like a human?" I asked.

"No. Dragons are too stubborn for that." A ghost of a wry smile on Akeem's face, vanishing quickly. "But we think there are ways out of it."

"You and Aida…" I pointed out. "You bonded? And she was wild?"

"Yes, but Aida was older than your Zarr was when we bonded, and she had her other dragon sisters around her. A few of us, me and Heydar, bonded early to the dragons we befriended, too, so we could share our experiences, keep each other human, I suppose." He shrugged, and his face darkened. "Yet another reason why the Training Hall needs to change. You can't force a bond, and you can't strand the poor humans and dragons when they have built one."

"But – but how do I stop it?" Fear rippled through me as I realized that if I had done what I had almost done – flown off to the southern deserts with Zarr (*or Thump, as he had been then*) then that snarling and hissing woman of Haqq Oasis was probably exactly what I would have turned out to be.

"You have to remember who you are," Akeem said gravely. "Which means you have to *know* who you are, and know what you want."

"Oh." *That was easier said than done when you were an orphan two times over, found on the side of the sea by your foster parents, and then sold to Dragon Traders after your foster parents were killed.*

"Easy," Akeem said as if I were a horse he was soothing. "It's not as all-bad as that." He sighed, taking the scroll from my hands and pushing it back into the shelves. "At least it shows that you have bonded deeply and truly with Zarr." He crouched at my side and drew out some pots and bandages for my knee.

"Woah – what are you doing?" I said, flinching away from his touch, curiously embarrassed to have this young man tend to my injury. "I can do that myself."

"Fine." He looked up at me with his hazel-green eyes, nodding slowly as he offered me the poultice and the bandages. "This will reduce the swelling, and these will keep the sand from getting at it."

"I know that," I grumbled, suddenly very annoyed that this young man thought that he could go around thinking that he was the heaven's gift to hurt girls everywhere. I was a Dragon Trainee! I was Dayie, and I didn't need any man's help.

"Keep 'em," Akeem said as he rose from the floor. "And the wine and *Bhuti* too – that's the candied snacks – I'm supposed to keep you secluded in here until Talal comes anyway."

"Secluded?" I said in alarm. "But I'm not ill!"

"Talal seems to think you are," Akeem said seriously. "Just, *try* to be a little less dragon-y, even if you feel it, okay?" His look of concern made me more annoyed somehow. Like he thought that I owed him.

"How about *you* try to be a little less arrogant," I snapped as he moved to the door, and when I looked up I saw that he was wearing a half-smile on his face as if he was mocking me.

"What's so funny?" I said, but he had already closed the Reading Room door behind him, leaving me confined to my new prison, and feeling oddly embarrassed for no sensible reason whatsoever.

"Feral Witch executed in Tijj, Newriver… Dragon-child found in Beshanti Coast…" I spent the next few hours laboriously reading through the scroll that Akeem had pointed out, making myself more and more worried as the light of the sun moved through the skylight.

Was this what I was going to become? But it didn't make sense – even after what Akeem had told me. The dragons and the Riders that I had seen in Torvald didn't seem to show any spark of ferocity that this 'Dragon Blindness' caused. *Maybe he was wrong,* I thought. If anything, the Torvald Academy Riders had appeared almost unemotional, austere…

"Dayie…" The door creaked open and my next visitor turned out to be none other than Talal himself, still sweating and dusted with a grime of sand and dirt. "I trust that the Handlers looked after you? And that you are feeling more ah…*yourself* again?"

"I am." I nodded, leaning up from the divan, and hastily wrapping the scroll again.

"Ah," the older man's eyes looked down at what I had been reading. "I suppose it is good – the Handlers gave you that to read, did they?"

I nodded once again.

Talal's face was stern, but his manner wasn't completely unempathetic as he took the scroll from my hands and leaned against the table to look at it. I watched as he perused the first few entries and a heavy sigh escaped his features.

"Now, perhaps, you understand some of the dangers that we are facing here, and why I was insistent that you learn to be a warrior first, and a Rider second."

I nodded silently, although internally I was thinking, *They are the same thing, aren't they?*

"Dayie, what are we to do with you?" His voice sounded tired., and when I looked up I could see his eyes sharp on mine. "You have the face of a wildcat."

"I beg your pardon?" I said.

"You cannot hide your feelings. It is a saying of my home people, many miles along the coast here…" A look of sadness clouded his eyes. "All dead now, of course: Deadweed."

I nodded. "My foster parents were taken in the same way," I said quietly. "That is why I am here, why I want this to work — because of them."

Talal regarded me silently, before he nodded. "I can see that. Perhaps that is why I am not shipping you off to the Palace Healers for a more, uh, comprehensive treatment of your condition."

What? My heart fluttered in surprise.

"Of all of the students I have had, you have come to my hall with the most promise. You have already bonded with your dragon – anyone with eyes can see that – and your dragon has been howling the place down since I've had you up here."

"He has?" I said, stunned I couldn't hear him, and ashamed that I hadn't felt his anguish since I languished in this sedate and peaceful environment. *Had my fear of this Dragon Blindness caused me to block him out from my thoughts?*

"Yes, but he has settled now. Finally. The Handlers have seen to him," Talal said brusquely.

"In what way?" My tone was sharp.

"Have no fear, Dayie. We are not monsters here. The Handlers know when to apply food instead of the goad." Talal's tone had resumed the terse tenor that he usually employed as he folded the scroll and returned it to its place on the shelf. "But your alarm at the Crimson Red's welfare tells me much. That you are still not out of the woods yet. So tomorrow, I will be sending you on a different sort of mission, *outside* of the Training Hall."

"Can I take Z—*Thump* with me?" I said, quickly. For some reason I didn't want to let the leader of the hall know my dragon's true name. It felt like he hadn't earned it yet, given his willingness to separate true-born friends such as me and Zarr.

"No, Dayie – and that is the point. You *can't,*" the man said forcefully, straightening his jerkin. "Come on, up. You've had long enough in here to consider your position, and what you know we need you to be. Tomorrow, I will be sending you with a scout party of trainees and *different* dragons, where hopefully you will learn to not be so attached to one particular beast."

Impossible, my heart thumped. It was as if he was asking me to bond to another dragon. Once again, it was almost like Talal could read my thoughts clearly.

"You *will* learn how to be a Dragon Rider of the South, and you *will* do it in the way that we tell you." He opened the door, and I appeared free to return to my late afternoon of stretches and practices. For a moment I just stood there, stunned by the level of arrogance in Talal's voice. *He was ordering me around no better than Fan had,* I thought, barely able to contain my rage. *Was that the price that I had to pay for being here?* The rest of the trainees regarded me a cautious silence as I lunged and jogged alongside them. Even Nas, it seemed, was only too eager to avoid my eyes.

It was like everything I had achieved by getting here, by showing the world that I wasn't a mere servant, by proving I was something better than what they thought of me, had been destroyed in one stupid afternoon. I was no longer Dayie the fierce dragon-friend, but Dayie the outcast.

CHAPTER 19
DAYIE AND THE MENALI BRIDGE

"Scout team!" the man roared through the dormitories, banging open doors without a care as to what trainees might be sleeping.

Luckily, I was already awake – having not been able to sleep a wink last night as I fretted over Zarr being held somewhere far below us. I had tried several times to reach out to him with my mind – if that was what I had done, but every time I met with nothing but a drowsy feeling of numbness, and I couldn't be certain if that was coming from *him* or if it was coming from my own sleep-deprived senses.

Maybe this is for the better, I thought as I grabbed my things and hurried to the wash rooms – before instantly feeling guilty about that thought. The reports of half-crazed dragon-children, and 'feral witches' were still fresh in my mind, and they still scared me. It wasn't something that I wanted for Zarr, let alone me! I wanted him to lead a full and happy life – not to be hunted down because I couldn't control my emotions.

There had to be a way to bond with the dragons that wouldn't lead to this, I thought as I washed and dressed and joined the river of students making their way down the steps to the communal common rooms below.

And I am going to be the one to find it.

"Eyes up!" snapped the figure at the end of the tables where we usually ate, and I saw the servants were already bringing out breakfast rolls and bowls of dried fruits, as well as platters stacked with pastry and meat.

The figure at the end I hadn't seen before, however – he wasn't Talal, and he wasn't one of the Dragon Handlers, either. He was broad and big, *hulking,* even, but he moved funny, and when he lurched around the edge of the table to start cramming the pastries into his mouth, I realized that it was because his right leg ended at the knee, and instead there was a metal peg, ending in a sculpted three-clawed foot. He appeared to be a warrior – the heavy muscles and open battle-harness, exposing a chest thick with hair the white spider-lines of scars made that much clear, as did the heavy curving scimitar at his waist. He looked older than Talal, the top of his head shaved bald but leaving the hair behind his temples and ears, which was braided together to form two long braids down his back.

Was he...?

"Gorugal the Mighty," I heard a familiar voice whisper behind me, and I turned to see none other than Nas, looking stunned at our new mentor.

"Goru-*who?*" I whispered back at him, earning a disparaging stare from the youth who had once been my oppressor.

"Gorugal the Mighty. The first of the Seven," Nas hissed at me.

"That's right – and don't any of you forget it!" the first of the Seven shouted over at us, spraying food from his mouth over the platters and laden table as he did so. The man might not have any manners, but he had quick ears, it seemed. He surveyed us with blue eyes that glittered against his heavily tanned face, taking in our sizes and shapes as if he were inspecting stud horses.

"Hgnh." With a dismissive grunt, Gorugal the Mighty turned back to stuffing his face. "Lucky if any of you come back alive," he muttered to his breakfast, then, in a louder voice. "Well – what are you waiting for? Get your breakfast down you! There's no telling when we'll get back."

With that, the trainees beside me looked at each other a little shaken, and gradually moved to the table to start eating. Nas was keen to stuff his face as Gorugal was doing, but I ate one of the pastries and a handful of the fruits before putting more in my pockets for later. Maybe it was the ex-servant in me, but

I knew the value of keeping something back for yourself when others might not look out for you.

There were only a handful of us students here, I noted, with Nas and Latifa being those I knew the best. No Adir, no Jeona, and no Roja – I was very grateful to see! I wondered for a moment if that meant that Talal was endeavoring to keep us separated (me and Roja, I meant, as well as me and Zarr) for fear of one of us seriously harming the other.

Damn right I would.

"Good. Now – you'll need the dragon ropes, the cleavers, and the bags of feed out the front." Gorugal gestured to where at least half of the equipment was still on its racks.

Okaay... I didn't want to be considered slow and unready, so I moved to pick up a coil of the dragon ropes. Heavier than normal ropes, they were made from treated leather strands and hemp and capped with metal clamps at the end. They were supposed to be strong enough to manage a dragon, but Zarr could break one if he wanted to, I was certain.

Next came the cleavers. "What do you think we need these for?" Nas asked as we moved past the racks of sabers and spears to those where the much smaller hand blades were kept. The cleavers looked like mean, large, wedge-shaped blades that were thicker at the extreme end, and thinner towards the handle grip. Several were heavily notched.

"Get a move on!" Gorugal shouted from the open hallway

doors out to the arena, and when we joined him outside, we saw a line of satchels by the wall, bulging and heavy. Picking one up and slinging it across my shoulder, I couldn't resist untying the latch that held it shut, to see that it was stuffed full of bits of charcoal.

"Eyes front!" Gorugal barked once more. He already had two such satchels, one across each shoulder, adjusted to sit at his hips. I did the same with mine. "Now you lot, watch how it's going to go down. I haven't got time to be playing wet nurse to all of you, so I just want you to look and pay attention, got it?"

We nodded, and, when that wasn't enough, we chorused, "Yes, sir!" in ragged voices.

"Just *pay attention!*" he barked, clapping his hands as two lines of Dragon Handlers ran across the arena to the far end, where the gate at the entrance of the dragon caves.

"Gorugal, you old goat? What you doing – showing us up?" called another voice from the other side of the arena. And all eyes turned in alarm and awe to see three more figures crossing the sand. Each one of them was broad, and moved with the easy assumed authority that their battles had earned for them. There was none of the quiet readiness that I had seen from Akeem's Wild Company, these were three of the Seven, and they *swaggered.*

Well, where they still had the ability to do so. One of the

Seven with masses of wild black hair dressed with lots of bangles and teeth, lumbered on a solid boot that I realized wasn't a boot at all, but was in fact a wooden foot, attached to the end of his leg. The second and the tallest of the Seven was a woman with dark hair cut into a bob. She wore black leathers and a studded armor battle harness, and at first, I thought that she might be the only unharmed one of the group, until she turned to look at us, revealing one side of her face that was horribly pocked and scarred from fire. The final of these three was a man with much lighter skin but still with the same dark desert hair. He held one hand hunched and curled up against his chest–useless. Each of these new three, like Gorugal, had heavy scimitars at their waists, as well as what looked to be a variety of smaller blades, hand axes, and pouches.

"Tabit the Burned, Marshal the Crippled, and Oleg One-Foot," Nas whispered in awe as his heroes lurched, stumbled, pounded and yet swaggered their way across the arena. It was hard not to feel a little of the same amazement at them. They appeared to be larger than life figures, who clearly didn't give a fig how they looked to us, or what any of us thought of them.

I want to be like that, I thought. *I don't want to be Dayie the outcast. I want to be so good at what I do that no one will dare doubt me!*

They cast rudimentary glances over us, and the younger

Marshal with the curled hand just snorted with laughter, shaking his head.

"Easy," Tabit snapped at him, moving to cuff her companion with an off hand. "Don't want to spook the little darlings yet, do we?"

"What does it matter? You know what's going to happen…" Oleg the one-footed hissed, his voice low and guttural as they joined Gorugal, their battle-brother.

"This is them." Tabit sighed, and I saw that she and Gorugal the Mighty were clearly regarded as some kinds of captains or leaders of the Seven. I wondered who we should take orders from then.

"Yeah. Horse-piss," Gorugal spat into the sand. It was clear what he thought of us trainees, then, I found myself taking a deep breath to try and calm my rising anger. After all – isn't that just what Akeem and Talal wanted me to do?

"Ah well, but we need the blades, at least," Tabit considered, not even bothering to talk to us as she and the other newcomers continued to walk across the sand towards the opening dragon gates.

"You lot!" Gorugal bellowed at us. "What did I just say about paying attention? Look! This is how you mount your dragon. We use these," he thumped a heavy fist on the sack of dragon charcoal, "to feed the dragons — this stuff is like catnip to a mountain lion for dragons—and if that doesn't work then we use those." He nodded to where one line of dragon handlers had stood to one side of the gates, their goads in hand. I wondered if any of them were Akeem, but I couldn't tell from this distance.

"Now, if any of these brutes come at you," Gorugal bellowed at us, "then you throw the damned charcoal in front of it and run. Keep on throwing it until it's either lost interest, or you've run out of charcoal or…" he grinned and thumped his metal peg leg with one hand. "I'm sure you'll catch on. None of you are going to be getting on the dragons yet though—"

What? I coughed. "But that is ridiculous," I muttered under my breath. All of this seemed a little unnecessary in my view, anyway. Surely, we could just talk to the dragons and ask if they would let us up on their backs?

"Shhh!" Nas said from behind me, and his tone was the same one I remembered from our time in Fan's caravans. I half expected it to be followed by a nasty little poke or a shove, but nothing happened, thankfully.

"Just stay back!" Gorugal shouted, as the arena was filled with hissing.

Zarr? My heart immediately leapt to the entrance to the cave, as black, acrid rivers of smoke started to thread their way ahead of the reptilian horde. I was disappointed however, when the first dragon to nose through the murk was an old Stocky Green— the same one that Talal had ridden, as I recognized the pattern of faded and smashed scales.

The old dragon hissed as it lumbered, head low over the sands, pausing to raise its snout to sniff the air delicately. He was sensing for Talal, his bond-partner, and something made me turn my head in the direction that the dragon was looking, back to the galleries of the Training Hall, where there was a sudden bang as a wooden-shuttered window closed. Had that been Talal himself, unable to deny the bond he felt when his dragon arrived to greet him? Whatever the answer was, it seemed that the old Green was not allowed to have its way, as it suddenly hissed at the arena in defiance, and then skittered forward on stubby legs as another draconian head emerged from the dark. A Sinuous Blue, this one not as old as its predecessor, and moving with a lithe grace as it started swaying its head from side to side, like a cobra about to strike.

"Get em out!" Gorugal shouted, and the Sinuous Blue hissed in anger as it was goaded forward into the arena by the line of Dragon Handlers to make room for the final two dragons.

Another Stocky Green appeared, this one smaller and looking more bullish than Talal's dragon. *Headstrong,* I thought, but the final dragon was the smallest of the lot – about the same size as the Vicious Oranges, but its snout was shaped more like a beak, with a display of tines erupting from ridge and behind the ears as it snapped at the air impatiently. Its scales were almost a cross between the ultramarine color of the Sinuous Blue, and the viridian emerald of the Stocky Greens, only with a silvery sheen, and an edging of bright crimson scales like drops of blood around its belly and up its neck.

"That's a Sea Dragon." Latifa spoke quietly, and her eyes lit up with pride, although I didn't know why.

"No Vicious Oranges?" It seemed odd to me that these dragons that the Training Hall had been working with were all dragons from the edges of the Southlands – the Greens and Blues were predominantly northern-territory dragons, and as far as I was aware, the Sea Dragons belonged way over in the Western Archipelago, didn't they? But the Vicious Oranges lived *here,* in these mountains. Wouldn't it be easier to capture them?

"There's a mountain black, but no – the Oranges are considered too wild," Latifa said with a heavy look in my direction, and I thought back to our conversation on my first day. She knew as I did that the Wild Company were real, and that they rode naturally-bonded Vicious Oranges – but more importantly, she knew that the Wild Company were considered dangerous; put down as a myth by the Lords of the South.

"*Hoi!*" Gorugal shouted, already pounding across the sands to the nearest dragon–Talal's Green—one of the warrior's meaty fists flinging a handful of the charcoal stuff in front of him.

"*Ssss!*" Talal's Green dragon hissed, but raised its snout as if it were taking no notice of Gorugal, even when he was approaching to within a few meters from it.

"She wants to fly with Talal, not him." My heart jumped in anticipation. "What a fool," I muttered, earning a gasp from Nas behind me. "Well – he should let the dragon choose!"

It seemed that Gorugal wasn't the only one afflicted with this arrogance. Just behind him there was the sharp screech of indignation as the bullish Green and the serpent-like Blue jumped back, and I saw that they had been separated by the prods of some of the Dragon Handlers.

"No!" I gasped at the sheer idiocy of it. I wanted to yell, *Don't poke adult dragons! You'll only make them mad!* but I held my tongue. Who was I to tell them what to do? Maybe they were right. Maybe I *didn't* know anything about dragons – not compared to these people, anyway?

As the Sinuous Blue turned to snarl at the handlers, Tabit ran forward, behind the Blue and started clapping her hands loudly, once again distracting it from where I was sure it was going to try and snap at the Handlers themselves.

"Hey beautiful," I heard Tabit say, and was pleased that at least she was complimenting the Blue – but once again, I couldn't feel any of the connection between them like what I felt between me and Zarr, or Talal and the older Green. Sure enough, the Sinuous Blue thumped its tail in annoyance – it wasn't angry yet, but it was getting tetchy with all of this running around and prodding – that was, until I saw Tabit started throwing handfuls of the charcoal on the arena floor just as Gorugal had done.

"Skreep!" the Sinuous Blue darted forward to snap at the hunks of charcoal, a lightning quick move that again reminded me of a striking adder. As she did so, Tabit jogged backwards quickly, throwing another handful of the dragon feed to one side of her, luring the Blue further apart from its fellow dragons, and giving the other Dragon Riders freedom to approach the remaining two dragons – the bullish Green and the Sea Dragon.

"Easy there, you like that, don't you?" Tabit said, unintentionally backing towards where we trainees stood, and there was a ripple of alarm as we started to back away, spreading out around the arena. Apart from me, that was, as I continued to watch as Tabit threw more handfuls of what was clearly a treat to the dragons, and tensing her legs as she waited for her moment—

"Hyugh!" A grunt, and Tabit had hopped and leapt onto the base of the neck of the Sinuous Blue, landing awkwardly and grappling with the shoulders and wing pinions there as the Sinuous Blue screeched and threw its head back.

"The poor thing – she thinks you're attacking her!" I called out in horror, as the Sinuous Blue thrashed its tail, and, on its back Tabit struggled into place at the base of the neck between the shoulders, where a natural depression creating a natural saddle.

"That poor thing will crush you if you don't move!" Latifa was seizing my shoulders and dragging me back with the others in the sand as the Sinuous Blue lashed out again and again, throwing up great gales of sand.

"What are they doing?" I coughed and spat out the sand in alarm as Tabit shouted.

"Goads! I need goads and saddle over here!" Her voice jumped and leapt as the beast underneath her bucked. On the far side of her, it appeared that Gorugal had much better luck with Talal's Green, perhaps because the Green was the oldest, and most used to this? He was already sitting calmly on its back as Dragon Handlers threw up a flexible, lightweight saddle for him to catch and shuffle into position underneath him. "Ties!" Gorugal roared, throwing down the straps from the saddle for a pair of Dragon Handlers to dart forward to fix under the Green's neck. As they did this, Gorugal kept Talal's Green complacent by throwing more of the charcoal for it to feed.

"Sckreach!" Tabit's snake-like Blue appeared to be much feistier, however, and I watched, appalled, as a Dragon Handler approached on either side of it, using their goads to fend back the tail and the snapping head as Tabit threw more and more charcoal out in front of her. With every failed attempt to dislodge its unwanted Rider, the Sinuous Blue seemed to settle into a disgruntled sort of complacency, resorting to thumping and curling its tail rather than swishing it, and only hissing with an open maw at the goads that came near its face.

It was all so wrong, I knew, and yet someone threw Tabit a saddle and she (and *more* Dragon Handlers again) performed the same risky maneuver of getting them strapped and tied down. As soon as the saddles were on though, the bucking lessened and the Handlers jumped back as the dragons trotted forward, seeming to accept their new constraints, but clearly not pleased by them.

On the far side of the arena, Oleg the One-Footed was somehow sitting upon the smaller bullish Green while the Handlers calmly secured a saddle and the Green crunched down on Oleg's entire satchel.

"She likes her fodder," Oleg said pleasingly, and I wondered if *they,* of all of these Seven, had an almost-bond, or perhaps the bullish Green had just been hungry this morning.

But Marshal the Crippled wasn't faring as well as the others. Even though one of his hands appeared useless, that wasn't the problem. The hand didn't seem to affect him at all as he pranced and jumped, flinging charcoal one way and then another as he tried to corner the Sea Dragon that was desperately scrabbling at the high walls of the arena. She had gotten away from him. She was fast – not as lightning-quick as the

Sinuous Blue– but this Sea Dragon was consistently quick as she half hopped, half swooped around the back of the arena.

"Don't let her get airborne!" Gorugal bellowed.

"I'm trying!" Marshal snarled back, closing the distance, before having to duck under a sweep of teal and turquoise wings. I didn't think that the Sea Dragon had any intention of harming the human who wanted to be its Rider for the day, but I also didn't think that would stop it from clawing Marshal if he got in the way, either…

"Skreh!" The Sea Dragon was making frantic noises and there was smoke coming from its nostrils as it searched for a clear leap into the air.

"Students! Ropes!" Gorugal bellowed, and it was clear what he meant. We were somehow supposed to stop the Sea Dragon from flying by throwing the loops of ropes over it.

There's no way I'm doing that, I thought, even as Latifa and Nas raced across the sand towards it.

"No – don't!" I took a few steps forward, unsure even what I could do in this situation as Latifa threw her coil of ropes. They slapped across the Sea Dragon's back, slid down, and snagged on one of its back tines. Nas went next, and he threw with all the athletic grace that his mother had tried to instill in him, and the rope looped neatly over another back tine of the beast.

"There she is! We got her!" Marshal the Dragon Rider whooped loudly as he raced forward, intending to jump on her neck – but at the last moment, the Sea Dragon twisted, pulling Latifa off her feet on the ropes and buffeting Marshal to the floor as it awkwardly hopped over them.

It landed right in front of Nas, whose rope was still attached to its back, but slack.

"Nas!" I called out, and this time the fear really did spur my legs into action as I raced across the sand. He might be an oaf, but I didn't want to have to watch him get eviscerated!

But something was happening up ahead of me. The Sea Dragon had paused its pounce—a pounce that would have taken it *through* the youth who had been my bully. Instead it just hunched in front of him, lowering its head as Nas staggered, tripped, and fell backwards onto the dirt.

"She's going to eat him!" one of the twitchier trainees wailed.

But no, that wasn't it, was it? My pinwheeling legs slowed to a jog, and then, to a stop. There was something about that wide-eyed stare from the dragon, straight into Nas's eyes that reminded me of something. Hell, it more than *reminded* me of the first time that Zarr had looked at me with open eyes.

"No, she isn't," I said, feeling the thrill of something electric and hopeful – like the first blush of white spring flowers. "Talk to her, Nas," I said quickly. "Just talk to her..."

"Hu-hey…." Nas's worried voice said, but he, too, must have felt something going on, as he held out a hand towards the Sea Dragon.

"Skree-pip?" the Sea Dragon whistled in the back of its throat at him, before its eyes narrowed in alarm and anger.

"Gotcha!" Marshal had thrown himself onto her back, and the Sea Dragon was looking around, trying to see who was behind her – but she was more scared than she was angry.

"It's okay, girl," I whispered, nodding at Nas. "*You* tell her."

"It's, it's going to be okay," Nas said, and the Sea Dragon gave a snort of soot as if to say that it doubted that very much, but she wasn't struggling anymore. She merely hissed as the saddle was brought forward and attached to her shoulders. Nas stood, looking stunned.

"Good job, kid. Now outta my way!" Marshal gestured for Nas to back off, and I had to tug at his shoulder to get him to stumble back to the wall.

"I felt it, Dayie. I could *hear* her, somehow…" Nas was looking at me in wonder, and I couldn't do anything but grin.

"Now you know," I whispered back to him, as the four Dragon Riders of the Seven were still trying to cajole their mounts into some sort of order. Nas appeared bewildered beside me, and I wondered if I'd had that same mooncalf look on my face when I realized that my heart was given over to Zarr. Probably, I thought, my eyes sweeping back to the disturbed sand, littered with charcoal and the air heavy with the sound of rasping dragons.

What a strange place to find friends, I thought.

"Head's up!" Gorugal shouted from Talal's Green, and it seemed to me even though Tabit had the more natural authority of any of the Seven I had met so far, she deferred to Gorugal 'the Mighty,' and I wandered why. "We're heading out, so stay out of the way. The rest of you will be following on ponies. Try to keep up, don't get lost, and see if you can make yourselves useful when we get there!"

"Get where?" I wondered out loud, but no answer was forthcoming as Gorugal kicked the Green with his metal leg, earning a grunt as the old beast shook out its wings and started trotting forward.

Clash-clash! There was a crashing sound of a gong, and the main, heavy wooden doors to the Training Arena were opened, and Gorugal's Green trudged out first, followed by Tabit's still tail-phwipping Blue, then Oleg the one-footed, and finally Marshall on the twitching and nervous Sea Dragon, which turned to look back at Nas just before it vanished under the arch of the arena doors.

Zarr. I felt a pang of loss, like the homesickness that I used to feel for the small cottage of my foster parents. Seeing Nas's look of awe, I was happy for him that he had found a friend in the Sea Dragon, but also, I had to admit jealous too. Why couldn't I ride *my* dragon? I thought stubbornly, as a long hooting call echoed through the tunnels and corridors below.

"I'm sorry, Zarr..." I whispered, and once again that numb fog crept to the edge of my mind, just as it did whenever I tried to reach out to him. I wondered then if it was *him* who was blocking *me* – maybe he was annoyed at having been kept underground for so long?

"You heard them," coughed a familiar voice, and I looked up to see Akeem and another Dragon Handler pulling forward a line of thin-looking ponies from one of the doors, their eyes rolling and their nostrils flaring at all of this dragon scent.

"But where are we supposed to go?" I asked, frowning.

"Menali Bridge, trainee," Akeem 'the Dragon Handler' told me brusquely, putting on the strange accent as he did so. His whole fake persona still seemed ridiculous to me, as anyone could see that he was far thinner and younger than the other Dragon Handlers.

"Do you know why?" I asked him pointedly as the other students around me started to take to their mounts.

"I couldn't say, ma'am," he replied again – and I was sure he was mocking me. *Why doesn't anyone trust me around here?* "But I heard that there's an outbreak of Deadweed near there..." he said quickly, before passing over the reins to the pony that I was supposed to ride as he mounted his.

243

"And you two are supposed to be keeping us safe, are you?" I said dismissively. *Let him know that I am not impressed by his theatrics.*

"Oh no, ma'am," Akeem said, and this time I could definitely see a wry smile on his face. "That'll be for the Seven to do – although I doubt they'll even spare a thought for you," he added quickly, wheeling his steed away from mine hurriedly. Was that a warning? That we were on our own?

"Skreaa!" Our conversation was split by the sudden cry from above and the mighty snap of wings as Gorugal on the Green swirled above the arena.

"Come on," Latifa was urging her mount forward – we probably don't want to be late."

As it happened, there were almost no worries of being late for this mission.

"That bloody fool's taken them to the river," Akeem muttered from where he had dropped back to ride at my side on the wide, cobbled roadway that led out of the rocks behind Dagfan. We had been riding due eastwards for the past two hours of the morning, and Akeem and the other Dragon Handler had set a punishing canter in the early morning sun before finally letting the steeds take their own leads when he saw what Gorugal, Tabit and the other two were doing.

Whoops of laughter rose on the breeze where I stood, looking over the rocky edge of land at the broad Taval River. Gorugal was down there, still on the Green's back as the dragon paddled through the river like a scaled boat, submerging its lower body until just its snout, eyes, and back remained.

"I thought we were going to fight Deadweed?" I whispered back. The other trainees were watching the antics of the Seven with a mixture of jealousy and excitement – I guessed none of them had seen a dragon at play, and this display probably made them think how brave the Seven were to be with such gigantic creatures as they splashed about in the waters.

"We are," Akeem whispered back in a grimace, pretending to fix some of the straps on his saddlebags. "Menali Bridge isn't far, keep your eyes peeled." With that, he clucked for his steed to pick up the pace and canter ahead.

We passed the cavorting dragons and rounded the bend in the road. The land up ahead rose in a collection of rocks and a few scrubby southern trees. There was a dusting of grass and even woody, fragrant-smelling bushes to one side of us, and I could see how well tended the banks of the Taval River were. It's the lifeblood of the south, I reminded myself, noticing the small stands of posts and pennants that indicated watering holes and stopping paces.

But on the right of us, the lush landscape gave way to a more arid climate. The grasses became broken by sand dunes, topped with whip-like razor grass that could cut the horses legs if we were forced to ride through it, and beyond that, the orange-yellow haze of the deeper souths. Out there started the great southern deserts, which were mostly rock and shingles plains this far to the north of the Southern Kingdom, but soon turned into the burning golds of the Deep Sands, which stretched for weeks in every direction.

Which is why Deadweed is so dangerous to us down here in the South, I thought as I rode forward into the rising heat. The weed traveled along the fertile water-irrigated lands at the top of the Southern Kingdom, and if it took a hold then there will be nothing left for us to live on. We could flee to the deserts to try and live like the black-wearing Binshee Tribes of the deep deserts – but their way of life was harsh and unforgiving. How many of the thousands who lived in Dagfan alone could survive out there?

As those dark thoughts swooped around my mind, something changed in the air and my pony started snorting in an unsettled manner. "What's up, handsome?" I leaned forward to talk gently into his twitching ears. *"Mamma-la, Mamma-la,"* I whispered-sang, and earned a slightly warmer whicker in response.

But now I could smell it too – something sweet and fragrant carrying on the wind, which I couldn't put a name to. It didn't smell like the hearty and wholesome spices of the curries and tagines of the southlands. If anything, it was *overly* floral, like jasmine and honeysuckle combined with something just about to turn over ripe – an apple press left out in the sun; cut flowers left to wilt and molder on an altar…

"Deadweed!" I remembered the smell in an instant. It was the same fragrance that I had detected in the North, before the Dragon Riders of Torvald had burned it. It was somewhere nearby.

"What's got your goat?" Nas was saying, picking at his fingernails with his belt knife as he clipped along behind me.

"It's Deadweed, it's somewhere nearby…" I stood up in the stirrups, certain of what I was saying.

"Oh…" Nas paled, looking at me under heavy brows, and I could tell that it was the same look that he and his stepfather had used to give me when they were sure that I was 'funny' or 'witchy.'

"What's up with Dayie?" Latifa was calling.

"Just listen to me, we're in danger!" I said, one hand on the reins while my other drew the hatchet that we'd been given. Fat lot of good that's going to do, I thought grimly.

"What? No, we're not – the Seven will be here any moment," one of the other trainees scoffed.

"If they ever get off their behinds," I grumbled, earning a gasp from the rest of the trainees.

"You can't say that!" Nas said.

"Why not?" I said. "They're being lazy, while the Deadweed is spreading!"

"He's right, you *can't*," Latifa added, and from the way that she was looking at me in alarm, I could tell she was scared. *Are we not even allowed to criticize the Seven?* I thought. She was warning me to hold my tongue – but there was no time.

"I tell you that the Deadweed is nearby, even our horses can sense it – look at how skittish they are!" I pointed out that each of the ponies were stamping and throwing their heads. They clearly didn't want to go any further.

"I'm going ahead on foot." I made my decision in a split second. I wouldn't put my poor steed through this much terror, and I wasn't about to see it get injured for some foolish plan by the Seven. I mean, we hadn't even been trained *how* to fight the Deadweed yet, just told 'that was what we did' like we would automatically figure it out for ourselves.

But I had seen both the Torvald Dragons and the Wild Company use fire, I thought quickly. "Has any one got a torch? Tinderboxes? Maybe we can make some torches from these thicker bits of sand-juniper? Light them up, and I reckon they'll burn pretty good."

"Hey, we got these." Latifa patted the charcoal satchels.

"Good thinking." I nodded, unslinging the satchel from my shoulder and wishing that I had a flint and strike.

"Here!" It was Akeem, riding towards us even as all the other students had joined me on foot. "What are you doing down there? Get back on your ponies! We need to be able to move quickly!" he barked, only half-remembering to keep his guttural fake accent in place.

"Handler," I cleared my throat, "I'm not endangering the ponies, and we know that there's Deadweed nearby. We need some fire-striking material if we want to have a chance to fight it."

"Oh hells..." Akeem gritted his teeth as he looked up at the skies in annoyance, "the Seven are supposed to fight it. You're only supposed to watch and clear the burned remains, but I guess that we're on our own." He fumbled at his belt for a small pouch of lamp-oil as well as a handful of sharp, arrow-head like flints and steels.

"Here. Don't use the lamp-oil yet until we know what we're dealing with, but I want each of you to take a flint and steel," he said tersely.

"And who made *you* an expert in fighting Deadweed?" Nas said imperiously, standing up to glare at Akeem, before I saw the shock cross Nas's face as he recognized the man who had saved him and his stepfather from the Deadweed before.

"*You!*" Nas whispered, to my horror.

"I'm sure you know how this goes," Akeem muttered in a low voice, as Latifa and the others looked between us in confusion.

"Come on!" I clapped my hands to distract them from working out that Nas and I knew Akeem. "We need to find this stuff quickly, before it finds us! We scan the ground, move in groups of two, never out of earshot of the next pair. If you see it – holler!"

But I knew from experience, that finding the Deadweed wouldn't be the difficult bit, it would be the fighting it.

The riverside along the roadway was broken with crags and splinters of black rock, dusted with more of the stunted southern trees. Latifa and I had climbed up the rocks to get a look down to the water's edge, and I was just about to cross over the summit of the crag when Latifa suddenly grabbed my shoulder and pulled me back.

"Woah – look down!" she hissed as she pulled me back, and I swiveled to see there, nestled between the lines of rocks was a fleshy green tendril, tipped with cruel-looking barbs, was the Deadweed.

I shivered in disgust as it moved like an insect, inching forward as if it had been trying to creep up on us. The vine grew thicker and darker the further down my eyes went, giving way to deep leather-like green leaves as I traced the growth down the sides of the crags, getting richer and more verdant as it joined the body of the plant below, by the water's edge. It was so strange that I almost couldn't take my eyes off of it –as the creeping mass of vines *trembled* and spasmed organically.

As I watched, the barbed tip of this runner-vine reared up a few inches from the dirt, wavering in the air as if tasting it. And it was doing that towards us.

"It knows we are here," I whispered, feeling sick. "It can smell us."

"Don't be silly – plants can't smell..." Latifa was saying, just as the 'plant' shivered once more, and suddenly it attacked—

"*Get back!*" I screamed, jumping backwards as the vine that we had been looking at snapped forward. It moved faster than I was expecting, faster than Tabit's Sinuous Blue dragon had. I felt the hiss of air as it rushed past my face, and the terrifying wrench as it snagged on my tunic, which luckily tore as Latifa dragged me backwards.

Just like when Wera and Obasi died, I couldn't stop myself from thinking. I thought I had forgotten that memory – had *made* myself forget it by pushing it down so far that I didn't have to wake up crying in the night ever again— but I was wrong. There it was, the memory of those ugly yellow flowers rising over the rockpools and the vines lashing out-

No. Concentrate. Run, I told myself.

We stumbled down the slide of rocks, slipping on the shale and sand and grazing our hands.

"It's still coming!" Latifa sounded horrified as we jumped to our feet, to see the vine emerge over the headland, its leaves shaking and making an eerie, scratchy sound.

"Quick – the satchels!" I grabbed mine from my shoulder, before remembering that I had given the small pouch of lamp oil to Nas and one of the other students to use. Would we be able to set alight to a bag of dry charcoal just with flint sparks? *I don't think so.* "Take these, get over there and use the dried grasses for kindling." I threw my back at Latifa, turning just in time to see a large, mustard-yellow flower bud appear over the shivering mass of murderous green. *The flower heads,* I had watched them spit or spray something at the dragons, but I didn't know what it was – a pollen? Whatever it was, I didn't want to take any chances getting caught in it; hefting my cleaver I jumped forward, even as the vines curled in on themselves, ready to spring at me…

"Yagh!" I screamed as I swiped broadly across the tops of the plants, to an explosion of the fleshy leaves and, thankfully, the still-closed flower head. It fell back into the nest of vines, but now they were branching forward, heading for my legs.

"Dayie?" I heard in the back of my mind, a rising howl of dragon-rage and knew that it was Zarr, still many leagues away and unable to help me.

"Argh!" One of the vines had curled around my ankle, its sharp barbs ripping through the thin fabric of my trousers with ease and embedding into my skin.

"Get off me!" I swung down, hacking off the offending vine (to see, disgustingly, a half curl still attached to my calf) but no sooner had I done that, then there were three more rising like snakes on the other side of me.

No! I flailed and hacked, cleaving the growing tip off one and making it recoil backwards in pain. *So you can feel pain then,* I thought grimly, before jumping back as the other two reached for me.

This wasn't fighting. This wasn't even the tense combat of wrestling. I was just hacking and swinging wildly – no time to try to guess what my opponent was going to do, no thought of doing anything other than stopping it from getting a hold of me again. What was stranger, was that I didn't feel anything from the plant. *No, that's not right,* my panicked thoughts told me. *I felt something from it – but it wasn't anything like a normal plant.*

I had never stopped to consider how I 'sensed' the animals that I was supposed to be so good with. It was different from my mental conversations with Zarr—it was the way I was able to tell when a mare was about to foal, or whether the pony was distressed. These were always natural senses that I had thought everybody had, until I had been proven wrong. Now, though, as I felt a sickening nausea just being around the

Deadweed, I realized that my senses also extended to plants. That was how I had managed to survive through the wild forests of the North and on the long road South – even if I hadn't realized it, the plants and the trees had sustained me, had told me about themselves as I had moved through them.

And the only thing that Deadweed was telling me was that it was evil, and that it wanted to kill me.

"Dayie, duck!" Latifa shouted and I did my best to throw myself backwards. We were still on the edge of the rocky rise, and the downward slope helped me to roll and bounce (painfully hitting the rocks, though) back as there was a crackle and a *woosh!* in front of me.

"Here, up!" Latifa grabbed my hand and yanked me to my feet as I smelt burning and saw that the Deadweed above us was shivering and twitching, thin streams of smoke rising from it. Latifa had used the dried, resinous bushes and grasses of these lands to light the two charcoal sacks that we had between us, and had thrown them like a bola, scattering their charring and smoking contents over the approaching Deadweed. *But would it be enough to catch?*

WHUMP! In these arid and dry conditions, yes. We were almost lifted off of our feet once again as a sudden wave of hot air exploded out from the Deadweed as the flames caught the oils of the plant and the air. I *swear* that I could almost hear a chittering, whistling sound of a creature writhing in pain as the deep scarlet flames erupted hungrily along its growth.

"You genius!" I gasped thankfully as we staggered back to the roadway, and kept on going until we were a little safer on the other side as well.

"Don't thank me – it was your idea," Latifa said, wiping some charcoal dust from her face with one hand as she hefted her own cleaver in the other. "But I don't think it's enough to stop it," she said grimly, and I followed her glare as more shivering humps of vegetation appeared over the rocks further to the right and left of us, climbing up from the river Taval below, and out of reach of the fires.

"But the fire will take, surely?" I hoped, holding my own cleaver in one hand, which was glistening with a green ichor that must be the sap of the Deadweed itself.

"Maybe not fast enough." Latifa pointed to an impossible sight. I don't know whether my ally had seen Deadweed in action before, but I had. Watching it move was like looking at a nightmare made real – plants weren't supposed to grow that quick. We could see a distant thicket emerging as the sharp vines rushed forward, curling around every rock and desiccated shrub in its path, as the fleshier body of leaves then followed to swamp and overwhelm any obstacle, before new vines rose whip-like in the air to lance forward and continue the process once again.

"Oh no," I gasped, and there, rising over the fatter body-mass of the vegetation, I saw several of the yellow buds of the flowers. "They'll kill you," I said, knowing it with a certainty that came with seeing them murder my foster parents.

"The whole sand's-damned thing will kill you," Latifa muttered. At least she still had her sense of sarcasm.

"Yes, but those things – I think its poison, I don't understand it. I saw those flowers fire their pollen *at* the attacking dragons, like a human might throw a spear, or fire a bow."

"Then let's get out of here before it gets us then..." Latifa started backing away, and, even though I knew that we had to stop it somehow – I also knew that there was nothing we could do against such a beast.

Woosh!

Whump!

Shouts rose up further behind us, and we turned to see other, smaller fires explode hungrily into life at different spots along the bank of Deadweed. "It must be the others, they saw our fire and started their own?" I said, and we ran back to them to see if we could concentrate our efforts. Cut off like this in pairs, I knew now that we would each just get swamped.

We needed more people. We needed an army. We needed dragons! I thought in anger. Where were the Seven?

"I will come to you, Dayie!" Zarr breathed against my mind,

still far away and sounding just like a whisper of fire and smoke.

"No – don't risk yourself," I gasped, and Latifa looked at me oddly as we ran. Whatever Zarr's response was to that, I didn't know as I lost our connection just as easily as I had gained it.

"More kindling!" Akeem shouted, and galloping on his pony back up the roadway, carrying bundles of the resinous scrub-bushes to throw them onto a long bank of kindling and wood. The other trainees were there, Nas in the thick of it, heaping the nearest twiggy material into a wall across from the Deadweed.

"Dayie! Latifa!" Akeem shouted at us, signaling for us to go around the southern, desert edge as Nas started lighting the bonfire. It caught easily, and the rich, heady smell of oily desert plants rose into the air along with black smoke.

"It will keep it back for a little while, but we can't stop it from spreading down the river towards Dagfan," Akeem shouted as we emerged around the far side of the wall.

"You'll have to warn the city," I said immediately. "Or…"

He knew what I was about to say. *Call the Wild Company.* He nodded quickly. "Aida has been shrieking in my head to come, now I can let her if the Seven won't be here…" He wheeled his pony—

"SKREARGH!" There was a bellow of outrage and indigna-

tion as the sky was split by a jet of fire. Gorugal, Tabit, Oleg and Marshal had at last arrived, Gorugal and the older Green being the first to swoop against the plant, with the Stocky Green pouring its dragon flame across the line of burning weed that we had already set alight to.

"Took them long enough!" Akeem muttered, and I wondered if he was annoyed that he hadn't got a chance to call the Wild Company. Maybe this was the threat that he had been waiting for, a chance to prove to the rulers of the city that the Wild Company was real, and that they were no threat to the South.

Now Tabit was swooping, ducking down behind the bank of rocks that overhung the river, and gouts of flames rose from the cliff-edge as she attacked its base. That's more like it, I thought. Next came Oleg, flying more awkwardly and narrowly avoiding the pollen-spray of the flowers, and finally, as fast as a darting falcon came the smaller Sea Dragon with Marshal on its back. Akeem was gesturing all of us trainees to move back into the dunes, away from the fierce heat of the burning weed as Gorugal once again swooped on another attack run.

"Get what rest you can. Drink any water you have," Akeem said grimly. "Soon enough there'll be ten-times the work we've already done today..."

Akeem wasn't wrong it turned out, because as soon as the four Riders had finished burning the Deadweed, they landed to great plumes of sand and dirt out in the dunes and demanded to be attended to.

"Trainees! Get this dragon staked out!" Gorugal roared angrily, his face dripping with sweat as the Green ambled slowly across the sands to lie down, fully outstretched on the hot dunes.

Do we need to? I thought as Akeem directed us to where we had piled the dragon ropes, and showed us how to use what trees were left to tie guide lines from them to the saddles of the great beasts. To my eyes, all of the dragons looked exhausted and only too happy to collapse on the hot banks of land, and I would be more concerned with giving them water than I would be making sure they were secured.

"They did well," I murmured as I ran towards the Green with the line of the heavy rope playing out behind me. "We should be rewarding them."

Which, surprisingly, was exactly what Tabit thought as we got the dragons on their leashes. "Where's the charcoal?" she snapped at Latifa as she jumped down to the sand and start unbuckling her part armor with a groan. "We need to feed them."

"Uh…" Latifa looked over at me for a moment, and I could tell that she didn't want to be the one to tell one of the Seven that we couldn't do what they wished. I took that choice away from her.

"We used them," I called out. "All of them."

"What?" Tabit looked over at me in annoyance.

"We used the charcoal satchels to fire the Deadweed. It was the only thing that saved us…" I said defiantly, putting a hand to pat Talal's Green distractedly. It gave a low, guttural growl that was *almost* a purr, I thought.

"Trainee. Come here," Tabit said, pointing to the sands.

"What did she do?" Gorugal was calling over from where he was liberally splashing himself with water. "She lost the charcoal?"

"She *used* the charcoal," Tabit spat back heavily as I approached, a part of me certain that she was going to slap me. If Fan had told me to do this, then that is precisely what would have followed – but Tabit just waited for me to stand across from her and glared at me in an assessing way. Her eyes met mine, and I swear that I could feel sparks.

"You were supposed to hold back until we got here," Tabit said coldly. "And then, after we have dealt with the problem, you feed the dragons and then go about hacking down the burnt Deadweed." She was waiting for me to argue, the better to judge my punishment – it was a trick I had seen Fan use many times, but I couldn't hold my tongue. Not now. Not when my friends' lives had been at stake.

"We would have been dead if we had waited for you," I returned, keeping my voice level.

"What is that supposed to mean?" Tabit hissed, leaning in towards me. I kept my ground. She was far more capable than Fan, I was sure, but I had endured a life of beatings. I could handle one more.

"It means that I don't think the Training Hall wanted us to throw our lives away," I responded.

"You're trainees. What does the Training Hall care?" Gorugal interrupted us, laughing at our confrontation.

I paused. The answer seemed obvious to me, at least. There were only Seven Riders, and there had to be twenty-seven of us trainees. Sooner or later, the Seven were going to die out here, and it was us trainees who had to fill their shoes. I elected not to point this fact out to them though.

"She speaks the truth," It was Akeem who stood up for me, speaking in his guttural, fake accent. "The Deadweed moved fast, and they would have been swamped *and* lost the charcoal anyway. It was my order to use it against the weed."

No, it wasn't! I frowned. Why was he taking credit for my idea?

"You fool," Tabit spat at him, and that was when I realized that it wasn't the credit that he was opting to take on my behalf, it was the blame. "We had it all under control. Now, as well as making sure that our dragons are un-pacified, and making our job more dangerous – you have all of this mess to clear from the roads." She nodded to where Akeem's wall of bonfire was still smoldering.

Akeem shrugged. He wasn't one to back down either, it appeared.

"I'll have words with Talal over this, mark my words – *Handler*," Tabit croaked, clapping her hands as she signaled to the other Riders. "No time to relax, we have to get these brutes back to the Training Hall before they get hungry, thanks to *them*," she shouted, earning a groan from Marshal and a growl of annoyance from Oleg, who was busy massaging his foot-less ankle, before strapping back on his wooden prosthetic.

There were a few more mutterings and grumbles from the Riders, but no more punishment was metered out to us, apart from the fact that it meant that we wouldn't be seeing the dragons. I was almost pleased to see the back of them as we untied the dragon ropes and hurried out of the way for Goru-gal, Tabit, Oleg and Marshal to take back to the air once again. If anything, I felt sorry for Nas, who was looking up at the Sea Dragon with an expression like a lovesick fool at her sudden appearance and just as quick disappearance.

"Come on, trainees," Akeem grumbled, kicking the sand after they had gone. "We might as well bank up the fires."

It took us a long time – working well into the night and past midnight, but by the time that the fires had died down, Akeem had shown us how to hack at the blackened char of the murderous weed until it was a mess on the earth, and then how to scuff sand over it to half bury it. Even then, I still felt uncomfortable around its dead remains, and at any moment I still expected to see its green shoots bursting from the soil, and searching for my flesh.

CHAPTER 20
DAYIE AND THE UNDERGROUND
SCHOOL

The next few days in the Training Hall passed in a blur of more exercise drills, more time spent trying to get the Riders onto the dragons as they emerged from the dragon caves, and more fighting drills. Nothing was said to us trainees of our recent mission to Menali Bridge, and so I had no idea if Tabit had kept her promise to tell Talal about our 'insubordination.'

"I think that they're too busy," Latifa confided in me a few days after the Menali Bridge encounter, just after we had helped see Gorugal, Marshal and Tabit out of the arena on the back of dragons. This time it had been Tabit on Talal's Green, and Gorugal on the younger bullish Green, and Marshal stayed on the Sea Dragon (much to Nas's annoyance). It was clear to me that Nas had bonded with the Sea Dragon, and, if the way that the Sea Dragon looked and made excited pheeps and chirrups at him when it saw Nas go by, I was sure that the feeling was mutual.

"Too busy getting everything wrong?" I muttered as I stooped to pick up the haul of dragon rope that we had to throw – this time on the younger bullish Green to stop it from snapping at Jeona.

"Huh. Your words, not mine." Latifa looked away hurriedly, but she was smirking. Something about our recent battle had thawed our relationship somewhat. I was even starting to think that she might see the dragons and this place in the same way that I did.

"But I heard that Handler of yours talking to the others in the equipment stores the other day. He was saying that Deadweed has been increasing its attacks up and down the coast and has been spreading up the Taval River again."

Just like what happened at Menali, I thought. "So, the Riders are being sent out to stop it all the time?" I surmised. "Good, I suppose." Everyone knew that the Deadweed was much more of a danger near the coast, where the land was wetter. So far, Dagfan had managed to stop its incursions into the inlets and tributaries of the rivers – but it was getting harder as every day passed.

"Apart from there's no one left here to train us," Latifa groaned, before looking at me from under her shaded eyelashes speculatively. "Unless, of course…"

"Unless what?" I finished the ropes and stacked them on the cart. Just a little bit more sweeping of the arena to do, and then we could return to the relative shade of the halls, and continue our indoor weapons practices.

"Unless you speak to that Handler of yours," she said.

"What?" *She meant Akeem, of course.* "Who do you mean?"

"Don't pretend," Latifa said, another sly smirk on her face as she added her rope to the pile. "I've seen the whispered conversations that you two have shared. And he's handsome enough, that's for sure…"

"What?" I could feel myself blushing, and not just from embarrassment – also from outrage. Those 'conversations' that I had managed to snatch with Akeem had for the most part been arguments, where I had been pressing him to approach Talal about the Wild Company, and he had been refusing every time.

"Oh, you keep on fooling yourself white girl." Latifa even laughed this time. "I don't care. All I care about is training, and it seems to me that Handler we're both talking about knows his way around a battlefield, and as well as that he has the keys to the dragon caves. We should start practicing ourselves with the dragons, if the Seven haven't got the time to help us."

"That's… that's…" I stammered, astonished that this idea had come from the stern and usually reserved Latifa of all people.

But if we were already in trouble over using so much charcoal – won't this be worse?

Then again, I remembered what life had been like under Fan. *I would always be in trouble,* so I might as well be in trouble for doing something that could help us survive and perhaps save other people's lives.

"That's a good idea is what it is," another voice broke in between us, and I turned on the spot in alarm to see that it was Nas, already shirtless and drying himself off with a towel. He had filled out a little in just the short time that we had been here, and maybe it was me, but he seemed to have lost that cruel sneer that he used to wear so often. If anything, he appeared almost like an entirely different person now than who he had been before.

"C'mon, Dayie," I was surprised to hear him say. "I've seen you with your dragon. You got a connection with it alright, and that guy – not that I trust him – but he seems to do most of the training himself here anyway."

Nas was right, I knew. It was Akeem and the other Handlers who actually taught us the various sorts of knots that we needed to know, and the different names for the pieces of tack and saddle equipment that the Seven used.

"What are you saying – that we just set up an alternate Training Hall within the Training Hall?" I pointed out the stupidity of their comment. Which then made me feel even

267

more ashamed. *This was exactly what I had been wanting, wasn't it?* I thought. But why should *I* be the one to take all the risks? And why did everyone seem to think that *I* had anything to do with Akeem?

"You don't want to ask for his help," I heard a faint voice say in the back of my mind, with a ghost of draconian humor.

Zarr, I thought warmly to him, and the relief I felt at even being able to hear him given our erratic connection over the last few days made me overlook what he had said.

"It's true. Too stubborn. Just like a dragon." Zarr said, his voice tattering away into the dreams and anxieties of my own mind, leaving me alone and bereft.

Zarr... Come back! I thought at him, even casting my eyes to the sand at my feet as if I could will my thoughts through it with sheer determination alone. But there was nothing, no sound in my mind, and I suddenly became terrified that this was how it was going to be from now on – or maybe even worse than this! The Chief of the Training Hall had been keeping me and my dragon apart for so long, that now I was scared that it was weakening our bond.

Is that what Talal meant to do? To make us all like his Seven? Unbonded, and unable to realize if we were?

"Dayie? Come back to us, Dayie!" Nas scuffed the sand with his boots, clearly annoyed. I shook my head, looking first at my two friends and then at the long gate that covered the entrance to the dragon caves.

"Okay," I said through gritted teeth. "Tonight. Bring only those you think can keep their mouth shut."

"You have to let us try," I hissed at Akeem as I handed him another section of the leather harnesses and saddles. It was early evening, and they had already rung the dinner bell and so all of the other trainees had abandoned the arena for the cool shade of indoors. It gave me just a few minutes amidst the chaos of trainees shouting for dinner and jostling for their preferred seats to talk.

"Not now, Dayie," Akeem muttered from the darks of his hood, moving to the back of the open gallery to stack the saddles that we had been polishing, and hang up the strings of harnesses from their hooks at the back. I followed him into the darkness, to be instantly surrounded by the smell of leather and preserving oil.

"Akeem, you have to listen to me. The others are going to try and do something themselves anyway, I'm sure of it. And how many of them are bonded – apart from sand-brained Nas, that is."

"Nas is bonded?" Akeem looked at me sharply. "The boy you came in with?"

Boy. It was funny to hear Akeem call him that, because from the looks of them, both Akeem and Nas were of a similar age – twenty-one, maybe? Twenty-three? But Akeem didn't *act* the same as Nas, not at all. Akeem was calm and competent where Nas was nervy and brash. Akeem stared hard at the Seven when he was being questioned, as if he wasn't scared of them – whereas Nas had only been too eager to prove himself to them.

Why am I comparing the two? I thought with a shake of my head. My thoughts were all over the place these days. I needed to focus.

"Tonight," I said.

"It can't be tonight." Akeem shook his head dramatically. "You don't know…"

Who on earth did he think that he was? I thought. "Stop treating me like a girl!" I burst out, advancing on him and prodding him, hard, in the chest. Through my rage, the look on his face was priceless. His mouth dropped open, aghast and embarrassed, and he even took a step back before his back thumped up against the wall of saddles.

"I – I don't think of you as a girl," he said softly and seriously, his eyes trained on mine. My stomach was full of butterflies, as if I were flying on top of Zarr – and I don't know whether that was a good thing or a bad thing.

"Tell me then," I asked. "What's so wrong about tonight?"

"The princes. The Lords of the Southern Realms are coming to Dagfan for a Council to decide what to do about Deadweed. They should already have arrived, and I am sure over the next few days they will want an inspection of the Training Hall."

"So what do you care?" I pointed out. "I'm talking about *tonight,* under cover of darkness – just like we did before. You let us down into the dragon caves, and I'll teach the others everything that I know how to befriend a dragon."

"*Everything* you know?" Akeem's mouth twitched into an almost smile, and I could have hit him.

"Yeah, I know about dragons!" I said, feeling suddenly very, very frustrated with him. Why was he treating me like someone less than him—like a girl? I could feel myself blushing.

"It's too dangerous," Akeem tried to say again, in that maddening slow and patient way that I had heard Rahim use a few times when he thought I was being stupid.

But I knew I had the upper hand. "Look, half of the Seven are already away, right? Fighting the Deadweed along the coast?"

Akeem nodded. "They could be back at any time."

"They could," I pointed out, "but knowing them, they probably won't. Why fly all through the night when they can rest up in some village somewhere and be treated like heroes?" It was a good point, and I was proud of myself for thinking of it at the last moment. I would have told him that I had heard the Seven had all been turned to cream cheese if it meant that I could get down into the dragon caves to see Zarr again.

"It has to be tonight, it's our best chance of being alone with the dragons," I said, and that was a fact that even stubborn Akeem couldn't ignore. I stepped back, straightening my jerkin and feeling oddly self-conscious. *Had I made a fool out of myself?* "Whatever. I am going to be at those dragon gates tonight, a watch after midnight, with whomever of the trainees I can trust. If you're *not* there, then we'll just have to find some other way to break our way in."

"Fine, fine. No need to threaten!" Akeem dusted his hands, glowering at me. "Watch after midnight. Just don't make any noise."

ACT 3: DAYIE, THE WITCH

CHAPTER 21
DAYIE, SWEETBALM

"*Dayie?*" It was Zarr's voice, as soft as the sigh of moonlit sands. It drifted into my sleepy thoughts, so naturally that I couldn't tell whether it was another one of my dreams. But of course, it wasn't.

"I'm coming," I whispered into the dark, opening my eyes to see the high stone ceilings above, and to hear the rustle of blankets nearby. It was dark, but I was sure that I had heard the soft chime of the midnight bell, meaning that it was after midnight. Looking over, I saw the glint of Latifa's eyes from the shadows of the dormitory, and I nodded. It was time.

As quiet as a mouse, I slipped from the bunkbed to join Latifa and Jeona as we hastily dragged on our clothes and prepared for what was to come. We didn't wear any shoes in case we made a noise, and we ghosted out of the dormitory and to the stairs leading down to the common hall.

The Training Hall was a different place at night. The shutters had been left open to allow the cool night air in, which also allowed the moonlight to cast bluish and eerie glows through the abandoned halls. Familiar shapes I thought I recognized turned out to be something else – I gasped when I thought I saw a guard waiting in the corner – but it was only where one of the Seven had stacked their helmet atop a stand.

"Psst!" I heard from the shadows of one of the alcoves, and two shapes detached themselves from there. Nas and Adir.

"No one else?" I whispered, earning a quick headshake from Nas.

"No one I could be certain wouldn't blab," he whispered, the moonlight casting his face into deep highlights and shadows.

Well, probably for the best, I thought. I didn't even know how many dragons there were down below us, and there was only one – Zarr – that I had any confidence wouldn't scream the place down when we tried to approach them.

But that was a part of why we were doing this, I had been thinking. If the Seven weren't going to train us, then we would train ourselves. And if Akeem was right and the Deadweed was getting worse every season, then we needed to know what we had to fight with. How many dragons did we have, really? How many would be willing to bond? How many were too far gone – either too ferocious, or too feral?

But more important than any of this, I just wanted to see Zarr again.

Our group of five whispered our way to one of the side terrace doors— I had decided to use the more direct approach rather than risk trying to get everyone out of the windows and down to the arena below. The last time *I* had done that, I had almost busted a knee – and I didn't know what I would have done if any of the others had got injured.

Then again, they're approaching dragons, part of me wanted to laugh (I guess it was the nervousness); what could be more dangerous than that?

The sand was still warm when we stepped out onto it, and I directed the others to edge along the arena walls, staying out of sight of any of the Dragon Handler guards that might be up there. When we had crossed a full quarter of the oval, I pointed to the pillars of rocks that sat on their own like a petrified forest. We used those for close-quarters fighting and scrambling, dodging behind them and then having to avoid other people in a game of fierce 'tag' which had been fun, but didn't seem like it would help us ride dragons.

Nas was the first to break cover, sprinting across the sands to the pillars where he turned and slid to the floor in their shadows. I held my breath, half expecting a shout – but thankfully none came. Then ran Abir, Jeona, and finally Latifa and me. We made it into the pillars and hurried to the far side, where it was just a short run to get to the dragon gate.

Which was still closed.

"Akeem!" I muttered in annoyance. *Please don't tell me that he had got cold feet!* I bit my lip, wondering what to do next. Had I meant it when I had said that we would find another way in? *Yes.* But how?

"Nas," I whispered to him, patting him lightly on his shoulder. "Do you remember when Fan showed us how to pick locks?"

"Of course," Nas said after a moment's pause. Was his voice a little thicker at the mention of his birth-mother? Had I done a stupid thing reminding him of her? There was a sudden glint in the night, and I realized that I was looking at two long and thin knifes held in Nas's hand.

"I've even still got my stilettos," he said with a grin, and, sparing a look above us, ran across the sand to hunker down in front of the gates.

"Dayie? You are close!" I could hear Zarr much better now. I wondered if that was the secret of it? That I had to be as close as possible in order to hear him?

"Maybe. It's been a long time since I've seen the sun…" Zarr breathed at the back of my mind, and I instantly felt a burning wave of indignation, shame, and rage. How on earth could I have ever thought that being separated was good for him, or us?

I was being selfish, I realized and I was glad that the deep shadows of the night hid my fierce blush. I had been too concerned with how *I* might have found a home here, how hard it was for *me* to prove myself – when all along I should only have been thinking about Zarr.

"Not only," Zarr advised me, and once again I felt hurt at just how grown up he sounded. When did he become so wise?

"Day!" I was shaken out of my misery to see that it was Nas, and he was beckoning, holding the central gate just a little ajar.

"He did it!" I felt glad, not jealous at all of how he had excelled at lockpicking. Just a few months ago, I might not have been so magnanimous, when I was still with Fan's cara-van. I patted Latifa on the shoulder first. If there *were* any guards down there in the caves, then I wanted her up front rather than Abir or Jeona. Latifa was tougher and quicker than the others. And, because she had been the one to first suggest this, despite all of our arguments – I felt like I could trust her.

My friend gave me a grin that shone white in the dark, and ducked as she ran, slipping inside as Nas held the heavy gates open. The dark swallowed her in an instant, and I forced myself to breath steadily, counting to ten before I sent Jeona, and then Abir before finally crossing the arena myself.

I reached the gates with a roll, holding out my hand to take the gate from Nas, but his face was not filled with excitement or joy.

"Dayie – you should know. The gates were unlocked when I got here," he whispered, before ducking inside.

Unlocked? Maybe Akeem *had* held up his part of the bargain after all. But then, where was he? There was only one way to find out, as I followed Nas and the others inside the cool interiors, and eased the gates shut behind us.

Darkness. Darkness and the smell of recent fires. The nearness of the great dragons washed over me in an almost physical wave. All of my senses sharpened, and even my eyes seemed to pierce the dark. My hearing told me of the subtle movements of the other trainees around me, the way that they were all anxious in one way or another, from their rapid breathing to the way that Abir jostled about.

And I could sense the dragons too – almost like the way that I could feel Zarr in my mind, but less strong than my connection with the Crimson Red. I couldn't tell precisely where each dragon was, but I could feel their large, brooding reptilian presences in the same way that you might feel the distant mountains where you are walking through their foothills.

"It's going to be alright," I breathed to my compatriots, making some attempt to ease their nerves. I don't think I was very successful as I looked at the whites of their eyes as they peered at me in the dark.

"Take each other's hands," I told them. "I'll lead the way..." I turned, following my newfound senses, and walked down the smooth stone ramp and into the dragon caves.

"They're close," I breathed, squeezing Latifa's hand encouragingly behind me. It was dark down here – almost pitch, but I wanted to wait until the glow of any torches that we might light wouldn't be seen from the surface. Until I remembered being under the earth a long time ago, seemingly years ago, though it was actually just a season ago.

The Earthlight! I fished through my pockets to see if I had thought to bring it with me. I felt the crystalline nub of the rock in the corner of my jerkin and was glad that this was the one – my old jerkin from my days with the caravan— that I had thought to wear on this mission. It had been my one and only 'gift' from Fan, (I didn't count the clothes that she forced me to wear) and even this lump of rock wasn't really a gift, but a tool that she had begrudgingly entrusted to me in order to make sure I survived the tunnels in the Dragon Mountain of Torvald and got out with the egg she needed for her livelihood.

The Earthlight crystal looked like an odd-shaped crown of bluish spikes that started to glow as soon as I had brought it out into the dark.

"Woah – Earthlight," Abir said, entranced by it.

"Yeah," I said, handing it over to him. "You can hold onto it if you like." He would probably appreciate it more than me anyway, as my memories of it were tainted by Fan. The smaller youth held it gratefully up, revealing our surroundings: a wide but low-ceilinged cavern, with darkened iron-work grills over tunnel openings.

"Is that—?" Abir had a chance to say, just before his unasked question was answered anyway by a deep, guttural sound from the darkness.

"Sssss....!" A thin rivulet of dark smoke escaped from between the bars, curling up to the ceiling where it vanished into venting shafts through the rock above.

"Uh...Dayie?" Abir asked warily, as one giant golden eye opened in the dark, and it seemed to glow, it was so bright and intense.

"Gren," Zarr said in my head. The Crimson Red wasn't here, in this cavern, but he knew all of the dragons that were.

"Gren?" I whispered into the dark. "You mean Green?"

"Sssss!" The hissing sound only increased from the darkness.

"Gren. Her human doesn't know what her name really is. That annoys Gren," Zarr whispered, and I suddenly realized who it was that we must be standing in front of. The largest, oldest dragon in the Training Hall that I had seen both Gorugal and Tabit ride – *Green,* or *Gren*, Talal's dragon.

So they *were* bonded! I knew that I had been right in what I had sensed between the Chief of the Dragon Hall and this dragon. How annoyed she must be to always being ridden by someone else – and someone as oafish as Gorugal, of all people!

"It's okay, Gren..." I said easily, taking a step forward to the grill.

The hissing sound grew louder.

"Uh, Dayie – I don't think that one's going to work out..." I heard Abir say behind us, but I had a different view. There was something about the way that Zarr had talked about her, and the way that Gren had been steady and methodical in her acceptance of everything that she had been asked to do in the arena up there.

"She's the oldest," I whispered, and *knew* it, too, in the same way that I knew that Zarr was just a little way away.

What was it that Akeem had told me? That dragons in Torvald had their own Den-Mothers? Queens? Yes, that was it. But down here they didn't. Every one of these dragons at the Training Hall had been stolen from their nests and raised here, suffering the same fate as what my Zarr was suffering right now. Isolation. Managed and controlled interaction, both with humans and with other dragons.

"And the one person she's given her heart to cannot even hear her..." I murmured, crouching down a few feet away from the bars, and extending my hand to *almost* touch their iron.

"What's that?" Latifa was a few steps behind me, and my newfound widened and developed senses could tell that she was tense, ready to yank me back at the moment that Gren opened her mouth. Not that there was anything that we could do down here if Gren decided to release her dragon fire on all of us. I couldn't run that fast, and this whole cavern was like an oven anyway.

"It's *her,* Gren," I said, feeling a wave of annoyance and hurt radiating off from the Stocky Green as though she were a fire herself, and her emotions were her heat. "I think she's the key."

"What is Dayie talking about?" Jeona murmured from the back worriedly.

"You're the oldest, aren't you?" I spoke, not to the other trainees behind me but to Gren herself.

"You're the oldest here, and you deserve some respect," I repeated.

There was a scrape from the shadows ahead of me, and her one eye grew larger, coming closer to the edge of the blue crystal light so that her shattered and heavily scarred maw appeared. I could make out the heavy crud at the root of her teeth, and smell soot and charcoal on her breath.

"Where's the charcoal?" I whispered back, not taking my eyes off Gren, and I heard a rustling as the precious satchel of the stuff that the dragons seemed to adore was passed hand over hand to my shoulder, where I set it carefully down at my side.

"Here you go, Gren. Eldest. Powerful. Wisest," I whispered, taking up a large lump of the black and sooty stuff and moving to roll it through the bars. As soon as I moved there was a hiss from the dragon as she was still wary around my movements, and her head disappeared into the darkness once more.

Just when I thought I had blown my chances, I heard the sound of a crunching, and the eye opened again, half-closed this time, and the snout pushed forward just a little, not quite touching the bars.

Good. I thought. That is probably as good as we're going to get it so far, anyway. "Everyone, I want you all, in turn, and very slowly, to give the great and mighty Gren here a lump of charcoal, and then follow me," I said.

"Why?" Latifa asked. "Is this a part of the dragon training?"

"Yes," I said gravely, slowly rising and stepping back. I didn't turn my back to Gren, not because I thought that she might release her flames on me, but because I thought it might be more respectful this way. "Go on, Latifa. You're brave. You next," I urged her as I stepped past her, moving to the edge of the wide opening to the next cavern, where I waited for the rest of the would-be Dragon Riders to do exactly as I had done, one at a time, and one after the other.

When Latifa stepped back to join me, she looked up at me in the dim blue glow with a question on her face. "The dragon caves here don't have a matriarch. A queen. A mother, right?" I said sadly. "Every dragon here is an orphan," I said, but what I meant was *everyone* was.

Latifa nodded.

"So, maybe we need to make one. And I can't think of a better candidate than the bonded dragon to the chief of the Training Hall, and the oldest dragon here." Just saying the words *felt* right. I don't know how you go about trying to create a dragon nest from scratch, but I was sure that I was on the right track.

And we have to get rid of all of these bars, too, I thought. But one step at a time.

That was when my heightened hearing picked up the crunch of sand. It wasn't coming from Gren or any of the other dragon's caves, and it wasn't the scrape of a claw across the floor, either. This was the soft *crunch, crunch,* of booted feet on the gritty floor – and it was coming towards us from the entrance way.

"Be quiet!" I warned the others. It was too late to hide the glow of the Earthlight, but if the game was up, then we might as well *look* as though we weren't up to anything…

"I heard you halfway back to the gate, which you left open…" came an annoyed mutter. I was starting to recognize Akeem's disgruntled mannerisms, and into the light stepped the young man, his heavy cloak pulled over him, and a bag over his shoulder.

"You took your time," I said, before my mind caught up with what he had just said. *We left the door open.* "But that wasn't us. The gate, I mean. You must have opened it earlier and forgot."

The look on Akeem's face, even cast in an eerie blue was one of total alarm. "Do you know how much trouble we would get into if we left the gates open?" he whispered in horror to me. "The gate security is the number one job of the Dragon Handlers. There is simply no way that I or anyone else would ever leave it open."

But you're not a Dragon Handler, are you? I could have said, but didn't. Just the one scandal per night, I thought. "Then what are you suggesting?"

Akeem's eyes slid to the wide tunnel that slid downwards to the rest of the caves. "We can't be alone down here," he said apprehensively.

"We have to leave," said Jeona. "Before whoever it is comes back."

No! I had to bite my tongue to stop from screaming in frustration We were so close! The very next cave was the one that housed my Zarr! Had we gone to all of this risk and effort to not even perform the simplest of training?

"Dayie?" Akeem's eyes were on me. Again, he was giving me that open, frank stare that made me feel, uncomfortable. Like he was waiting for *me* to make the decision. "You're the Dragon Handler," I said stubbornly. "What do *you* think?" I turned to the tunnel leading onwards. "Because *I* am going to go see my dragon, and the rest of you can do whatever you want to."

"Oh hell," Akeem said from behind me, as the rest of them seemed paralyzed as I used my heightened senses to navigate the darkness down the short corridor, until I felt the space open up on all sides around me. At that point I didn't need any heightened senses, dragon-touched or magical or whatever they were – my heart led me as straight as a released bird to the patch of darkness where I knew that Zarr lay.

"*Dayie!*" Zarr opened his eyes, and their soft golden glow showed his noble and graceful snout, the curving horns that had only been nubs just a scant few weeks ago.

"*They itch,*" he confided in me, and, with tears in my eyes I put both hands through the bars to scratch the base where the horns erupted from his draconian hide. A moment later I heard a deep and repetitive purr as his eyes half-closed once again.

Zarr appeared sleepy, and some of it must have fed into me because I suddenly felt my eyes growing heavy, too. But it wasn't just the joy at us being reunited, I shook my head to try and think clearly. No, this was something else.

"Akeem?" I said drowsily over my shoulder.

"I'm here," he said, and he was, crouching to my side with a speed and attentiveness I hadn't credited him with. "Is he okay? Is he hurt?" I liked the way that Akeem's first questions were for Zarr, not for me or for our safety. *Maybe he really does understand a bit about dragons,* I thought.

"He's—" *yawn* "sleepy."

"It is night..." Abir whispered from the darkness behind us, meaning it to be a joke, I thought, but it fell flat.

"It's the Sweetbalm we give them," Akeem said, moving his head to examine the look of Zarr's eyes, nose, and teeth.

"Sweetbalm?" I said, I knew of that name somewhere. "That's a herb, isn't it?"

"A drug," Akeem said. "It makes a particularly good tea after a long day of stress and fighting, but in dragons its effects multiply. They feed that along with the charcoal to keep them docile." I could hear the barely suppressed rage from his voice.

How dare they do this to my dragon! The fury that swept through me was so total that I was almost certain that *I* would be the one who would be spitting fire! "Open it up," I said immediately to him. You can do that, right?"

Akeem nodded, and, sensibly, he didn't dare argue with me. He produced from his cloak pockets a heavy wrap of cloth, before opening it to reveal a large iron ring, on which was hung many finger-length black keys. I couldn't count how many there were there, and nor could I work out how Akeem knew precisely which key to insert into the gate. There had to be at least twenty, maybe thirty or forty keys on that ring – did that mean that there could be as many as forty-odd drugged dragons down here, starving for human contact?

This is cruelty, I thought as I waited impatiently for Akeem to turn the key in the lock and for the door to creak open. I knew it in my bones. These creatures might be fed and watered, and they might even be comfortable – after a fashion – but this was no way to keep an intelligent, social creature like a dragon.

"Zarr," I breathed as soon as Akeem had held the gate open and I swept in to fold his great snout in my hands and bump my forehead against his.

"Thump," I teased him, earning a deepening of the purr from his chest.

"Woah…" I heard the reactions and whispers of the other trainees behind me as they watched 'the crazy girl hug a dragon' but I didn't have time to explain to them that dragons weren't the monsters they thought them to be. Well, they were very dangerous beings, clearly, but danger and strength were different from monstrosity, I knew. Humans call criminals and murderers and bandits 'monsters' which I guess is an accurate term – but they also call everything a monster that scares them. Desert lions. Mountain wolves. Storms. Illness. A dragon was capable of being cruel, just as it was capable of causing vast amounts of damage and devastation – but that did not mean that they could not also be empathetic, caring, loyal, and very good friends.

If the others hadn't worked this out by now then there likely wasn't enough time in the world to explain it to them. I disengaged from Zarr to move along his side, marveling at how much he had grown. His head was almost the size of my entire torso – meaning that he stretched from nose to tail tip for a long way. My eyes immediately went to speculate on this cavern, peering into the darkness to inspect this home he had been forced to live in. It was still big, even for his size, and there were sleeping platforms of stone carves at different heights into the softer sandstone walls. *But it still wasn't big enough for a creature that could ride the wind,* I thought. There was a layer of fresh straw (some of it blackened to char, I could see) and there were also more of the small vents in the rocky ceiling where his smokes must be filtered out of the caves.

"Come on, Zarr, I'm getting you out of here," I declared, just as there was a jostle of alarm among the other students behind us.

I rushed forward just as Akeem clanged the gate shut and turned the key.

What!? "Akeem!? What the hell are you doing?" I gasped as he backed away from the gate, a look of worry in his eyes. *Had he turned on me? Was this all some great trap?*

"Someone's coming. Get down and stay out of sight!" Akeem hissed at me before he jumped back into the darkness, the blue crystal light flaring off. Where were the other trainees going to go? Had they fled the tunnels? Were they going to leave me down here?

Which I didn't mind, I suddenly realized. I would be here, with Zarr – and as I, too, heard the approaching voices, I snugged myself down under one of Zarr's wings and begged him silently not to give me away.

"Of course not. It is only the plant people," Zarr said in a little dreamy sort of voice.

"The who?"

"Plant people. Take a sniff, you will see," Zarr assured me, and then I understood what he meant. The *Plant* people, as in flowers and herbs. I took a long and soft breath through my half-open mouth, catching the notes of dragon, soot, meat, and then a fresher note in the background. Something fragrant almost like pine or lavender – but not quite that endearing.

"Here he is," a man's voice said, and I could have sworn it

was Talal. He had approached, not from the outer caverns where his own Gren lay, miserable, but from deeper in the cave system itself. Talal's voice was tight as if he didn't want to speak, or was finding it difficult to.

"By the sacred sands!" Talal's unseen companion gasped, and a cold ripple of ice spread through me. I knew that voice. I would recognize it anywhere. It was a woman's voice, and one that I had hoped never to hear again in this lifetime.

Fan Hazim.

"So, Trader, what have you got to say for yourself?" Talal muttered heavily. I think that even I could tell from the tone of his voice that he wasn't happy about consulting with my nemesis. *Of course. Who actually likes talking to that woman?* I thought.

"What do you mean? Nothing to do with me. The last time that I saw this little newt it was an egg!" Fan contested hotly.

"But this girl – this Dayie – she was in your employ, wasn't she?" Talal said.

Well, 'employment' must have a very wide meaning then in that case... I balled my fists to keep from screaming in fury at her.

"She was a charitable gesture on my part," Fan muttered back.

"I could have let that backward village lynch her, but no, I thought I would save her from a life of boredom and beatings and offer her a new one on the road, not that it would do any good for either of us in the long run, as you can see…"

An irritated sigh from Talal. "Whatever. Are you telling me that you saw this Crimson Red as an egg not a handful of months ago?"

"Well, unless that spiteful little girl of mine had another egg up her sleeve, then yes, that is precisely what I am saying!" Fan said, causing me to squint my eyes in hatred. I tried to keep calm by listing all of the many ways in which I was going to tell her precisely what I thought of her.

"Then why is it growing so fast?" Talal said. "I might be able to make something up to tell the others here, but they're going to catch on sooner or later. Not even the northern dragons grow this fast!"

"Tell them what you like, Talal. I'm just a humble Dragon Trader, all I do is risk my life and the lives of my family to retrieve the future of the Southern Kingdoms—"

"Horse crap," Talal said, and I had to swallow my laughter at Fan's disgruntled squawk of indignation. "Whatever the circumstances were, she got this egg on one of your missions. So, I think that I have a right to know what is so dangerous about it. Will this Crimson Red keep on growing? Are we looking at another King Dragon?"

King Dragon? What is one of those? My ears pricked up.

"You bought the girl and the dragon too remember, not my concern..."

"It is if you ever want to be rewarded with another contract again," Talal countered harshly. "And, I don't have to remind you that I have your son here too..."

"...Nas?" Fan's voice waivered for a moment, and, for just a second I almost felt sorry for her, before she snarled, and I heard her spit on the floor. "He left me. I don't care about him. I'm sure there are plenty of other street urchins out there who need a job..."

She's lying, I thought. She had to be. No mother could be that cruel, could she?

"Whatever you want to tell yourself, Fan. But you will never see another coin out of Dagfan unless you start giving me some answers to what is happening to this Crimson Red here. I cannot afford to have an 'incident' here, and that girl of yours that came with the Red? She's already afflicted with Dragon Blindness. She won't be able to think straight around her dragon at all, until I train it out of her – and even then – she may be too far gone." He paused "You know the stakes."

There was a moment of silence, in which I could have bet Fan was scratching her hair as she measured up just how much this information would be worth. Fan, it turned out, was predictable in her greed.

"I know that the Deadweed gets stronger every day. I know that you have your southern lords in the capital for some big Council," Fan said, her voice going low and seductive. "There is *one* thing that might explain this, of course… *One* thing that could put a stop to all of these problems of yours…"

"Out with it, Trader."

"It's not my secret to give. I will need assurances. *Monetary* assurances," Fan wheedled. "Or else I'm not going to get you any more of this Sweetbalm!"

"I told you. Plant people," Zarr said drowsily.

It was Fan who was harvesting the herbs to drug the dragons? I could feel my blood boiling. It seemed as though she had expanded her career somewhat in the last few months we had been apart. It must have been a way for her to recoup her money at having lost both of her two (un)willing workers so recently – one of them her very own son!

"Fine. A hundred gold?" Talal said.

"A hundred! Pfagh!" Fan tried to bargain. It was something that she was good at – but it appeared that Talal was even better.

"Don't test me, Trader…" he growled at her. "Like I said. I can find other Harvesters, other Traders. This place doesn't rely on you, you know."

Another grunt of annoyance, and I could tell that the deal had been agreed, because the very next thing that I heard was, "It's the girl. Dayie."

No, Fan, don't...

"What about her?" I could hear Talal say gravely.

"She's the one making the dragon grow. She's always had the gift." Fan sounded disgusted.

"What gift?"

"Can't you see, Dragon Chief? That girl's a witch. That must have been why she was so cheap when I bought her. Her home village was ready to string her up, because they had seen the way that she had ensorcelled their animals, trees, every living and natural thing that she came into contact with!" Fan spit.

"She's a witch..." Talal's voice was but a whisper. I couldn't even tell if he was being angry or not.

What have you done, Fan? What have you done?

"Aye, she is. You should drag her out of here immediately before she causes any more harm, and give her the Witch's Punishment. You know what I'm talking about, Talal." Fan's voice sounded perversely excited. "Drowning, burning, or stoning. The only three ways to kill a witch. Just look at what she's done here already – how do you know that she isn't growing this Crimson Red so big so that she can take over the hall herself? Start a whole new reign of terror down here, a few leagues away from Dagfan!"

Oh Fan, you are cruel... I thought. All of these lies. She must know that even if I *was* a witch, I would never do what she was saying. I just wanted to be with Zarr, and I wanted to help fight against the Deadweed. But I also knew enough to know what it would look like to Talal if I were found down here, especially after being accused of insubordination with the charcoal. Talal would believe Fan, surely, especially if he caught the others. The others—what must they think of me now the truth was out?

"I've never seen much evidence of this 'gift' of hers, Trader. But she *did* suffer from Dragon Blindness not so long ago." Talal's voice was unsure.

"There, you see! Dragon Blindness. She probably doesn't even know what she is anymore. Probably thinks that she's a dragon herself. Or a Dragon *Queen...*" Fan's words were sly. "You should do it now. Wake her from her bunk. Drag her out of here, for all the world to see..."

I was sickened by the level of hatred that I was hearing from her. I knew that Fan hated me, of course – I had the wrong skin color, I was too tall, too clumsy, not fast enough, or a thousand other things that she would blame me for. But wanting me lynched? Stoned? *What had I ever done to deserve this?* Did the other trainees see me in the same way? Were they hiding out there in the dragon caves even now – hearing all of this and having their minds poisoned by Fan?

"She hurts you?" Zarr roused, wakened by my strong

emotion. He growled, a deep, rattling sound that shook not only his chest – but mine where I hid.

"Enough of this, Trader. I will deal with the girl in my own time and in my own way. Now, you have your money, so hand over the Sweetbalm. Look, the dragon is rousing…" Talal's tone was fierce, and this time even Fan dared not argue with him.

"Just don't tell me that I didn't warn you, when a new evil sorceress rises here, in the very heart of the southlands!" Fan said, as she rummaged around with what must be bags or packs, until finally a sweet and lemony fragrance filled the air. It *was* a nice scent, I had to admit – one that was filled with spring and the first flush of light, warm rains that brought out the desert flowers.

But there was also some other note to it, my still heightened senses informed me. There was something over-rich and cloy-ing, that made me wrinkle my nose, and almost sneeze. Like cut flowers left too long in the sun…

"There. Enjoy yourself, wyrm!" Fan said, followed by a light thud as she threw something into the cave. Peeking under the darkened shadow made by the edge of Zarr's wingtip, I saw a large garland like a wreath of off-yellow flowers with tiny bud-like flowerheads, and the smell of the plant washed over me forcefully.

"Ah. Smells sweet…" Zarr murmured, and his growling inter-

rupted, tried to restart, but hitched in his chest. *"Maybe I won't eat them after all, not just yet. I'll just have a little rest first..."*

No, Zarr – you have to fight it! Ignore it! I said, even though my own eyes were getting droopy as well. The herb was having a far stronger effect than I would have thought—on me, too. I had never known a plant whose simple smell could make a dragon or a human fall asleep – but there it was, and I was struggling to lift my eyelids. It was so warm here, nuzzled against Zarr. And I was trapped anyway. Maybe it wouldn't bother anyone if I just took a little doze...

"There, see? As docile as a little lamb," Fan cackled. "I'm the best Dragon Trader, Talal. You wouldn't believe the stuff that I can get my hands on..." I heard her boasting as their voices started to fade away, accompanied by the receding crunch of their boots.

But, in the grip of the strange herb, I found that I simply couldn't care...

CHAPTER 22
DAYIE, AND DEEP BAY

"Dayie? Wake up!" Someone was calling, and for a moment I thought it had to be my dream-dragon: a huge, Crimson Red creature many times the size of a mountain that was surrounding me and keeping me safe.

Keeping me safe from the flowers, I thought muzzily. They were everywhere, large, yellow flower-heads that writhed and twisted, and were trying to overgrow my dragon.

"No, just leave me be…" I mumbled, until a hand shook me awake.

"Dayie, sand's-dammit! You have to wake up *now!*" The urgency in Akeem's voice broke through my heavy thoughts, and I blinked to see that it was the Captain of the Wild Company, leaning over me and looking worriedly into my eyes.

He has pretty eyes, I thought dreamily, and was almost about to tell him so when he upended a pouch of cold well water over my face.

"*Pagh!*" I spluttered and coughed, all tatters of the dream fading from me as I sat up. "Get off me! Why on earth did you do that?" I almost shouted, catching myself when I remembered where I was. I was still in the dragon caves. In Zarr's cell, as a matter of fact. It was lighter in the caves all around – there was the guttering orange and yellow flames of the torches outside. *How long have I been asleep?*

"Zarr…" my thoughts turned to worry. How was he? The Crimson Red was similarly trying to rouse himself beside me, the broad curve of his reptilian belly pressed against my back, he flapped one of his wings sluggishly and raised his head to look around at me under half-lidded eyes.

"*I kept you safe. No flowers,*" he thought at me. Had we shared the same dream?

"*Of course. We share everything,*" Zarr informed me, opening his maw to emit one great, long yawn.

"Oh no – no, this isn't right…" Akeem muttered, reaching for his pockets to draw out a small pot of something that smelled sharp and pine-scented. In a moment he had waved it under my nose, making me sneeze.

"Hey! Stop doing that. What's wrong with you?" I said, irritable.

"You've slept too long. It's almost first light," Akeem said, looking first from me to Zarr, and then around the cave. With a growl, his eyes rested on the bouquet of Sweetbalm and he tore off his cloak to throw it heavily over the plant. "I should have known that would affect you worse than it does other people. You are still young in your bond with your dragon." Akeem threw a glance back at the entrance to the cave. "Come, we haven't got any time, and I need to get you back to your room before the others find you in here. Last night..." he said worriedly, shame coloring his face.

The memories of last night's failed 'schooling' of the others swept back to me. "Are they safe? They didn't get caught?"

"No, no one got caught, but when I returned to see if I could get you out of here, Talal had doubled the security on the dragon gates, and then was busy in his map room all night," Akeem said. "I was sure that he had discovered you and was keeping you locked down here."

"Then why..." I asked, wide eyed. I couldn't believe I had come so close to being discovered!

"I talked to the other guards, and they said that Talal was concerned over Zarr. *Very* concerned. Something spooked him, and I need to find out—"

"I know," I said, and relayed the information that I had over-heard from last night's conversation with Fan. *She thought I was a witch. She's pressuring Talal to have me killed, all because I'd dared to defy her and had escaped her clutches?* I couldn't even begin to understand how Fan would go to such lengths. What had I taken from her? What had I ever done to her?

Maybe it was Nas, I thought. Even though Fan professed to not care about her son – she had said so to Talal before –I had heard her voice catch. *She must think I took Nas away from her?* "And the worst part of it all is," I said nervously, "*I* think that I might be a witch too."

Akeem fell silent and drew back a little from me to rest lightly on his haunches. I feared that this might be it; the end of our uneasy alliance. I was surprised when he cleared his throat, "I don't give a damn what you are, Dayie."

"What?"

"Look, it's like this…" those clear eyes of his sought out mine. "When I was first starting on my path, everyone thought I was mad. No one believed that it could be done – befriending the wild Orange dragons. They said that the Vicious Oranges were too that; too wild; too feral. They said that anyone cavorting with dragons would be cursed, or would bring death and destruction on their peoples… But they were all wrong."

I didn't quite follow. "Are, are you saying that I'm *not* a witch? Then how do you explain Zarr's growth? My way with animals? The fact that I could sense all of the dragons down here?" I swallowed nervously.

"I am saying, Dayie," Akeem's expression was serious, "that it's not *you* who is wrong, but the other people. The small-minded people. The likes of Fan and, sands help him, Talal. What do any of them know about witches? Apart from the scary stories they've read in story books? They probably know as much about witches as they think they do about dragons – which is to say not a lot at all!"

I couldn't hold that sharp gaze of his as I felt a rush of embarrassment, nervousness, and gratitude all at the same time as he continued.

"Listen up and listen good, Dayie Dragon-Friend, when I was trying to work out how to ride, befriend, even to get near a dragon, I discovered a lot that other people said was mad or make-believe. There are old tales of Dragon Friends being able to do incredible things. Able to call on the elements, able to heal people, able to share thoughts or to see much farther than their normal eyes ever could. The people of Dagfan call that stuff witchery – and sands help *me*—I think I've even experienced *some* of this in my own connection with Aida, my companion."

"But…" I felt that I had to point out. "You still didn't want me to join the Wild Company. Why, if it wasn't because you thought I might be a witch yourself?" I said.

"I, I--" It was Akeem's turn to look away, and for his face to darken with embarrassment. "I was wrong," he said, and I saw how much it cost him to admit this. "I may know more about dragons than the Training Hall does, but that does not mean that I know any more about women. My people – the Binshee – they do not let the women ride dragons, thinking that it is too dangerous for them. When I saw you with the dragon, I was sure that it wouldn't work out..." He shook his head violently. "No, that's not quite right. I was alarmed. I was shocked at how a girl – and one so young – could have already built such a close bond with a dragon. It challenged everything that I had been taught – and so now I have to ask for your forgiveness, and to say thank you, Dayie Dragon-Friend."

I nodded, feeling oddly shy at his honesty. Maybe I had finally found someone who knew what was happening to me, with whom I could share this strange adventure with.

"I thought I was going mad. I thought I was bewitched – and then I realized that I didn't care. I was still myself, and someone else. I hadn't given into the Dragon Blindness as the scary stories said I would. How does any of us know what you are experiencing isn't something to do with your bond to Zarr?" he asked, his voice forceful with passion. There was an anger in him that burned as he talked—a rage I admired. It was a cleansing, indignant, purifying sort of anger. Like a dragon's, I thought.

"Thank you," I said quietly.

"Don't thank me," Akeem whispered. "We still have to get you out of here, before Talal decides to do anything that he will later regret..."

"And Zarr," I said immediately. Last night had changed things for me. There was no way that I was going to leave Zarr down here with the others. If I had my way, I would open all the dragon's gates right now, and I was just about to suggest so when Akeem cut me off.

"Impossible," Akeem said. "I can hide you, or claim that I found you in the halls, or that you asked me to mend a piece of equipment – but a juvenile Crimson Red?"

"Who's calling whom juvenile?" Zarr was quickly regaining his senses, and I realized the herbs must be wearing off.

The herbs. The thought hit me. Akeem was right, if we took Zarr out of here, I didn't know if he was awake enough to fly. Would Talal get the Handlers to throw their heavy ropes at him to try and pin him down? Would he tell the handlers to fire on us? Or, sands forbid – even use the other Seven against us?

"Maybe there is a way…" I looked at the hump of Sweetbalm under Akeem's cloak. "We could pretend that Zarr is ill? He's stumbling and weary, and while everyone is fussing, we could spring into action?" I said, realizing how weak my plan sounded.

There was something about those herbs. My eyes kept on pulling back to where they lay, hidden. Something was nagging at my mind, and it was about the way that they had smelled. Sweet, floral, but also cloying and overripe…

"I'm not sure that'll work, but I'm willing to give it a try if you are," Akeem said, and I was surprised at his decision. He must really be worried about what Talal was going to do.

The herbs smelled like Deadweed! I suddenly realized, and Akeem must have seen my face fall as he looked aghast.

"What's wrong?"

"Well, I told you that I have a connection with living things…" I explained my suspicions to him; "It's that plant, Sweetbalm. There's something wrong about it. It doesn't, I don't know, *feel* like a normal plant. It smells like something bad… Like Deadweed!" Akeem frowned, but then nodded. Without saying a word, he bundled the cloak and its toxic plants and took them into the main chamber outside. He carefully unwrapped them, using his dagger to poke and pry at the bouquet. Even from this distance I could see that the dried flowering heads had been tied together with twine to form a thick brush, but they seemed to have lost some of their potent smell overnight as Akeem worked.

Schnickt! He cut the twine and the bundle fell apart, revealing a dark secret. There, in the center was a large and wilted flowerhead that was completely different from the Sweetbalm. It was a yellow globe. It was Deadweed.

"Gah!" Akeem sprang back, throwing his cloak over the parcel. "What is Talal doing? That idiot!"

"It's Fan," I said, knowing it to be true. "She must be trying to harm the dragons somehow. Maybe she wanted them ill, so then *she* could cure them…" That sounded like her, I thought. The existence of that Deadweed flowerhead would also explain the extreme affects that the herbs had on the dragons. The 'remedies' the Training Hall had been using had been secretly leaking Deadweed pollen into the air!

"I'll kill him," Akeem said, shaking with fury as he stood up. "But first I'm going to get rid of this." He kicked the bundle of herbs together and gingerly picked up the wadded poisonous plants together, before looking over at me. "Get yourselves ready. Dawn is breaking, and we have a small window of opportunity while the hall is still waking up. I'll burn this and check if the coast is clear – there is no way I am going to let any dragon near it-- and then we're getting you out of here…"

I nodded that I understood, and he had already gone, running out of the chamber and back up in the direction of the arena beyond.

"Well, Zarr. Looks like we're going to join the Wild Dragons after all," I whispered, sliding back to rest against his belly.

"Better than this hole in the ground," Zarr said wearily, his jaws snapping as he yawned once again. Another wave of shame and regret washed over me as I thought how long he had been down here in the ground.

"I'm sorry," I said. "I thought it was for the best."

"Maybe you should think less," Zarr said, and I wondered if

that was a dragon joke, but either way he was right. The Crimson Red lifted himself up on his hind legs, and wobbled. *Maybe my earlier plan of him pretending to be sick* was *right,* I thought in alarm.

"Zarr? Are you going to be okay? We will need to fly, and fly fast…" I explained. I didn't know what Talal was going to do when he saw us emerging from the dragon caves, and I needed Zarr to be able to respond quickly.

"Fine. I'm Zarr," he said, one of his back legs now giving out as he slid to a seated position and yawned once more.

Oh no. The Deadweed must have affected him more than I had realized. *Maybe it was the ongoing exposure over days?* I thought, reaching a hand to pat his side. "It'll be okay," I promised him. All we had to do was to wait for Akeem, and then we'll be out of here…

"What's taking him so long?" I muttered under my breath again, as I paced Zarr's personal cavern, clenching my hands and unclenching them, wishing I had my weapons on me, and not just this silly little belt knife. It had felt like hours had passed since Akeem had gone with the bundle of Deadweed. The other dragons were stirring. The sun surely had to be up! If I had to fight my way out of here – what good would that do?

"You have me," Zarr said, his eyes drooping heavily as he turned to regard me.

"True," I said, not wanting to let him know that I was just as worried for *his* safety as I was worried about mine right now. What would happen to me and Zarr once we had escaped the Training Hall? Would we be hunted like the reports I had read in the scroll; a witch and her dragon? They would certainly think of me as a dragon thief, stealing from 'their' Training Hall. I even worried about Latifa and Nas. They had put their futures on the line to come down here. Would they be able to stay? Would they want to? *And was Zarr strong enough to fight if he had to?*

"You're thinking again. I'm a dragon." Zarr opened his mouth and lolled his red forked tongue in a gesture that I was sure was him laughing at me.

Again, Zarr had a point. Even if he was still feeling groggy – he was still a dragon. *Who would dare to stand against him?* I tried not to think of the answer to that question as I stepped out into the cavern chamber beyond and then beckoned the dragon after me. "Come on. Try and keep quiet," I said as Zarr lifted his head and hissed a little. He took a step, and then another, blinking his eyes and sniffing the sanded cavern floor as his tail lashed behind him.

"I'll show them all…" Zarr said, and I could feel the fire burning in his eyes as he took another step, and then another

until he was completely out of the cavern that had been his unwanted home.

"Let's go," I said, leading the way up the slope that led to the next cave, and hearing the rattle of the other dragons nearby.

"I'm sorry," I whispered in their direction. "I wish I could free you, but I don't have the keys…" *And none of the dragons were strong enough to break their bars,* I thought as Gren's large and mournful head looked back at me from her cave.

"Lady Dragon," I cleared my throat, approaching her as Zarr waited, sniffing the cavern walls for a moment. "I apologize for your captivity." I did my best to curtsey, keeping my eyes on the older Stocky Green behind the bars the entire time, letting her know that I respected her. "I will endeavor to free you," I said, although I had no idea how.

"You won't free me, human, if you run off with your young bull!" said a cracked and old voice in my mind, making me blink in amazement. Gren had spoken to me! This was the first time that I had ever heard another dragon, and I was amazed. Even if she was rebuking me.

"I will find a way, Gren, I promise…"

"Ha! Don't make promises you cannot keep. A very human failing," Gren hissed. She was annoyed, and I was the nearest human to take it out on.

Feeling suitably rebuked, I nodded as Zarr lowered his own

snout, and then I watched as he turned his head to expose his neck to the older Green in a curiously puppyish gesture. He was telling her that, even with her behind bars, he still regarded her as the superior here. *Yes,* I thought. *Gren is the Matriarch, even if Talal doesn't recognize it yet.*

With a final, worried look at the caves, I nodded up to the bright, dazzling light of the sun leading down the final ramp to the arena and just hoped that Akeem had left it open as I ran ahead and gave it a push...

Creeak! It moved, swinging out over the sands that were curiously empty of, well, everyone. I couldn't see any Dragon Handlers, just as I couldn't see any trainees filing out to start a new day's worth of exercise and combat drills. In fact, I couldn't even *hear* anyone.

"Where is everybody?" I asked as I stepped out onto the sand with Zarr following along behind me, his eyes blinking in the light.

"Free!" he said in my mind as he whistled and rasped, unable to remain silent as I had asked him to. He shook his head as if the sun hurt his eyes, wobbled on his feet and very slowly as if they were stiff from misuse, he opened out his long red wings-

"STOP!" Someone bellowed, and all hell broke loose.

Clash-Clash-Clash!! The dragon gong was being pounded, and the shutters on the Training Hall were flung open, and, even worse – I heard the scrape on the top battlements all around the Training Hall's high walls as guards emerged from their hiding places. It *had* been too quiet after all, and this was why Akeem had not returned …

From every open window – and there had to be easily fifty or so of them—the nasty, stubby forms of the Dragon Handlers' crossbows pointed down at us in a complete circle. From the walls the danger was even more dire – there were the much larger flat-carts of the arbalests being winched into place. Those things fired bolts the size of harpoons, and it would only take one of them to kill Zarr – and I could count easily twelve.

"Do you think that this is the first dragon that we've had try to escape!" a voice shouted, and I searched the windows for its location. *There.* It was Chief Talal, wearing his full armor and looking down at us. "We're a Training Hall, girl, sometimes our beasts go rogue, and we are ready when they do!" he spat. "But this, clearly, is the first time that we have had to turn our weapons on one of our own trainees."

"Witch!" Someone shouted from the walls, and I looked around to find the source of the insult. One of the Handlers—it seemed Fan's poison had spread beyond Talal. *But at least I couldn't see any of the Seven up there,* I thought quickly – not that it gave me much consolation. The Seven, with their dragons, would be even worse a foe than these crossbows, I thought. Maybe.

"Dayie?" Zarr was rapidly trying to fill his lungs, bellowing

them out and back, in an attempt to summon his dragon flame. I didn't even know if he *had* any flame yet, as I hadn't seen him use it…

"Wait," I held my hand out to him. *He'll die if he attacks,* I thought. *I have to make them see another way.*

"You are wrong, Chief Talal!" I called out. "You have been misguided and misled by sour counsel!"

"Are you denying that your merest presence has the strangest effect on the living things around you? Are you denying that this Crimson Red is your plan to take over the South?" Talal shouted.

"Take over the South?" I spat back. "What are you talking about – I'm trying to defend it!"

"*Witch! Liar!*" another voice shouted from the balconies, and my cheeks burned in shame. Not because of what they thought of me, but because somewhere the other trainees stood inside, probably confined to their dormitories, listening to their insults.

But then I remembered what Akeem said. It's *they* who were small minded. Who didn't know anything. *I* was the one just trying to be myself. "I don't deny I have bonded with my dragon," I called out. "Just as every one of you should do with your own chosen dragons!" I made sure that I was standing facing Talal, as I said pointedly, "Even you, Talal. Gren pines for you down there, and you refuse to ride her! Are you so scared of your own bond?"

There was a moment of silence from the high window, and then a snarl of fury. I guessed my words had hit their mark. "You will be taken from this place, Dayie, where no one here will have to listen to your heresies again! But your dragon stays."

"No."

"No."

The Crimson Red and I both roared at the same time, making several of the crossbowmen waiver in their posts. An angry dragon – even a drugged one – is a very alarming thing.

"Then you leave me no choice but to—"

"SKREAYARCH!" The sky was split by a thunderous roar and a shadow fell across the arena. I heard shouts – even some screams – as the shape of a dragon flashed fast and low over the walls, narrowly avoiding the arbalests to land, scrabbling and with a giant spray of sand on the arena floor. I recognized the mane of tines behind its horns, and scales the color of teal and turquoise.

It was the Sea Dragon, and, sliding from its saddle and hitting the floor was one of the Seven, the Rider named Marshal.

"What is the meaning of this?" Talal bellowed – but we had no time for theatrics. I ran across the sand to him, holding my hand up to the Sea Dragon as I did so. There were guards with bows and worse up there – but I couldn't let that stop me. This Sea Dragon was distraught, and it needed help.

"Mamma-la, Mamma-la," I sang, wondering if my little relaxing-song would work on him. It did, and the Sea Dragon sat on its haunches like a cat, its exhausted head dropping to the floor.

"Gone..." croaked Marshal as I reached him, cursing that I didn't have any water on me.

"It's going to be okay," I said to him, before wondering if it really would. I seemed to be making lots of promises today that I wasn't sure that I could keep... The Rider looked haggard, and his face was smeared with dirt and blood. He had been scratched over every part of his body it appeared, and there was a bubble of spittle at the side of his lips, as if he were feverish. I wondered if the only thing that I *could* do down here on my own would work...

"Mamma-la, Mamma-la," I continued, singing the song I remembered from my childhood which had come with me from out of the storm waves where Obasi and Wera had found me, but which I didn't know where it had come from. My voice was thin and reedy to start with, but swelled as I closed my eyes and remembered the calming, curative tones.

Marshal sighed, and he seemed to stop shaking so much. It had worked! On a human, as well! But he was still awake enough to grip my hand in his one good one. "They're gone," he tried again, in a stronger voice. "Gorugal. Oleg, Tabit. All the people of Deep Bay. Gone."

"Easy now, Marshal." I smoothed his hair back from his face, wishing that I had water. The horrors of what he had witnessed – whatever he had witnessed – had turned him from a cruel and arrogant young man into a youth. "We'll get to the bottom of this, don't you worry. You need to rest…"

"Get away from him!" I heard the angry tones of Talal as a door banged and he was racing across the sands towards us, flanked by more Dragon Handler guards. "What is the meaning of all this?"

It was Marshal who answered him. "No time," he croaked. "Deep Bay has been destroyed. The others…? The Deadweed has them!"

CHAPTER 23
DAYIE, DRAGON-INSTINCTS

The arena was in uproar. More of the Dragon Handler 'guards' spilled out onto the sand, followed by a team of the healer-specific staff with their lighter tabards.

"It's not just his wounds," I told the healers as they slid to the sand next to me and Marshal, bringing with them water and bandages, and pots of unguent. "I think it's an infection. Or Deadweed poison." I said the last words carefully, making sure that Talal, standing over me with his sword already drawn, heard. *The same poison that Fan was using in her 'Sweetbalm' remedies for the dragons...* Talal's eyes didn't even flicker, just glared at me in rage. *He mustn't know what Fan has been dosing her 'cures' with,* I thought. *And if he doesn't know the depth of Fan's malice, then there might be hope for me to change his mind about me. If I told him...* But there wasn't any time for me to argue my case now, as Talal cut me off.

"Right, this doesn't change anything…" Talal started to say, nodding to the Dragon Handler guards standing around, obviously wanting them to seize me and drag me off.

"*Sssss!"* Zarr stamped one of his feet on the sanded arena heavily, sending up puffs of grit into the air. It was clear that if anyone wanted to grab me, then they would have to deal with a very irate Crimson Red dragon, too.

"Ah…" I saw Talal look around. He might have enough guards to overpower me, for certain. But there were healers here too, and half of the arbalests had been raised, for fear of injuring the Sea Dragon.

"You need us, Talal," I said in a low voice as I looked up at him. "I'm not your enemy, and I am no threat to you." Which perhaps wasn't strictly the truth, as I *did* want to free the dragons below. "But things have to change." I cleared my throat. "Starting now. Deep Bay has been overrun with the Deadweed, and you've lost almost half of the Seven. You need anyone who can fly a dragon. Which is me."

Talal's face screwed up in annoyance, as he tried to figure out what to do, but his hand was swayed by a sudden shout as a small knot of people burst out from behind the Handler guards trying to hold the doors to the galleries.

"Stop!" It was Nas, Latifa, Abir and Jeona, and they were

pulling on their training gear, and even had sabers, scimitars and ropes already on their belts. They must have seen Marshal land, and figured out that something was deeply wrong.

"I confined you all to your dorms!" Talal barked at them.

"We want to help," Nas said breathlessly, and I could see his eyes moving to the Sea Dragon who whistled encouragingly at him.

Yes.

"We can fight." It was Latifa who answered next. "If you let us."

Talal looked back to me, to the trainees, and then to the fevered form of Marshal One-Hand on the floor, surrounded by the healers. "The lords are arriving soon. We haven't got time for this."

"You haven't got time to *not* defend the South," I said severely. "Think about this: what a great opportunity this is to show the Southern Lords just how many Dragon Riders you have!" It was a gamble, but Talal's shoulders slumped and I knew I had won the argument. He was caught between two terrible outcomes: having to try and separate me from Zarr, which would cause bloodshed, scandal and mayhem before the Southern Lords, or sending untrained Riders to fight the Dead-weed. At least with the second outcome, he could lie about harboring 'a witch' at the Training Hall, I thought a little derisively.

"Fine," Talal snarled, sheathing his sword. "But only because we need that Crimson Red with us. And I will be riding with you, so if I see any suggestion of you trying to harm the South, I will..."

"Sckrrrr..." before he could threaten me, Zarr growled deeply, lowering his head into the space between Talal and me. It was enough to make the chief step back.

"I understand, chief," I said, standing up. I had learned to be impeccably polite around dangerous people, thanks to Fan. *I need him to see that I can be trusted. That what I have to say, about my powers, about the dragons – and about Fan – can be trusted.* "You won't regret this decision." I nodded.

"I hope not," he muttered, turning on his heel and barking orders. "Handlers! Open the dragon caves! Get the ropes! The charcoal and saddles! Summon the remaining Seven!"

"Chief – leave *us* to handle the dragons," I said sharply, acting on instinct. Latifa and Nas immediately stepped to my side, with Abir and Jeona not far behind. Wisely, they didn't have their weapons drawn so the chief knew that we weren't trying to threaten him, but presenting a united front.

"Dayie – this isn't the time for experimental practices," he said in horror.

"Please, chief," I said, and Talal snorted in disgust – probably thinking that we were all going to die anyway. He stormed away, back to the equipment sheds as the Healers carried

Marshal out, and the Handlers rushed to comply with their leader's orders.

"Dayie?" hissed one of the Handlers, and I turned to see Akeem, looking remorseful. "I couldn't come back down to you – as soon as I got out of the caves there were guards everywhere – but it looks as though you didn't need my help." He spoke low and quickly, our conversation hidden by the frenzy inside the arena. "I'll bring out the dragons…"

"We can help," Latifa said this, springing to Akeem's side.

"Wait!" I said, thinking about everything I had seen down in the caves. The way that the dragons were kept separate, what Zarr had said about respecting Gren. "Bring out Gren first," I said quickly. "Give her charcoal, food, water. Make sure she knows that she is first, and let the other dragons follow her," I said. "And don't let the remaining Seven mount the dragons yet. We need to show them that this can be done without bullying or fear."

Akeem stood for a moment, his face stunned as he looked at me.

"Well? What are you waiting for?" I said. Had he seen something? Was something wrong?

But a grin spread across his features. "That's it! What I have been trying to achieve for months – to make the Training Hall work like a proper nest! You're a genius!" He was already backing away to fulfill my wishes. "And Dayie?" he called back. "I'm glad you didn't die."

"So am I," I said with a smirk, feeling reckless and slightly giddy. I didn't know if I had earned a reprieve for myself, or just a stay of execution. It would all depend on how well we fly, I thought.

"You won't fight alone," Akeem said earnestly. "As soon as you are clear, I'll be calling the Wild Company. If we can help, then we will."

"We'll need it," I assured him. "I'll need it."

"Just follow your dragon," he said, a parting shot of advice. "Zarr will know what to do."

I know he will, I thought, reaching out a hand to pat Zarr on the snout, before turning to the others. "Nas? I want you by the Sea Green."

"Nandor," Nas said happily. "Her name is Nandor. She told me."

I opened and closed my mouth in wonder, but the urgency of the situation didn't give me any time. It seemed a good omen. "But don't try to saddle her yet. I want Gren saddled first, got it?"

Nas nodded – and I thought that this was probably the first time that he had ever agreed to follow my suggestions.

"Latifa?" I said. "On the Sinuous Blue. The one that Tabit sometimes rides." *Rode,* I corrected, still unable to imagine that Tabit was gone – as horrible as she was, I had admired her strength.

"Aye," Latifa nodded.

"Abir – the bullish Green," I apportioned the dragons to each of the four trainees who had come down the caves with me, working on a gut instinct about who would match each one. There was already a loud hiss from the open gates as Akeem had wasted no time in racing to bring up Gren.

"And who will ride Gren?" Latifa asked.

"Only one person in this entire Training Hall has the right to ride Gren," I said, looking back to the doors where Talal was already re-emerging, now dressed in part leather armor, with a long metal lance in one hand and a small, round helmet. He looked like a different person, and I wondered how often he got to fight and fly. I watched as, without thinking, Talal made his way towards the older Stocky Green.

"Gren," I called out to him. "Her name is Gren, chief,"

"What? *Green,* you mean." He shook his head irritably.

"No, if you please, sir, just call her *Gren.*" I could only hope that Talal would listen to me – which I highly doubted, given that he had wanted me to be dragged off for being a witch not an hour ago, but I held myself back and watched as Akeem crossed the sanded floor, throwing handfuls of charcoal in front of Gren as she lumbered into the sun and sniffed at the air. Her head swiveled to Talal, who jerked as if poked. *He knows they are bonded,* I saw. *He just doesn't know if he can accept it...*

"Go to her, chief!" I muttered under my breath, willing the connection to work, and, miraculously or through emergency, Talal broke through the wall of his ignorance and did so, walking towards her and even picking up a lump of charcoal to throw into her open maw.

Snap! She crunched on the tidbit and gave a deep, guttural purring sound. Already Akeem had brought forward the saddle – no ropes—and offered it to Talal wordlessly. I saw the chief look askance at this odd gesture, but then he stepped forward gingerly to place it on Gren's waiting shoulders all the same. Within a short while he had the seat secured, and the stoical Gren endured this all without so much as a hiss, as she had been waiting for this day to be reunited with her rightful Dragon Friend. As soon as Talal was mounted, I signaled to Akeem and Latifa. *Next.*

Akeem in turn beckoned the Dragon Handlers to start throwing charcoal, and there was a distant groan as the next dragon appeared –the Sinuous Blue that Tabit had so often rode. I was a bit more nervous about this pairing, as I couldn't tell if Latifa matched the Sinuous Blue's temperament more so than Tabit, but given the trouble I had seen the older woman have a few days ago, I figured that no bond had yet been forged.

Besides which, I could *feel* that Latifa's reserved stoicism would be a good match for the Sinuous Blue's sharp temper. The Blue lashed her tail and her long, humped body writhed across the sand, but she was more subdued then last time she'd been brought to the arena. She sniffed at Gren, who snapped back – which appeared to be enough to put her in her place.

"She recognizes her Matriarch," Zarr advised me, and I agreed.

"Okay, go," I nodded to Latifa, as Akeem handed her the saddle and Latifa approached the Blue.

"Ssss!" the Blue reacted badly at first, raising on her haunches to rear back from the proffered saddle, but Latifa, the sharp-witted and indomitable girl, amazingly stood her ground and glared back. Another snap from Gren, and the Sinuous Blue slowly, ever-so slowly, lowered its shoulders to the ground to accept Latifa's handling.

It's working! I was overjoyed. I had seen the way that the dragons had calmed down as soon as they had been saddled before, so I knew they had that training to accept the Riders– but previously the Riders had to fight to get them to accept it. This changes that, I thought with a grin. You *ask* the dragons to accept the Riders, and you *show* the dragons that they have nothing to fear. Which was where Gren's actions served as an example for all of them.

"Nas?" I nodded, and he was only too happy to approach the Sea Dragon – Nandor, whose saddling went faster than any of the others. They appeared to enjoy each other's company, and I was glad for them. It would probably do him some good, to have some dragon-logic.

But I knew that it was too early to count my dragon-eggs just yet. The last dragon (a Stocky Green) was too fretful and wary, until Abir offered to double-up with Jeona as the Torvald Riders did. The wary Green seemed to appreciate that, as I guessed that it thought that it was going to be in safer hands with two humans.

Last of all came who was left of the Seven, both of whom were Riders that I had never seen before, and both of whom were as skittish and as contemptuous as the two remaining Greens that they approached. *Only two.* With Marshal wounded, and with Gorugal, Tabit, and Oleg missing (not dead, I prayed) there were only two of the Seven left – which meant Talal was one of the Seven! I realized, feeling stupid. Of course he was.

The first to successfully mount was a dark-skinned, rangy-looking man who was clearly from the deep southern deserts. He wore the same armors as the others, but his face was decorated with dot-like tattoos. He didn't speak much, and his Green appeared similarly taciturn. The final Rider was a fair-haired woman, which surprised me. I rarely saw other fair people in the South, although her blonde features and sun-tanned features were still nowhere near as pale as my white hair and pale skin. She wore her blonde hair back in a braid and had on metal shoulder pads, like the northern Torvald Academy Riders wore. When she finally mounted and turned in her saddle, I saw that she had one ear missing, and in its place was a mass of scars instead.

"Right," I sighed. We were all set, all apart from me. "Zarr?" I said, as Akeem passed me the final saddle.

"I'm ready to hunt!" he crowed majestically and took the saddle easily. When I was settled, with Akeem pressing into my hands the final pouches of supplies and bandages to affix at my side.

"Dayie," he said quickly to me. "You know much, but I probably have more experience flying into battle than you. Let Zarr have his head – let *him* lead *you* on the approach. Learn to anticipate, and work with your dragon..." His words were serious, as were his eyes.

"Thank you," I said. "After, if we survive – you're going to have to teach."

"If we survive." Akeem nodded, moving away from me.

I looked over to see what we had accomplished; Talal, Latifa, Nas, Abir and Jeona, the two remaining Riders and me. Seven to ride out, to replace the Seven that there had always been here.

"We fly!" Talal shouted, as Gren lumbered forward towards the open gates, picking up speed, pounding and charging as she did so. A ripple of fierce joy spread down the line as each dragon followed the next in line, cantering, running, charging, before—

Whoosh! When it was our turn to leap in the air, Zarr did so with an exaggerated pounce, and his wings unfurling to either side of me with just a slight wobble. It might not have been the most perfect takeoff that the Training Hall had ever seen, but it would do for me.

We flew towards the coast, towards fire and battle.

CHAPTER 24
DAYIE, THE BATTLE

D eep Bay was a little more than a rounded curve with a high wedge of a rocky promontory hooking around a sanded beach. The place formed a naturally secluded mooring for long boats, and past the rocky wall I could see the wide expanse of the Great Southern Pelagic ocean. Set back from the beach were the many twisted avenues of a walled town, with lots of flat-roofed houses like Dagfan, but far smaller.

Or at least – that is what Deep Bay *should* have been had it not been for the Deadweed.

Almost the entirety of the bay was clogged with a thick mass of green vegetation that shivered and rippled with the incoming tides of the waves. As we swirled overhead, following Talal and Gren's lead, I was certain that I could even see the heads of the vines shivering and straining, dotted with the yellow gourds of the plant heads.

And the coastal townlet of Deep Bay hadn't fared any better, either. The Deadweed had spread up, stretching long fingers of vines over the beach and up to the houses of the town itself. Whole streets were filled with the green stuff and entire squares were thatched and blanketed by the vegetation.

And elsewhere – the sign of scorched and burned areas outside the town showed where the previous Dragon Riders had fought. They had been trying to save the town, I thought, as I saw the pattern of burn marks all along the beach and even the outer walls of the town, but they hadn't been ruthless enough. They couldn't stop the town from being engulfed.

"The beach!" I shouted across the airs at Talal, who was stowing his lance at his side and instead reaching for his saber. He turned to regard me with glittering eyes, clearly feeling alive now that he was flying on Gren once again. I could well agree with the sentiment, as flying on Zarr filled me with a sense of purpose and direction that I had thought that I had lost. This was where I was meant to be, I thought, and not for the first time on that flight.

The flight itself had taken less time than I had presumed that it would – as the coast was many days travel away by foot— but Zarr and the others had risen higher and higher into the air, to glide and soar over the burnt orange lands far below. The wind had been surprisingly cold, even given the fierce sun's heat – not that I minded.

"What?" I heard Talal shout back to me.

"The beach – the vines!" I shouted, pointing to the four thick 'fingers' of vines that connected the seaborne Deadweed to the town-colonizing one. Talal nodded that he understood and raised one fist in the air. It was a Rider signal, I realized, as the two remaining trained Riders of the Seven slid behind him in an attacking run towards the beach.

"You ready for this, Zarr?" I breathed.

"Of course!"

I tried to do as Akeem had told me, letting the dragon have its head to follow the two Riders however it wanted to. Which was actually a sage bit of advice, as I had very little experience of how to navigate these airborne currents.

"For the South!" Talal roared, as Gren dove downwards with a rush, resulting in a steep dive that bellied out just above the buildings, and, as the Deadweed wavered upwards to try and snap at him - Gren opened her maw and released her dragon flame.

Woosh! A great gout of a deep red fire and smoke swept across the first tentacle of inter-knotted vines – itself as thick as a fallen tree and made of many smaller vines rolled together into one. I had seen Gren in action before, and marveled at how such a large beast could fly so quickly.

But this time, something different happened. A high-pitched keening erupted from the Deadweed, hurting my ears with its deafening screech.

"By the sacred sand's! What is that!?" I shook my head as Zarr wobbled and lurched on his own flight path. It was the Deadweed, somehow it had found a way to emit this noise – and if it hurt *my* ears, then I knew that it would cause havoc to the hearing of the dragons. I raised my eyes, tearing up in pain as our four-dragon flight of Gren, the two Riders and me split apart and flailed awkwardly in the air. One of the other Greens released its dragon flame all the same, spilling it onto the water-borne Deadweed, creating a sudden gout of steam as the fire warred with the wet foliage – and ultimately lost.

"Fiend!" Zarr roared, coughing and belching to try and release his own flame in agitation, but all that came out were belches of black smoke.

The was part of the Deadweed's plan – if such a thing can be said to have a plan, I thought. *It emits that noise to disrupt and distract the dragons…*

"No good!" Talal was shouting as he managed to swoop back up into the safer airs over the bay. "We'll have to—"

"Dayie!" Someone screamed, and I turned around in my seat to see that it was Nas. The youth who had been my oppressor had lost control of Nandor the Sea Dragon, and he was spiraling out of control, to the far side of the where the town joined the beach.

"Nas!" I shouted in alarm, and even as my heart leapt to thoughts of his safety, so too did Zarr throw one of his wings down and turn towards them. Was this how you ride a dragon? I thought. You think *with* them?

*"Don't think, Dayie – **feel.**"* Zarr's voice was a growl of pain as the high-pitch screeching of the Deadweed below us continued. Below his talons I saw vines suddenly darting up to dare to try and reach us – but Zarr's erratic and awkward flight as he suddenly swerved to one side, then to the other, dropped a few feet then rose ten, kept us from being caught.

Then, just as we reached the end of the beach, I saw the fleshy-leaved vegetation rise up before us in several places at once, and we were already flying too low and too fast to avoid them.

"Zarr!" I screamed.

WHOOSH! I didn't know what unlocked it, but Zarr's head jerked forward at the last moment, and from his open roar game an explosion of smoke and fire, clearing the way for us to break through the restraining wall of the Deadweed, and straight into the sands beyond.

"Aaagh!" The shout was yanked involuntarily from me as we crash-landed.

Zarr managed to catch the ground with his two back claws, sending up dirt and sand in equal measure – but he still wasn't used to flying and had kept his wings open as he hit the dirt. They powered us forward, flinging us into the air again as he jumped and spun, snapping his wings closed to skid across the earth.

"Sckrarr!" he barked indignantly, shaking his head in front of me.

My head was spinning and my back hurt, but I didn't have time to be ill or injured. Nas had been brought down somewhere around here-

"Help!" came a shout from a little way away. Nas had been thrown by Nandor and had tumbled across the sands in front of the walls of Deep Bay, where vines of the Deadweed were even now racing towards him. *Where was Nandor?* I thought, before I heard a mournful cry from *beyond* the walls. Nandor had landed *inside* the town.

"Zarr – we have to save them!" I called desperately, and he broke into a loping, slightly limping run towards Nas with me on his back.

"Dayie!" Nas had turned over, kicking at the first of the tendrils that snapped at his boot, only for it to latch onto his ankle, and I heard him scream. I well knew how much that hurt, as I still had pock-marked scars across my calf from Menali Bridge. I shouted in horror as I saw Nas being dragged back towards the vegetation-filled gates, desperately scrabbling and clawing at the dirt and sand as he flailed and kicked.

"No"! I shouted in horror, helplessness filling me – and again those memories of Obasi and Wera filled my mind. *Had they felt like this, when the Deadweed had engulfed them?* There had been nothing I could do to save them. I had been too young, but the shame haunted me at every step. I screamed helplessly, but Zarr beneath me reacted. He jumped, snapping his wings out just a little to aid his pounce and landed *atop* the vine, easily crushing it with his talons and ripping it to shreds – but now *we* were also being attacked and surrounded by the vines-

"Nas, get up!" I shouted, swinging down from the saddle to extend a hand to my adoptive brother. His leg was bleeding, and his eyes were wide with terror, but he managed to push himself from the ground and leap up, throwing forward his hand to me-

"Gotcha!" I caught it, throwing my weight backward so that he could scrabble to the back of my saddle. No sooner were we settled than Zarr let out another roar, thrashing with claws and tail at the vines. He was strong enough to shred them but not precise enough to cut them at the root – and already his claws were bloody from the many wicked thorns that the

Deadweed had – thorns that could even pierce the weaker places between dragon scales!

"Zarr, we can't fight it. It's too much. Please!" I begged the dragon to jump back as the wall of vegetation grew larger before us, as more and more vines spilled over the walls to add to the onslaught.

That was how the Deadweed overwhelms you, I thought for just a brief moment of clarity. *It swamps anything that is moving.*

But the Crimson Red was already enraged, and I saw how painfully young the bull was still. He was whipping his claws and his head back and forth in a frenzy, and from our connection I could only feel rage and hate – and pain from the many small cuts that he was enduring.

I can't get through to him, I thought in horror. Zarr was too angry. He had spent too long down there in the dragon caves...

"Nas? Draw your weapons! Any weapons you have!" I un-did the saddle belt that attached to my belt, and drew my saber as I crouched up on the back of the Crimson Red, and Nas rose with the same knife that Rahim had given him just a few months earlier. We stood back to back, as the Deadweed grew tall all around us, and prepared to strike.

At least we'll go down fighting, I thought.

"SKREYARCH!"

The roar of dragons filled the air, and the vegetation-wall before us shimmered in a heat wave, before bursting apart from fire. A trio of dark shapes flashed across the skies, flying low and fast and banking and turning, spiraling over each other. And from their undersides, they looked like a dusky, burnt orange.

"The Wild Company!" I shouted, as Zarr managed to break from his rage and pounce back from the wall of flames. But there was no time to count our victories.

"Nandor's still in there!" Nas shouted from behind me and thumped back into my seat. He was right, we had to get in there to save the Sea Dragon. I peered through the smoke and flames, and, with a trick of the smoke, I managed to see her

"There!" Nas shouted, seeing his dragon at the same time. Nandor was scrambling to hold onto the minaret of a tower with heavy tendrils of the Deadweed wrapped around its tail.

"Come on!" I shouted, and Zarr knew precisely what we had to do. He leapt forward, over the flames and the wall and suddenly we were swooping above the overgrown village of Deep Bay itself. It was like the town had been abandoned for centuries, not days. A thick carpet of waving green infested every street and blurred every contour of the houses.

Zarr roared, and there was another explosion of flames from his maw, hitting the base of the minaret and the small plaza that it had once stood over. Nandor screeched in a mixture of alarm and joy, the flames working to weaken the grip that the Deadweed had on her tail as she thrashed free. Great, sizzling globs of greenish dragon-blood fell from her tail behind her as she joined us in the air, and flew across Deep Bay, swerving to avoid the poison-spitting flowerheads and the grasping tentacles.

I could see distant firestorms at several places around the town and along the beach as the other dragons tried their best to contain the Deadweed – but it was like containing a box of spiders –every time Talal and the others burned one of the 'root' tentacles to the beach, another two (albeit thinner) ones jumped out. And on the other side of Deep Bay, where the members of Akeem's Wild Company and the trainee Riders were attempting to fight back the Deadweed, it just grew outward in the opposite direction.

"We can't win…" I cried dismally. "We need more dragons. More flame…" I was shaken to my core.

"No, Dayie," Nas said behind me, his hands still gripping onto the saddle as we hadn't had a chance to return him to Nandor yet. "We need magic," he said, and I knew that he meant me.

"I haven't got that kind of magic," I informed him.

"Yes, you do." His words came out desperate. "You have a

way with living things. This Deadweed is living, don't you think?"

"But…" I shook my head, confused and scared. *What if Nas was right?* I could sense the Deadweed – and that it felt wrong to my heightened senses somehow. It didn't *feel* like any normal living thing. *Or rather, it didn't feel like any normal plant,* I clarified. If anything, it moved and acted exactly like a living creature. I thought that I could even sense a sort of malevolence from it, no, *a hunger.*

And if it had a hunger, a need, an impulse – then did that mean that I could calm it?

I opened my mouth and held out my hand towards the vegetation below, willing myself to try to reach out to it, heart-to-heart, mind-to-mind.

"Mamma-la, Mamma-la…" I started to sing that small, sing-song tune that I had written through my very bones. It was a soft, lilting tune like a folk melody, or a lullaby for a teething baby. I sang it again, raising my voice.

Was it working? I risked looking over the clouds of reaching green as I sang. The Deadweed was still everywhere, still hungrily devouring the buildings.

Please work! I sang harder, trying to remember what about the song had always made *me* feel calm. It was the way it had been sung. With tenderness. Like the caress of a mother over her sleeping babe.

*But could I think like that about the evil, murderous Dead-
weed? The very same weed that had taken and killed my foster
parents?* My song choked in my throat. Maybe I couldn't do
this. Maybe I just wasn't strong enough.

"You ARE strong, Dayie Dragon-Friend" said Zarr's voice.
*"That song. It's like our dragon speech. Something more
powerful than human tongue. Something older,"* Zarr told me,
although I could sense his confusion too. He hadn't had
enough time around older dragons to learn enough dragonlore
to tell me, but I knew without a doubt that he was on the right
track. I cleared my throat, and started again.

"Mamma-la, Mamma-la," I tried to remember where it came
from. The song and the Deadweed both had come from the
sea. The crash and the rocking waves—

"It's working! Look!" Nas called out in astonishment, and my
voice faltered as I looked down to see that the Deadweed had
stopped its fast advance through the city. The flower buds and
the vines were waving in a slightly drunk, sleepy sort of way,
as if sedated.

"Keep going!" Zarr advised me, and put some more effort into
it this time, trying to sing to the whole patch of the Deadweed,
and not just what lay beneath us. It was then that I started to
feel it – the magic that was flowing through me from some
unknown place, filled with a mother's warmth. It hit the Deadweed in waves of consideration and stern restriction, the way

that a mother dragon might have to nip and contain a wayward newt.

And, miraculously, the Deadweed responded. Its vines waved sluggishly and died down, curling back in on themselves as the plant seemed to go dormant, the flower heads retracting into the body of the plant and the leaves curling over themselves as if sleeping.

"Now!" I distantly heard someone shouting through the hazy feeling of the song. Akeem. He was shouting for all the dragons to use fire if they could, to attack now, as the Deadweed had stopped attacking them.

As I sang, great gouts of flame appeared before my eyes like pillars of light, and joined to form a brightly glowing wall that swept across the beach and the two Deadweed-tentacles on Deep Bay, utterly consuming it, and cleansing it.

When we landed, I staggered on my feet, suddenly exhausted although all I had done was sing to the Deadweed. I was half-expecting Akeem to be the first to find us, but he wasn't. It was Talal and Gren, landing near in the dunes and racing across the sand.

"You did it!" Nas turned to me and said, breathless and excited, and as confused as I was as we both sank to the floor. "You found a way to stop the Deadweed!"

"Does this mean they're not going to exile or kill me?" I

murmured, thumping my back against the tired and panting bulk of Zarr behind me.

"It means that we need to find a way to hide your talents," Talal responded seriously. "We can't have the Southern Lords knowing we used magic to beat the Deadweed. They will see what you did here today as witchcraft – just as bad as the Deadweed is itself. But we don't have to tell them what happened. We can say that our Training Hall tactics worked..."

More lies, I thought wearily. Had all this been for nothing? "We need to change." I murmured up to the Chief of the Training Hall, too tired to care if I should stand, salute, or even call him 'sir.' "The Training Hall needs to change."

"Oh, I can see that, Dayie," Talal said. "And who better to help me than Rider Dayie of the Seven?"

That forced open my eyes, making me shake my head in astonishment. "You are really going to do that? To elevate me to one of the Seven?" I opened and closed my mouth.

Talal the Chief Trainer gave me a small smile, rolling his shoulders as he looked speculatively back at the burning township of Deep Bay. "I think, after seeing you in action, I want you on my side the next time we have to do this."

I wasn't sure if that was a compliment or not, but I knew that I believed him. We *would* have to do this again, and we hadn't destroyed the Deadweed that was fast taking over our world, however much we had slowed it down, for now.

THE END

Thank you for coming on this adventure with me to explore the new Southlands of Three Kingdom's World! If you like Dayie and Zarr, Akeem and Aida, Latifa and the other cast of the Training Hall, then please follow on for the next exciting instalment of Deadweed Dragons! And I love hearing from you, dear readers – please leave feedback at the market-site you purchased this book from!

END OF DRAGON CALLED
DEADWEED DRAGONS BOOK ONE

Dragon Called, 24 April 2019

Dragon Magic, 29 May 2019

Dragon Song, 26 June 2019

PS: Keep reading for an exclusive extract from **Dragon Magic** and **The Dragon Tamer.**

THANK YOU!

I hope you enjoyed **Dragon Called**.

Please don't forget to leave a review.

Receive free books, exclusive excerpts and be kept up to date on all of my new releases, when you sign up to my mailing list at AvaRichardsonBooks.com/mailing-list.

ABOUT AVA

Ava Richardson writes epic page-turning Young Adult Fantasy books with lovable characters and intricate worlds that are barely contained within your eReader.

Her current work is 'The First Dragon Rider' Trilogy.

She grew up on a steady diet of fantasy and science fiction books handed down from her two big brothers – and despite being dog-eared and missing pages, she loved escaping into the magical worlds that authors created. Her favorites were the ones about dragons, where they'd swoop, dive and soar through the skies of these enchanted lands.

Stay in touch! You can contact Ava at:

f facebook.com/AvaRichardsonBooks

a amazon.com/author/avarichardson

g goodreads.com/AvaRichardson

BB bookbub.com/authors/ava-richardson

AVA RICHARDSON

DRAGON MAGIC

DEADWEED DRAGONS BOOK TWO

BLURB

They must either stand together, or the Kingdom will fall.

The combination of Dayie's magic and dragon's fire has halted the advance of the Deadweed. But it is not defeated. Now, a new enemy lurks on the horizon: Water Wraiths sweep in from the sea, cutting their way inland, and assisting the invading plant's onslaught deeper into the land.

Killing everyone in their path.

The new strategy against the Deadweed has proven effective, but Dayie grows weaker each time she uses her powers. It can only be a temporary fix. When she and her dragon Zarr are invited to train with the High Mountains' Dragon Riders, Dayie eagerly accepts the opportunity. But it's far from a warm welcome as the tight-knit riders of the High Mountains distrust the outsider and her unusual power.

When the High Mountains leader suggests a compromise, a schism in the ranks threatens to tear the group apart. The loyal few must convince both dragons and riders of the Southern Kingdom to join forces against the Water Wraiths.

But Dayie won't be much use to them if she can't figure out how to balance her magic usage and avoid depletion.

To survive the growing menace, the Dragon Riders must set aside the things that divide them and unite.

Before it's too late.

Get your copy of ***Dragon Magic***
Available 29 May 2019
AvaRichardsonBooks.com

EXCERPT

Chapter One:

Dayie, a Dragon's Games

"Hold eye contact!" I shouted across the packed earth of the Training Arena, worry clutching at my belly with its icy claw. Ahead of me stood my fellow trainee, the dark-haired girl Latifa, a few years older than me but looking uncertain as she half-crouched in front of the Sinuous Blue that she had been attempting to train.

It was a clear day in the south, and that meant it was *hot*. The heat was making us all exhausted, but it was having the opposite effect on the dragons. They loved the heat– my Crimson Red dragon, Zarr, (now larger even than Gren, the oldest Stocky Green we had here) was clutching the walls of the amphitheater of the Training Hall, half-holding his gigantic scarlet wings out to catch the heat. Further away was Nandor, the smaller Sea Dragon bonded with Nas – the boy I had grown up with, happily lashing his tail and setting up swales of sand and dust while Nas tried to approach her with a bag of charcoal.

The heat filled the dragons with an eager, excitable energy – but in Latifa's Sinuous Blue (*Bitey,* as she had started to call her), it only made her even more agitated than normal.

Thwap! The Blue whipped out her long tail – prehensile and curling like a cat's, only with cruel barbs instead of fur.

"Hey!" Latifa jumped back, staggering in the sand and – *oh no* – she broke eye contact.

"SHREYKH!" The Blue hissed and pounced forward, her giant golden eyes narrowed to a cruel squint—

"STOP!" I shouted, starting forward as I felt Zarr's contentment dissolve into alarm against my mind.

With a heavy thump, the Sinuous Blue (*Bitey...*) had landed with both paws to either side of my friend Latifa, whose usually stoic demeanor was broken with a sharp scream of alarm. Sand exploded outwards, covering the scene as I heard gasps from Nas, Abir, Roja and the other trainees from the side of the Training Arena, and shouts from Talal Sal, the Chief of the Southern Kingdoms Training Hall, from his balcony up on the walls above us.

The Sinuous Blue's head darted downward, into the swirling sands.

That's it. She's going to eat her – the certainty rushed through me as I ran forward and felt the explosive wave of air around me as Zarr was already swooping down – doubtless to protect me from the madness of charging a fully-grown dragon with just a wooden stick in my hands.

"Get off me!" Latifa shouted – and, as the dust settled, I saw that the Sinuous Blue had indeed wrapped her jaws around my friend, but she was holding her between her teeth, and hissing a deep and guttural growl.

Oh, this is bad, this is bad... I thought. One false move or accident and the Sinuous Blue could easily puncture a limb.

"She's playing." Zarr landed with a heavy thud on the sand of the arena, earning a sudden increase in the serpentine growls coming from the Blue, as if worried that Zarr would take away her toy.

"Playing!?" I burst out as I skidded to a halt, not knowing what to do. "It doesn't look as though she's playing, Zarr…"

"Dragon playing," Zarr said. *"She's making up her mind whether to eat the girl or not."*

"Well, tell her not to!" I said in exasperation, balling my fists as sweat dripped down my brow. To one side of me, Zarr started to whistle and twitter to the Sinuous Blue, thwapping just the end of his forked red tail in the sand. Beyond him, Nas was trying to soothe the Sea Dragon Nandor, who was hissing and snapping at the air in alarm at the commotion.

"Just let her go, easy now…" I cleared my throat and reached for the song in my mind that I knew would calm her down. It was the only thing that might work – although I knew that we couldn't rely on it all the time. What would happen if I wasn't around to help each trainee with their dragon? *But now you have no choice, Dayie,* I told myself.

There was a snort of hot, sooty air from the Sinuous Blue before I could get a chance to release my magic, and with an agile little head bob, she casually flipped Latifa over onto the sand and sprang back to sit on her haunches and casually preen her belly scales with her long snout – as if saying *'look at me, look at what I can do, anytime I want!'*

Which was what was worrying me, actually. "Latifa? Are you okay?" I rushed to her side as Zarr continued to whistle at the Blue, taking the dragon's attention off of me as I grabbed the young woman's arms and helped her to her feet, pulling her back as I did so. I couldn't see any blood, and she wasn't screaming from the pain of broken or fractured limbs, thank the sands.

"Yes, yes – I think I'm okay…" She pulled at the hem of her cotton trousers (like mine, they were cream-colored and light, helping us survive in all this heat) to reveal a half-circle of deep welts around her calf. "She didn't even break the skin," Latifa said, wonderingly, looking up with a frown at the Sinuous Blue she had been trying to befriend. From her expression, you would have thought she was going to go and scold the dragon for scaring her – but I could feel the girl shaking against my side – and I wasn't surprised, too. It was a scary thing, having a dragon decide whether to eat you or not.

"As if you would know if I decided to eat you." Zarr turned a lazy eye at me, his forked tongue unrolling from his open

maw. *"If I had wanted to, I would do it and snap! – you'd be gone before you got a chance to squeak!"*

"Just try it, wyrm," I muttered in annoyance. Why did Zarr think this was all a great big joke? As much as I loved him, the Crimson Red was definitely a boy dragon. Ever since coming back from the battle of Deep Bay two months ago, he had been acting like a yearling goat just coming into his prime.

"Okay." I turned back to Latifa. "Get some water and let the healers see to your leg all the same." I patted her on her back and let her limp off to the side of the arena where the galleries of stone opened out to the sanded floors, before making my way to the covered-over water buckets myself.

"Dayie?" It was Abir, the smallest of our trainees but the one who was the friendliest. "What shall we do with Bitey? Shouldn't we be trying to get her back down into her cave until she's calmed down?"

He had a point. I turned back around from the water butt, my forearms and head drenched, and looked skeptically at the scene. Today had all been about trying to befriend (or re-friend) the older dragons that stayed here in the Training Hall; the ones that the Seven had, or still did ride. But of the Seven, we were down to just four. *Five,* if you included me. At the end of the battle for Deep Bay against the Deadweed, Chief Talal had officially recognized me as a Dragon Rider. Mostly because, as he had said, 'I want your powers working for me!'

And that was why he and the others were putting up with me making all of these decisions.

But it wasn't an unlimited freedom though, was it? I couldn't avoid remembering. Chief Talal had made it very clear that his patience wasn't total. *'You can try out your training methods, Dayie,'* the chief had told me. *'Because the sands know that we need them to work. But if you haven't managed to build a fighting force out of our trainees before long...'*

I had to make my ideas work. The older dragons of the Seven were the most set-in-their-ways. Gren (the oldest Green, and budding Matriarch of the little nest I was trying to build here) was stolid, slow, and stubborn. She would let others ride her, but she would never fly as well or respond with any enthusiasm unless it was Chief Talal with her. *Which was a good thing, if I could convince Chief Talal that MY way of befriending and riding the dragons was better.* The chief still thought his training methods were better – bribe, shout, entreat, and threaten the dragons until they could accept *any* rider, while I knew that they would work best only with the bonded. What Chief Talal was trying to do was unnatural to both the humans and the dragons and this had been my attempt to prove it – by getting the older Seven dragons to ACTU-ALLY bond with the trainees, step by step, and bit by bit.

Only it clearly wasn't working very well, was it? I thought of Latifa very nearly becoming a dragon's dinner.

"I guess..." I started to say, watching the Sinuous Blue as she had moved from preening her chest scales to sprawling across the sanded floor, resting her long neck on the sand and watching us tiny humans under lidded eyes. *She's laughing at us,* I thought in annoyance. As much as I loved the sight and the sound of dragons – I couldn't even imagine how I survived the long years of indentured captivity with the Dragon Traders without this joy in my life – but they could sure be a pain in the butt sometimes. Maybe it would be easier to get Bitey into the caves when she was a bit calmer…

"Leave her." A voice broke into our conversation. It was Akeem in his heavy leather harness of the Dragon Handlers, walking at the head of a gaggle of the stocky, well-built men and women who worked to 'manage' the dragons here. He was still holding onto his ridiculous disguise, I thought with mild irritation. Akeem, the Captain of the Wild Company of Binshee Dragon Riders, was still masquerading as a Dragon Handler here, even though Chief Talal and half of the trainees now knew that he was something much different.

"She already didn't respond well to today's practice…" I pointed out as Akeem stepped up to us, nodding to the other Dragon Handlers to go about their normal tasks of sweeping the arena and distributing charcoal and water to the dragons' present. I copied his example, asking Abir to give us a few moments alone.

"She's acting up," Akeem said softly as he moved to wash his hands beside me, still pretending to half the Training Hall to be nothing more than a Dragon Handler. "You won't get her to do anything now until she wants to. Best to just placate her and let her sleep in the sun for a bit…"

I felt that I should argue with him – here he was, walking into the arena and casually countermanding my suggestions, but he had a point. If *I* were a dragon – wouldn't I rather be lazing up here in the sun than being told what to do by humans? *Especially if I had spent my life being told by humans to do this and that.* "Maybe we should bring *all* the other dragons up. Gren, the other Stocky Greens, and Sinuous Blues…" I pointed out.

Akeem's dark eyes sought mine out and held me for a moment before a crooked half smile moved across his sharp features. "You're not wrong," he said.

Well, gee thanks for letting me know! I scowled at him. Apart from when he was ignoring me, it seemed that Akeem's next favorite hobby was making fun of me.

"But we'll need everyone on the ground. Handlers, trainees, ready to step in whenever they start spitting at each other," Akeem said, scratching the stubble of his chin. "And then, of course, is the trouble of them flying away…" He made this last point teasingly, because it was an argument that we'd had many times before. The dragons of the Training Hall were going to fly away, and there was nothing that we could do about that – and the last time that they had done so it had taken us two days to coax one of the Blues back. Our answer had been to bring them up in pairs, threes, or sometimes fours at a time, when the dragons were so busy with the human Handlers and Trainers (and each other) that they didn't seem so interested in escaping.

"In shifts," I sighed heavily, repeating our pattern and feeling defeat. Akeem was making a point. That our training methods were terrible, and nothing like those of the Binshee Tribe. Akeem had told me that they wouldn't dream of keeping their Vicious Oranges in caves or pens until they were 'needed,' and that their Vicious Orange dragons could always come, go, and hunt as they needed. *But what can I do?* These were not High Mountain dragons. I had to work with the dragons that we had here, and that meant trying to iron out the difficulties and the stubbornness and build trust, one step at a time. "We let all the dragons up in shifts, and I guess that *Bitey* and Nandor gets the first."

Akeem's cocky smile faded, and I saw his jaw harden as he looked up at the circular walls all around us. "You're right," he acceded to me, "but I wish that you weren't."

"Nothing new there, then…" I said under my breath, only half teasing, but his expression didn't change. "What?" I said, feeling more than a little put out. *What, he could tease me and I couldn't tease him? How self-important was he?*

"Look, Dayie – there's something that I came to talk to you about. Something *not* about the dragons, for once. I have to leave the Training Hall, head away from Dagfan and back up to the High Mountains." He used the old southland's name for the mountains that cut across the top of the southern deserts and formed our natural barrier with the northern queendom of Torvald.

"The Fury Mountains?" I said. That was the more popular name for them. I should know, I had grown up in their shadow. Before, of course, the Deadweed had come and killed my foster parents.

"The *High* Mountains," he insisted with a flicker of a grimace. That was Akeem all over. He would use the old names and the old language of the south all the time. No one talked like that anymore which didn't help his camouflage one bit, and was one more thing that annoyed him.

"Something's happening back at home – my people…" he said brusquely.

"The Binshee Tribes?" The black-robed tribes lived high in the mountains but travelled far and wide. They kept themselves apart from the other southerners, only paying lip service to the Council of Lords.

"Yes. There's a…a *challenge*. Look, it's difficult to explain right now, but I have to go. The fate of the Wild Company depends on it." He swallowed nervously. Whatever he was about to say next appeared to cost him dearly. "And, well – I think that you should come with me."

"What?" I coughed, looking at him as if he were mad. *He*

knows all the work that has to be done here! We're only two months out from the Battle of Deep Bay, and the Deadweed is still spreading! We're down three of the Seven; aside from Gren, the old dragons haven't bonded to anyone yet; hardly any of us know even how to shoot a bow or throw a lance from dragon-back yet...

"It's important," Akeem said through gritted teeth. "Not just for me and the Wild Company... but for the dragons as well. You'll be able to see how the Binshee do things. How *we* train. There's only so much I can teach you like this, through hasty conversations by water butts." He looked disparagingly around us. Already we had spent too long here, talking to one another. Someone would notice. One of the guards would notice, and start asking questions.

"But, how can I leave – the others need me..." I said helplessly.

"They need a tutor who knows what she's talking about!" Akeem suddenly said, looking fierce and annoyed, but the way that he wasn't eager to meet my eyes made me think it was because he was annoyed with the situation and not only me. "Talal recognized you as one of the Seven, which means that you and your dragon are free to come and go. I have Aida out in the wilds beyond Dagfan, and we can leave tonight."

"But – what do I tell the others? Latifa, Nas? Abir and Jeona?" I said.

Akeem looked once more at the large reclining Sinuous Blue in the center of the arena, who had now clearly stopped all training for the foreseeable afternoon. On the far side Nandor had clearly taken inspiration from the larger Blue and was perching on the pillars of rock that stood in the arena, avoiding Nas's reaching arms beckoning her down. "Tell them that you're going to find an answer to this mess."

Get your copy of ***Dragon Magic***
Available 29 May 2019
AvaRichardsonBooks.com

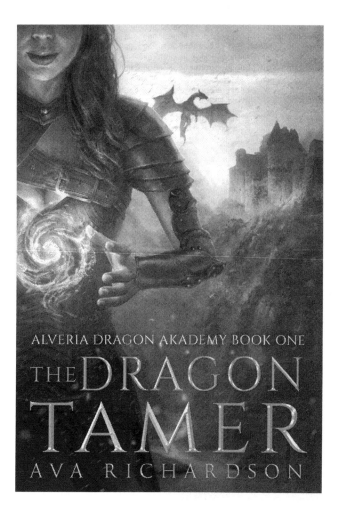

ALVERIA DRAGON AKADEMY BOOK ONE

THE DRAGON TAMER

AVA RICHARDSON

BLURB

A kingdom divided cannot stand. For those caught in the middle, it means death.

For centuries humans and dragons existed side by side in Alveria, bonded by their care of one another. But no longer. After decades with no viable eggs, humans far outnumber dragons, and the survival of the species appears bleak. The outlook for everyday humans is little better as rogue dragons raid and torment villages. Yet it's far worse for the tamers, beaten and killed simply for serving the noble dragons.

But eking by at the bottom of Alverian society isn't any easier for seventeen-year-old Kaelan Younger. Harder still when her loyalty to the dragon crown is no secret. But when her dying mother reveals a horrifying truth about her identity, Kaelan is thrust into a world for which she is ill prepared.

Faced with a new life at the proving grounds for humans and dragons alike, Kaelan must reconcile not just her past but embrace the future laid out before her. When her responsibilities as an Akademy tamer collide with her feelings for a powerful dragon shifter, it will take everything she has to prepare for the danger threatening them both. The fate of the dragons she has sworn to serve rests in her hands.

Now Kaelan is no longer an outsider.

She's the enemy.

Get your copy of **The Dragon Tamer** at
AvaRichardsonBooks.com

EXCERPT

Chapter One

Kaelan Younger cradled her basket under her arm as she skulked through the small, shaded market. She had to cradle it because it was full of eggs she needed to sell if she was going to buy the ingredients needed for her mother's medicine, and she had to skulk because she'd technically been banned from this particular market.

Ducking her head, she scoffed—quietly—as she wove between the vendors who were setting up shop. She was still upset about her banishment, especially since the incident that had caused it hadn't even been her fault. Accidentally break one guy's ankle, and suddenly the whole town turned against you. No one cared that she'd been stopping the jerk and his friends from pickpocketing a helpless old man, or that she'd technically done nothing more than give the boy a single light shove. He had gotten out of the incident scot-free—well, minus the broken ankle, which he'd more than deserved— while she'd been exiled to the lesser market.

Which was right next to the pigpens. In the mud. Where no customer with more than a few half-pennies in their pocket would venture. If she wanted to sell her eggs and herbs for enough money to buy the expensive, imported ingredients for the medicine her mother needed to live, she had no choice but to sneak back into the greater market.

Kaelan ducked her head and gritted her teeth, trying to concentrate on finding an unoccupied stall rather than thinking about her sick mother. Every time her thoughts ventured to the broken-down mountain cabin where Ma lay helpless in bed, Kaelan's stomach flopped over and her head went fuzzy with anxiety, and she'd need all her wits about her if she was going to get a prime price out of her goods. Not to mention avoid getting caught, which would mean the confiscation of everything she'd brought to sell.

She couldn't help the ugly and unwanted stir of resentment that always followed on the heels of her anxiety, though. The truth was, Kaelan was sixteen. She'd be an adult in a bare handful of years. She should be ramping up her studies as a healer-in-training, thinking about what she wanted to do with her life. Maybe even, if she was lucky, sneaking off to make out with some hot village boy in a broom closet. She shouldn't have to be here, risking her future and her reputation for the sake of selling a few eggs.

She shook off that last thought, ashamed, and shoved the resentment away. Ma needed her, and Kaelan would come through for her. And that was all there was to it.

She spotted a tiny stall in the very back of the market and darted towards it. It wasn't an ideal location, but it was right next to a vegetable vendor whose plump potatoes might bring a few extra customers their way. She made sure her ratty hood was pulled down far enough to hide her black hair and green eyes, and then she set her basket on the low table.

It was too early for the typical morning crowd to make their appearance yet, but she didn't have to wait long for the first trickle of potential customers. All she could see were two torsos, their heads cut off by the hood that draped over her eyes, but she could tell from the shiny buttons and fine leather that they were well-off. She pulled her hood back just a touch and worked up a charming smile which she'd practiced extensively that week since it never came naturally to her. "Good sires," she started off her sales pitch... but they'd already turned away, toward the vegetable vendor's stall.

Worry fizzed in her veins. It was still early in the morning, so she had plenty of time to make her sales, but every moment that passed heightened the risk of discovery. Maybe these customers could be swayed by a discount and she could get out of here quickly. "Good sires!" she called again, raising her voice this time and lifting her hood a little more so they could better see her hard-won charming smile.

The men—no, boys—turned away from their perusal of the potatoes and glanced at her. The worry in her veins turned to lead, freezing her in place. "You," she said, in a less-than-charming tone.

The boy in front—he was about her age—gave her an ugly smile, looking her up and down. His artfully tousled red hair bobbed with the motion. He swaggered back over to her stall and crossed his arms, probably trying to look tough, but the splint on his ankle ruined his pose.

"I thought I smelled a dragon-lover back here," he said, sneering. "I wonder, does the chieftain know you're in the greater market?"

I may be a dragon-lover, but at least I'm not a pickpocket, she wanted to reply, but didn't. The boys in town had taken to calling her that name—a slur for someone loyal to the dragon-blooded royal family—ever since her family had moved there. It didn't matter. It wasn't worth getting upset over. What she *did* have to worry about, though, was this jackass or his friend telling the village chieftain that she'd broken the terms of her banishment.

The vegetable vendor glanced over, giving Kaelan a long, suspicious look. The rest of the vendors were still preoccupied with setting up shop, but if this guy turned this into a confrontation, they'd all be on her like flies on a carcass, hoping for some juicy new gossip material. If she didn't convince the boy to move along quickly, her chances at a clean getaway would be shot.

Her mind skittered. What was his name? She couldn't recall it. All the guys were the same here, at least as far as she was concerned: a bunch of self-righteous jerks, bullies and proud of it. "Don't you have anything better to do than make trouble for me?" she tried, knowing it wouldn't work. "Surely I'm not worth wasting your time on."

The boy's ugly smile dropped. "Funny thing," he said. "Normally, I *would* have something better to do right now."

The other boy leaned forward, his sour breath wafting between them. "Knattleikr practice was supposed to be this morning," he said. "But thanks to your little stunt, Bekkr here is off the team till next season, and he was our captain. Which means the town's lost its chance at attending finals. You're now officially the least popular person in Gladsheim. So, if you ask me," he said, reaching out a finger and poking her arm hard, "making trouble for you *is* the best use of our morning."

Her heart sank, but before she could say anything in her own defense, Bekkr cut in.

"Actually," he said to his friend, "I think you do have something to do right now, don't you?"

The boy frowned, but then his eyes widened in understanding. He sent a leering smile at Kaelan before he trotted back toward the center of the market.

There was only one place he could be going—to tell the chieftain she was there. Hissing a curse under her breath, Kaelan snatched up her basket and wheeled for the side exit, but Bekkr caught her by the arm.

"Where do you think you're going, dragon-lover?"

Her temper flared and she yanked her arm away. "Stop calling me that!"

His eyes went mean and squinty, the way all her tormentors did when she lost her temper—because that was their goal.

She huffed out a breath, frustrated with herself for taking the bait. She should know better by now.

"Why?" Bekkr taunted. "That's what you are, right? Well, let me tell you something, *dragon-lover*. You're not welcome here."

As if she hadn't figured that out on day one. Dragons and the dragon-blooded ruling class weren't popular in Gladsheim, nor were those loyal to them. The way these villagers looked at it, dragons used up the kingdom's resources and gave the common folk little in return. Kaelan had never agreed with that outlook, in part because she knew dragons provided many irreplaceable benefits to the kingdom. The other part of her feeling on the subject was, admittedly, due to her own fascination with the creatures.

She shook herself. She had to get out of the market before the chieftain had her goods seized. She tore herself free from Bekkr's grip and wheeled around to face the vegetable vendor. "I'll give you a thirty percent discount on these eggs and herbs," she said quickly, evading Bekkr as he grabbed for her again. She kept her eyes on the vendor. Her offer of a discount would mean she'd only be able to afford broth for dinner again, but at least it would leave her enough to pay for the medical ingredients she needed. "You can sell them for much more than that and make a profit."

The woman squinted at her. "Don't need no eggs or herbs," she grunted, and then turned away as if Kaelan was invisible.

Kaelan groaned. What now? Should she try one or two more people in hopes of getting a sale here, or run before the chieftain arrived? Realistically, she knew she should run. It was the smart choice. She still had a chance at making a sale in the lesser market even if it made her next to nothing. But just as she turned to flee, Bekkr's hand snaked out and yanked her basket away. "Hey!" she shouted, trying to grab it back.

Bekkr smiled, holding the basket up out of her reach. Damn his tallness. "Say Queen Celede is a worm and I'll give it back."

Her blood boiled at the derogatory nickname for dragons. When the boys goaded her, it made her angry, but she was used to it. She'd be damned if she'd stand by and let him mock someone else, though—especially a descendant of the dragons she admired. "Queen Celede is a good ruler," she said staunchly. She had no idea if it was true, of course. She'd never been to Bellsor and never so much as seen the ruling family, but she was a loyalist at heart, and plus, at this point she was liable to disagree with anything this jackass said on general principle.

He raised an eyebrow, took one egg out of the basket and dropped it. She yelped and scrambled to catch it, but it hit the ground too quickly, splattering yolk all over the hem of her cloak. She fumed helplessly as he picked up another egg and held it aloft.

"One more chance," he said. "How about Prince Lasaro this

time? Everyone knows he's not fit to rule, anyway. None of the royal brats are."

Her temper snapped. She took two jerky steps forward and shoved him, much harder this time than she had when she'd broken his ankle. He stumbled backward, that stupid grin slipping off his ugly face as he had to drop her basket and the egg to reach out and catch himself on a table.

She grabbed her basket and stood above him, raging. "You," she growled, "are *nothing*. All of you, including those other boys you hang out with, you're *nothing*. I don't even have to know Prince Lasaro to know he's twenty times the man you are. Now stay down before I break your other ankle."

She didn't dare look up, but she could sense everyone in a five-stall radius training their attention on her. Now that she'd made a scene and ruined all chances of escaping notice, she tucked the basket under her cloak in hopes of at least making a quick escape with her remaining goods intact. If she got out fast enough, and if there were already a few customers in the lesser market, she *might* still be able to sell her goods for maybe a third of their worth. If she was lucky.

She started to turn and nearly impaled herself on a dragon's skull.

Get your copy of **The Dragon Tamer** at
AvaRichardsonBooks.com